The Spy and the Mobster's Son

Also by Keira Andrews

Contemporary

Honeymoon for One
Beyond the Sea
Ends of the Earth
Arctic Fire
The Chimera Affair

Holiday
The Christmas Deal
The Christmas Leap
The Christmas Veto
Only One Bed
Merry Cherry Christmas
Santa Daddy
In Case of Emergency
Eight Nights in December
If Only in My Dreams
Where the Lovelight Gleams
Gay Romance Holiday Collection
Lumberjack Under the Tree (free read!)

Sports
Kiss and Cry
Reading the Signs
Cold War
The Next Competitor
Love Match
Synchronicity (free read!)

Gay Amish Romance Series
A Forbidden Rumspringa
A Clean Break
A Way Home
A Very English Christmas

Valor Duology
Valor on the Move

Test of Valor
Complete Valor Duology

Lifeguards of Barking Beach
Flash Rip
Swept Away (free read!)

Historical

Kidnapped by the Pirate
Semper Fi
The Station
Voyageurs (free read!)

Paranormal

Kick at the Darkness Trilogy
Kick at the Darkness
Fight the Tide

Taste of Midnight (free read!)

Fantasy

Barbarian Duet
Wed to the Barbarian
The Barbarian's Vow

The Spy and the Mobster's Son

by Keira Andrews

The Spy and the Mobster's Son
(formerly *The Chimera Affair*)
Written and published by Keira Andrews

Cover by Dar Albert
Formatting by BB eBooks

Copyright © 2012, 2017, 2023 by Keira Andrews
Print Edition

The Argentine Seduction
Written and published by Keira Andrews
Copyright © 2013, 2017, 2023 by Keira Andrews

ISBN: 978-1-988260-96-9

This is a work of fiction. Names, characters, businesses, places, events and incidents are either the products of the author's imagination or used in a fictitious manner. No persons, living or dead, were harmed by the writing of this book. Any resemblance to any actual persons, living or dead, or actual events is purely coincidental.

Acknowledgements

My gratitude to Gio for the invaluable assistance with all things Italian. Grazie! And thanks to Amy, Anara, Lisa, and Rachel for their help and support.

Table of Contents

CHAPTER ONE

A S HIS FATHER'S booming laugh echoed off the marble archways, Sebastian took another gulp of champagne. It fizzed pleasantly in his throat, and he beckoned a waiter, plucking his fourth glass from the man's tray.

Another server appeared as if out of thin air. "Arancini?"

Sebastian waved off the offer of deep-fried cheese-and-rice balls and leaned back against a column. He stood on the landing of the large staircase, watching the hundreds of party guests below. The great hall of his father's mansion was carved in Carrara marble of white and grayish blue, with ornate columns and sculptures throughout.

By the fountain in the center of the hall, Sebastian's older brother, Beniamino, stood at their father Arrigo's side. They spoke animatedly to one of the local politicians, a particular favorite among the many who were regular guests at the mansion. Perched on the shore of Lake Como, surrounded by the Alps soaring to blue skies, the mansion was Arrigo's pride and joy. Second perhaps to his regard for his firstborn son, but Sebastian felt it was a toss-up.

The floor-to-ceiling glass doors leading to the terrace were closed against the surprisingly robust June heat. Even in late evening with the air-conditioning working overtime, sweat gathered at the nape of Sebastian's neck, and he tugged on the collar of his tuxedo. Oh, what he'd give to be able to sneak down to the lake for a dip.

"Why don't you come down and meet Signor Scali?"

Sebastian hadn't noticed his brother's approach. "I'll leave it to you, Ben. You know you're better at all that."

Ben hitched a shoulder. "Yes, but I'd much rather be spending time with Signor Scali's niece, Valentina." He nodded across the room toward a young woman in a beaded sea-green evening gown. As he caught her eye, she smiled coyly, wrapping one of her long, loose blonde curls around one finger. Ben groaned softly. "I've seen her every chance I've had this summer. She's exquisite."

"Yes, she's very pretty." Left him utterly cold, but Sebastian could at least appreciate the girl's beauty.

"Let's hope her uncle will be kept busy. And perhaps she has a friend for you, Basi."

Sebastian's stomach clenched, and he drained his glass. "Perhaps. But I'm fine on my own. Thank you."

Ben's expression clouded. Square-jawed, with dark, wavy hair and a strong nose, he was the spitting image of their father. Sebastian, on the other hand, favored their fair mother, with green eyes and golden hair. On more than one occasion, usually in the midst of a frightening temper, Arrigo had questioned Sebastian's paternity.

"Basi, it's the best way to move on. You've moped around for a month. Father's patience wears thin. If you still want to go back to Harvard this fall, you'd better show that you've learned your lesson. You're twenty now. Time to be a man. You were just"—he waved his hand around—"experimenting. Now it's out of your system, right?"

Wrong. "You think he might let me go back?" A glimmer of hope flared. After the embarrassment Sebastian had caused, he didn't think his father would let him out of arm's reach again. He'd been waiting for his father to force him into a job at his company. *Probably thinks I'm too useless.*

"If you play your cards right and listen to your big brother.

Come join me and Valentina after you've finished brooding."

Something clicked in Sebastian's mind. "Wait, is that Valentina *Bruno*?"

Ben nodded, a goofy grin on his face. "I think she likes me, Basi. *Really* likes me."

"Isn't her father the…"

"*Businessman* from Naples? Yes. But I don't care what her father does. It's nothing to do with her. And just *look* at her."

Sebastian chuckled. "I've never seen you so head over heels before."

"You should try it, Basi. I'll see if she brought a friend." With a wink Ben was off, weaving through the crowd before Sebastian could tell him not to bother.

Taking another glass of champagne, Sebastian wondered how much longer he had to stay before he could slip away to his room and get out of the tuxedo. He didn't know why his father cared if he was at the party or not—it wasn't as if Arrigo paid the slightest bit of attention to him.

Still, he'd insisted Sebastian attend, and with Sebastian's luck the one time his father actually wanted to introduce him to someone would be tonight. Plucking a smoked salmon delicacy from a passing waiter, he watched his father holding court. As always—in public—Arrigo was garrulous and lively, greeting guests with kisses and hugs.

His parties were always popular, drawing many neighbors and even guests from several provinces. The food and wine were plentiful and decadent, and as Sebastian took another gulp of champagne, he had to admit his father had excellent taste.

Down below, Ben was speaking closely with Valentina, and Sebastian groaned to himself. *Please let her be utterly friendless.* It would certainly be the capper for the night if he had to dance with some girl and pretend to be interested. *But maybe if Father saw, it would help. I could kiss her, even. For everyone to see.*

He imagined it for a moment and sighed. It would be a lie, and the mere thought of pretending to be what he wasn't made his stomach churn. No, he would abide his father and keep his true feelings to himself, at least at home, but he wouldn't be part of any charade.

Sebastian desperately hoped he wouldn't have to stay home for longer than the summer. He wanted to return to Harvard more than anything. Arrigo had allowed him to finish his first year of studies, despite the "incident," and when Sebastian arrived home, he'd briefly thought perhaps his father wasn't as upset as he'd expected. The sting of his father's hand and his purple-faced reprimand had quickly put an end to that notion.

In the weeks since, Sebastian had done his best to avoid Arrigo. He'd been so excited to get away from home and go to America. Although he and his father had never been close, Arrigo hadn't hesitated to send him to the school he'd requested. He knew his father saw what Sebastian had done as the ultimate betrayal. Not only of his generosity but of their family name.

Finishing another flute of champagne, Sebastian wondered if he should attempt to speak to his father. Make a good public showing. Perhaps if he did well tonight, Arrigo would soften toward him enough to allow him to return to school in the fall. Pushing off the wall, Sebastian took a deep breath and straightened his tie.

"Excuse me? Where's the bathroom?"

The question was asked in shaky Italian, and Sebastian turned to answer. However the words lodged firmly in his throat as he peered up into the warm, gold-flecked eyes of a beautiful man. "Huh?"

About thirty years old, the man was at least six-two, substantially taller than Sebastian's own five-eight. His tuxedo was sharp and fit snugly across broad shoulders and down over lean hips. He smiled tentatively. "My Italian isn't great. I'm looking for the—"

"Bathroom. Right. There are several. Dozens, actually."

"Ah, another American! I was beginning to feel lonely here." The man's smile bloomed, brightening his face and sending Sebastian's somersaulting.

"No, I'm not American. But I've been working on my accent since I was a kid. I watch a lot of American TV. I just finished my first year at Harvard." *Please let it not be the last.*

"You're Italian? Wow, your English is amazing."

"Thank you." Sebastian fought the urge to grin like an idiot at the compliment. "So, the bathroom." He pointed to the second floor. "If you go up and turn right, you'll find a bathroom halfway down the hall. Should be quieter than the ones on the main floor."

The man smiled. "Thank you. Up and right, and at the end of the hall."

"No, not the end. The middle."

"Sorry, I'm terrible at directions. I'll probably get lost on the stairs knowing me." He chuckled self-deprecatingly.

"I can show you if you want."

"You wouldn't mind?"

"Of course not." Sebastian left his empty glass on the ledge of the wide railing and led the way up the second flight of stairs and into the east wing. Away from the great hall, the house was much quieter, the sounds of chatter and the strains of the string quartet fading away.

As he stopped by the bathroom door in the long hallway, he sensed the man standing very close behind him. "Well, here you go."

"Thank you." The man brushed Sebastian's shoulder and arm as he stepped around him. "I'm Steven, by the way. Steven McBride." He extended his hand.

As Sebastian clasped their palms together, he swore sparks actually traveled up his arm and right down his spine. His throat was dry. "Sebastian Brambani. Well, Sebastiano, but only my father calls me that."

"Brambani?" Steven still held his hand. "So this is your party?"

"My father's." Sebastian pulled back and shoved his hands into his pockets. "What brings you to Como?"

"Business." Steven's gaze raked down Sebastian's body and back up again. He stared intently. "And perhaps pleasure."

As Sebastian tried to formulate a response, Steven ducked into the bathroom. Sebastian's mouth opened and closed again, his pulse racing. Did he just...was he...did he want...?

Peter's words echoed in Sebastian's mind. "It's all in the eyes. That's how you know. It's about the stare. The understanding. Trust me; you'll know it when you see it."

At the thought of Peter, the familiar ache stabbed and twisted. Longing, regret, and anger coursed through him, and Sebastian gritted his teeth as he pushed it aside. As he stood there dumbly, trying to get his mind under control, the bathroom door opened and Steven stepped out.

"Can you show me around the rest of the house? Or do you have to go back to your guests?"

Sebastian thought of his father and his expectations, and of Ben and pretty young women in glittering gowns. "Sure, I can give you a tour. Too hot down there anyway."

Dimples appeared in Steven's cheeks as he smiled. "Thanks."

As they made their way through the upstairs rooms, Steven listened attentively and asked insightful questions about design and art. At the end of the hallway, he paused by a watercolor painting of red stucco roofs. "Is this Florence?"

"Yes. Have you been?"

"Not yet, but I've always wanted to go. To Rome too, of course. I'd love to see the Sistine Chapel. Michelangelo is one of my favorites." Steven chuckled. "I suppose he's many people's favorite."

"My father owns a Michelangelo. A sketch."

"Really? An original Michelangelo?" Steven's face lit up.

Sebastian felt foolishly proud. "Yes."

"I'd love to see it."

"It's in my father's private suite of rooms, I'm afraid." He waved his hand to indicate the locked door beyond them. "I'm not even allowed in there."

"There's no way we could sneak a peek?"

"I don't know the security code. Sorry."

"Of course, I understand." Steven shook his head, blushing slightly. "I'm sorry to even ask; I'm letting my passion for Michelangelo get the better of my manners. Thank you for the tour. It's been a pleasure. We should get back to the party." He started to walk away.

"Wait, I can still show you..." Sebastian cast about, trying to think of something—anything—to keep Steven to himself for a few minutes more. But perhaps he'd misread the signals earlier, as Steven hadn't shown any further interest in anything but art. "Um...never mind. I'm sure you're right. We'd better get back."

As he turned, Steven's hand closed over Sebastian's forearm and he stepped in close. "Are you sure there's nothing else you want to show me?"

Heart pounding, Sebastian faced him. This close he could smell the musky scent of subtle cologne and maleness. "I...I..." Sebastian stammered.

Steven leaned down, his breath tickling Sebastian's ear. He murmured, "I can think of something." Then his hand closed over Sebastian's cock, which jumped to life.

His exhale more of a moan, Sebastian rubbed himself against Steven. It had been four long months since Peter had disappeared from school, and Sebastian had only had his own hand since then, too afraid of being caught to pursue anyone else.

But now there was another hand on him that was not his own,

and he rutted against Steven, yanking his head down for a kiss. As he slid his tongue inside the other man's mouth, Sebastian thought he heard a sound of surprise, but it was soon swallowed as Steven gripped his head and kissed him.

His dick was already hard and leaking against his tuxedo trousers, and Sebastian broke their kiss, panting. "Let's go…"

Steven squeezed him. "Where?"

Sebastian's room was in the west wing, and they'd have to pass the great hall to get there. His raging hard-on would be impossible to hide. "Any of these roo—" His words were strangled by a sharp gasp as Steven's hand stole into Sebastian's pants and wrapped around his shaft.

"Sure you can't get into the master suite?" Steven grinned. "Wanna make you come in front of a Michelangelo. You remind me of David. So beautiful." He nipped Sebastian's earlobe. "So hot."

Sebastian moaned. "I might be able to guess the code. But my father would kill me if he found out."

Withdrawing his hand from Sebastian's trousers, Steven sucked on his index finger. His eyes locked with Sebastian's as he slid his hand down the back of Sebastian's pants this time, finding his hole. He teased it lightly and whispered, "All the more exciting."

His thighs trembling, Sebastian bit back a loud gasp as Steven pushed the tip of his finger inside. He'd only been penetrated with his own fingers, but this was so much better. Thrusting against Steven's hip, his orgasm was building already, his balls tightening as the pleasure boiled up and—

Suddenly Steven's hand was gone, and he took a step back. Eyes glittering, he nodded to the closed door. "Come on. Give it a try."

Breathing heavily, Sebastian went to the keypad. Part of him felt a forbidden thrill at the idea of being with a man inside his father's private suite. He knew he'd only have one shot at the code—an alarm would sound even on only one false try. A security guard had been fired on the spot last year for making an input error.

With a deep breath, Sebastian punched in a sequence of numbers and pressed Enter. The red light disappeared, and a green one illuminated in its place. He exhaled, excitement thrumming in his veins as he pressed down the steel door handle.

"Shh! What was that?" Steven glanced around nervously. "I think someone's coming."

Sebastian's excitement was tempered with fear, and he stepped back from the door, letting the handle lock back into place. The red light on the keypad turned back on. He strained to listen beyond the distant sounds of the party. "I don't hear anything," he whispered.

Steven indicated the closest bedroom. "I'll wait in there. Maybe you should go back to the party for a minute and make sure you haven't been missed. I swear I heard someone calling your name. A woman."

Sebastian groaned. "Probably the girl my brother's lined up for me."

"Go tell her you're not feeling well." Steven kissed him, his fingers strong in Sebastian's hair. Then he rolled his hips forward, rubbing their cocks together. "I'll be waiting."

Sebastian practically ran, fortunately realizing before reaching the great hall that his trousers were still embarrassingly tented. He shucked his jacket and folded it over his arm, holding it in front of his waist. At the top of the staircase, he scanned the crowd for Ben and the girls.

Ben waved to him, and Sebastian resisted the urge to take the stairs two at a time, walking calmly instead. Ben slung his arm around Sebastian's shoulders when he reached them. "Ladies, this is my brother—"

A piercing alarm filled the air, and partygoers clapped their hands over their ears. Security guards appeared, storming up the stairs and disappearing into the east wing. Sebastian's heart thumped against his ribs. What if they found Steven? What if…

The alarm's shriek matched the icy chill that took hold. The code to his father's suite. Steven. "Oh, God." Sebastian rocked on his feet, and then he was off and running, his jacket flung aside, his brother's confused shout in his wake.

When he made it to the end of the main hallway, he rushed into the bedroom where he'd left Steven.

Empty.

Angry shouts emanated from his father's nearby suite, which was the last place Sebastian wanted to be. Still, he crept as close as possible and caught a glimpse of the suite's sitting room—and the open safe. With a terrible sinking sensation, he ducked back into the empty bedroom and rushed to the window, peering into the darkness. A wall surrounded the estate's grounds on three sides, but by the water's edge, he caught a flash of movement.

Steven.

Guards raced through the gardens and across the wide lawn. Sebastian's eyes widened as he realized they'd raised their guns. Shots rang out, but they were too late. Illuminated by the faint moonlight, he watched as a small motorboat sped off into the night. As the alarm was silenced, his father's bellow of rage took its place.

And in that moment, Sebastian really knew fear.

CHAPTER TWO

B Y THE TIME he approached the lakefront in the village of Bellagio, Kyle was ready for a nice cold beer. Preferably a Bud, but he was willing to settle for whatever European brew he could find. It had been a long walk from where he'd abandoned the boat, but at least his T-shirt and jeans offered a little respite from the heat compared to the stifling tux.

He was just about to curse Marie for being late when her lilting French accent floated over to him on the gentle breeze. "*Bonsoir*, my darling!"

Putting a smile on his face, Kyle opened his arms to her and kissed her passionately, caressing her through the soft cotton of her sundress. As he held her close, he felt Marie's small hand steal into the front pocket of his jeans and remove the three-inch vial.

"Oh, how I've missed you, *mon cher*." Marie sighed, gazing at him lovingly. A few years older than Kyle, she was quite a beauty.

With a final kiss, Kyle took her hand, interlacing their fingers as they strolled along the water, one of dozens of couples. At night the promenade became a lovers' lane, and Kyle nuzzled Marie's brown curls affectionately. She looked up at him with a loving smile on her beautiful face, dark eyes gleaming.

She spoke quietly. "Any trouble, Mr. Grant?"

"None," Kyle replied, his tone equally hushed, yet casual.

"The boy was no match for your charms?"

"Of course not. Putty in my hands." They always were. Men, women—didn't matter. He always got the job done.

Marie's moony smile remained, but he could hear the smirk in her tone. "One day I'd like you to meet someone who can resist you."

"But I've met you already, my sweet."

"Ah, but I fear you wouldn't be giving me your best work, given my deficiencies. Lack of a prick, for starters."

"*Chéri*, your balls are bigger and more fearsome than any man's."

She laughed genuinely, pressing into his side. "On that we can agree, Mr. Grant." They arrived at a small, two-story hotel. Standing on tiptoes, Marie whispered in his ear. "Wait for further instructions." With a final kiss, she melted away into the humid darkness.

In his small room Kyle gazed out over Lake Como. By now his abandoned boat would be found, although the rumpled tuxedo was safely disposed of in a pizzeria dumpster on the outskirts of Bellagio. Brambani's men would certainly be searching for him, but they'd expect him to leave the Como area as soon as possible.

There was no fridge in the room, so instead of a beer he had to satisfy his thirst with tepid tap water. Kyle stripped off his clothes and stepped into the shower, hoping for half-decent water pressure. It was passable, and he tried to relax under the spray.

His mind replayed the night's events. It had all gone smoothly, at least. Sebastiano Brambani had proved to be as pliable as expected and also as clever with numbers as Kyle's research showed. Kyle recalled the few hours he'd spent reading through the blog Sebastian had kept during his year at Harvard.

Not the typical writings of a wealthy son of a crime boss. Math had never been Kyle's favorite subject in school, yet Sebastian wrote with a passion, clarity, and wit that had intrigued Kyle and made him think about the subject in ways he'd never considered before. Cursory research was usually all he needed, but with Sebastian he'd found himself tracking down all the details he could. According to his research, Sebastian had done almost no partying at school, focusing his attention on studying and a friend or two.

As he rubbed shampoo into his short hair, Kyle mused that with that kind of stimulating mind and Sebastian's looks, it was a shame it hadn't been a longer assignment. He would have enjoyed taking a few days to get close to him. In his line of work, Kyle had seduced countless women, and it was rare to get to charm a man. And Sebastian hadn't disappointed him, proving just as bright and appealing as he'd seemed.

If there'd been more time, Kyle would have greatly enjoyed seeing if Sebastian was as creative in bed as he was with numbers. Shaking his head, he decided he really needed to find the time to get laid after the mission was completed. Clearly it'd been too long since he'd had a man if he was getting this distracted by the idea of a math geek with a pretty little body. Kyle groaned and reminded himself that Brambani's son was just a tool he needed to do his job, and he snapped his focus back to that night's mission.

He'd known there was no way around the internal alarm he knew had to be in the safe in Brambani's private room, but by gaining access to the room itself, he'd had precious minutes to crack the combination. It had been easier than expected, although of course the internal alarm sounded as soon as he removed the vial from the weight-sensitive interior. A quick shimmy down one of the house's ornate columns and a sprint to the water had been child's play.

Now he'd move on to the next mission. Move on to the next country, another city or town. He hoped Marie would have the assignment in the morning. He didn't like waiting or staying in one place too long. Made him restless. Always better to be moving forward.

As Kyle rinsed his hair, his mind stubbornly returned to Sebastian. He'd liked listening to Sebastian talk. Liked touching him.

Of course he hadn't been able to truly enjoy it at the time, not mid-mission. But he could now. What would it hurt? He gave in and allowed himself the luxury of a smile at the memory of the boy's surprisingly aggressive kiss.

His hand slick with another squirt of shampoo, Kyle spread his legs and leaned back against the tiles, letting his mind go. His eyes drifted shut as he stroked himself to hardness, remembering the sweet taste of Sebastian's mouth, the warm panting of his breath as he eagerly leaned into Kyle's touch.

Sebastian wasn't Kyle's usual type, which was older and experienced. Rough and ready, with no emotions to get in the way. But there had been an unexpected heat between them that had gone straight to Kyle's dick. He twisted his palm over his cock, squeezing his nipples with his other hand.

He thought of how tight Sebastian's hole had been on his finger. Despite his indiscretion at college, Kyle had a feeling Sebastian's ass was virgin. There was still an innocence about him that was unmistakable. The sound Sebastian had made when Kyle kissed him echoed through his mind, and he wondered just what other noises Sebastian would make. As Kyle sped up his strokes, he imagined bending Sebastian over and plowing into him.

He'd be so tight and hot around Kyle's cock as Kyle took him and made him beg for more. Sebastian would moan prettily, spreading his legs wider and pushing back as Kyle claimed him. Kyle would come inside him, or maybe pull out and fuck Sebastian's mouth, those full red lips wrapped around his cock as he—

With a ragged exhale, Kyle spurted onto the wall of the shower stall, shuddering with pleasure as he roughly milked himself. It was rare that he didn't have to fake attraction to a mark, but with Sebastian Brambani, there had been no imitation of desire necessary. If anything, Kyle had been forced to hold back; Sebastian's kiss had been almost distracting enough to make him wish he could forget his mission. Too bad he'd never have him properly.

Kyle snapped off the water and toweled himself. His was not a business of regrets.

THE RAP AT the door was so sharp with irritation that it could only be Marie. Once inside, her mouth was a grim line. "It's not the right compound. This is little more than pepper spray. Maybe he was expecting an extraction attempt and had a decoy in place. The Chimera prototype is still out there, and Brambani has it. Word is he's upped the asking price."

It was barely eight in the morning, but Kyle wanted that cold beer more than ever. Rubbing the sleep from his eyes, he pondered their options as he yanked on his jeans and T-shirt. "I could try the son again. Although getting to him would be difficult. Getting to anyone will be difficult now that Brambani's guard is up."

"Forget the boy. He'll likely be dead by noon." Marie paced the short length of the room. "And yes, Brambani's guard will certainly be up. *Very* up. We had one chance at this, and you failed."

Kyle clenched his jaw. "Failed? I was told the vial of powder would be in the safe. Other than what I extracted, there were only diamonds and gold bars." Something else Marie said registered belatedly, and his stomach strangely somersaulted. "You think Brambani would take out his own son?"

"Our contact says it was the straw that broke the camel's back. Brambani is a ruthless man. He killed his wife for less."

"But Sebastian's…"

Marie frowned. "What?"

Kyle didn't have an answer. Sebastian was a good kid? Lots of collaterals were good people, solid citizens. Nothing made

Sebastian different from any of those who'd lost their lives in the past—not his passion for numbers, or his clever way of writing, not his wide eyes, his aggressive kiss, or his tight, round ass. He was like any other guy who was in the wrong place at the wrong time, Kyle told himself.

Or like any other guy whose father couldn't accept him. With a deep breath, Kyle bit back the unwelcome memories of his own father's fury. He needed to forget the past and forget Sebastian Brambani.

"The boy's irrelevant." Marie continued pacing. "We need to figure out where Brambani's hiding the Chimera. Our sources say the sale to the terrorist cell is on for Friday. We have to get to the weapon before he can hand it over."

Five days. "Even if we find this prototype, what's to stop him from making more?"

Marie paused. "This is high level, but we've eliminated the source. The formula has been destroyed. Brambani doesn't know it yet; he's just the dealer. But if we don't get to the vial first, the buyer will be able to analyze the compounds and recreate it."

"Why don't we just kill Brambani before he makes the sale?"

"You know why. Politics, Mr. Grant. The Association has its reasons. And—" Marie broke off as her phone vibrated. She answered and listened. After about five seconds, she said, "Understood," and hung up. She glanced at Kyle. "We're out. Take the black Ferrari outside and drive to Geneva. You'll fly to New York from there." She reached into her purse and tossed him a set of car keys.

"No other assignment?" Kyle didn't like going back to his threadbare Hell's Kitchen apartment. He needed to keep moving. Keep hunting.

Marie already had a hand on the doorknob. "They're not happy. After Rio and then that fuckup extraordinaire in Singapore, you needed this one. If you'd successfully extracted the

Chimera, things might be different." She seemed to want to say more but finally smiled softly. "Get some rest, Kyle."

The hairs on the back of Kyle's neck stood to attention. "Marie…"

But she was already gone.

Downstairs a minute later with his battered duffel bag in hand, Kyle walked around to the hotel's small parking lot. He examined the underside of the Ferrari, the trunk, and the engine. No sign of explosives. Still he hesitated, Marie's farewell ringing in his ears. She hadn't called him by his first name once in nine years.

Turning on his heel, he left the Ferrari behind. He needed to catch a boat to the other side of the lake. He'd find the Chimera yet.

Kyle Grant wouldn't be put out to pasture.

THE SUN HAD been up for several hours, but the house was still silent. Sebastian strained to listen at the door of his room and couldn't even hear the staff going about their daily duties. He dressed in black slacks and a dark red button-down shirt. His father disapproved of sloppy clothing.

He'd spent the long night huddled on his king-size bed, waiting. While part of him hoped he was tying himself into knots for no reason, he knew it was extremely unlikely. He hadn't slept a wink as he imagined the ways his father might punish him. Sebastian had no doubt it wouldn't take long for Arrigo to discover his son's role in the robbery. Steven's image had undoubtedly been captured by one of the outdoor cameras as he made his escape, and surely someone had noticed Sebastian and Steven together.

Steven. At the thought of the bastard, Sebastian began pacing the length of his room. How could he have been so stupid? How could he have thought an older, gorgeous man wanted him? Steven—or whatever his name really was—had only been after one of Arrigo's treasures. He wasn't sure what Arrigo kept in that safe; perhaps his mother's jewels? He wasn't about to go and ask.

So he waited. After running through the hexadecimal approximation of pi, he calculated Fibonacci sequences. But he kept losing his place as images of Steven leaning down to kiss him flickered through his mind. He'd never been kissed like that before, and he couldn't help flushing with remembered desire. "Think of what Papa will say," he muttered to himself.

Yet his father didn't come. The silence was even more terrifying than one of Arrigo's rages, when his face would become red as a tomato as he screamed a litany of curses that would make a Napolitano street criminal cover his ears.

There was a quiet sound from beyond the door, and Sebastian froze, holding his breath as he listened. Then a furtive knock. "Basi?"

Relief coursing through him, Sebastian ushered his brother in. "What's happening? Is Father very upset?"

Ben's normally golden skin was decidedly ashen. "Basi, how could you be so foolish? Is it true? Did you open the door to Father's suite?"

"I… How did you know?"

"How do you think?" Ben exclaimed. "You think Father doesn't have eyes everywhere in this house?"

"I'm sorry. He just wanted to see the Michelangelo."

"Your lover?"

"No!" Sebastian's cheeks flamed. He and Ben had never directly discussed what had happened at school with Peter. They'd sidestepped around it agilely. "I don't even know him!"

"Yet you let him into Father's private rooms."

"I…" Sebastian searched for a response that would not incriminate him further.

"How did you know the code?"

"I guessed."

"You guessed?" Ben's eyebrows shot up. "How on earth did you guess?"

"You know I always have a good memory for these things. It was just a sequence of numbers and dates that are important to Father. Your birth date and the founding date of his company."

"The founding date of his company?" Ben shook his head, amazed.

"But, Ben, I was going to go in with him! I wouldn't have let him steal anything! He thought he heard someone calling for me, and I closed the door. It was locked."

"Clearly he watched you put in the code."

"Yes, he must have." *Lying bastard.* "Do you think he was after Mother's jewels?"

Ben shook his head. "Basi, how can you still be so naive? Jewels are the least of Father's concerns."

"Then what was stolen?" The acid in Sebastian's stomach churned.

"Apparently the thief didn't get what he was looking for. I don't know what it was. I do my job, and I don't ask questions. I know Father's business is about much more than energy, but he hasn't trusted me with details yet." He took Sebastian by the shoulders. "Basi, you must plead for mercy. Promise that you'll never look at another man again. Date Valentina's sister. Marry her, for fuck's sake. Whatever it takes."

"But…"

Ben's fingers dug into Sebastian's flesh. "Do you want to end up like Mama?"

"Mama? That was an accident. The road was slick, and—"

With a groan, Ben stepped back and ran his hands through his hair. "You really are that naive. Basi, she found out about Father's new business dealings. How do you think we went from living in a four-bedroom house in Milano to this?" He waved his hands around. "This palace?"

Sebastian realized he'd never considered it. "But…Father loved her." Sebastian had been twelve when she died. He still remembered every moment of the day when he woke to find seventeen-year-old Ben at his bedside, his brave brother's face terrifyingly tearstained.

"Yes. He did. But she was going to leave him. He couldn't allow it." Ben's throat seemed suddenly thick with emotion, his voice gruff. "She shouldn't have been so foolish."

Sebastian's head spun, his legs like jelly as he leaned against the bed. "He…he *killed* her?" He found himself on his knees, stomach roiling as memories of his sweet, wonderful mother raced through his mind. "You knew?"

Ben swallowed thickly. "Not at the time. There are a lot of things about Father—about the things he does—that I wish I didn't know. Believe me, Basi, I wish I didn't have to tell you." He crouched down and brushed back Sebastian's hair. "I wanted to keep you out of all of this, but I thought you'd figure it out by now."

"He killed her." Sebastian said the words again, still unable to believe them. *Is this a nightmare?* "How? She was…she was so *good*."

"She was," Ben agreed. His voice cracked. "Too good."

"Didn't you love her?"

"Of course I did, Basi! And I love you too. That's why you've got to—"

"I don't understand—how can you work with him?" Anger flashed through his veins, and he shoved at his brother. "How can you even *look* at him? *How?*"

Without a knock, the door flew open. A man Sebastian recognized as one of his father's security guards towered in the doorway. "Come with me."

Rage gave way to terror. "Ben?" Sebastian's voice trembled. He wanted to hide behind his brother as he had so often as a child.

Ben pulled Sebastian to his feet. "Remember what I said, Basi. Please, do whatever it takes." Ben pressed a kiss to his forehead. "Go on. Don't make him wait."

"What's he going to do?"

"I don't know. I really don't. Just promise anything he asks. Please."

The hallways of his own home seemed foreign as Sebastian followed the guard. Instead of going to his father's office, he was led to the basement. He'd never been below before, and his pulse raced as he followed the guard. In contrast to the opulence of the main floors, the windowless lower level was utilitarian and drab. He couldn't help but feel he was being led to the gallows, and he glanced behind him, gauging the distance to the stairs.

The urge to run overwhelmed him, but as he turned, the guard yanked his arm and propelled him farther down the concrete hall. *Maybe Ben's wrong. Maybe it really was an accident. His father loved his mother. He loved his children. Didn't he?*

Inside a small, airless room, Arrigo waited. A television hung on one barren wall with a single chair placed before it. At Arrigo's nod, Sebastian sat, his heart hammering in his chest. He pressed his sweating palms against his trousers as the guard stepped in and shut the door behind him.

"Father, I—"

"Silence." Arrigo's tone was quiet and controlled. Calm.

Sebastian clasped his hands together to keep from shaking. A moment later the TV flickered to life. Frozen on-screen was an image—recorded from a ceiling-level video camera—of Sebastian and the man he'd known as Steven. They were in the hallway outside Arrigo's suite.

They were kissing.

The image was unfrozen, and Sebastian tingled with shame as

he watched himself rubbing against Steven desperately, kissing him with loud noises recorded on the surveillance. Surveillance Sebastian had never known was there. He knew there were cameras on the grounds, of course, but had never spotted any inside. Were there cameras everywhere? In his own room?

He dropped his head. "I'm sorry, Father."

Hard fingers gripped the back of his neck as Arrigo forced his head up. "Look at yourself. Disgusting. A dog in heat."

"Please forgive me." The image froze on-screen once again, with Steven's hand down Sebastian's trousers. Sebastian felt red to the tips of his ears. "I'd had too much to drink."

Arrigo's grip moved to Sebastian's hair, his fingers tightening. "I gave you another chance after you humiliated me with your roommate. After you let yourself be photographed."

"Peter was my friend. It was a party, and we were just…joking around. I know what the pictures looked like, but there was no need to have him sent away."

Arrigo let go of Sebastian's hair and stepped in front of him. "Do you know how many people saw those photographs? How you shamed me?"

"I didn't know they'd end up on Facebook! Father, please." In the back of his mind, Sebastian knew it was pointless to argue that he and Peter had only been friends after Arrigo had seen him with Steven, but in his desperation he could think of no other defense. "It was all a prank!"

"Your friend was only too happy to tell the truth. And to take the money I offered him to leave and never see you again."

Actual pain clenched Sebastian's chest. "No. He would never do that! You forced him!" He thought of all the phone calls, texts, and emails for months that had gone unanswered after Peter suddenly left campus. "He wouldn't do that to me!"

"Ah, Sebastiano. So like your mother you are. A dreamer."

He wanted to protest, to scream that it wasn't true, but in his heart he knew it was. As he'd gone to class the day Peter disappeared, Peter had given him a long kiss. "I'm only human, Sebastian."

"And now you let yourself be so easily seduced by this man." Arrigo jabbed his finger at the TV. "A *spy*. Fortunately he did not acquire what he came for."

A sliver of hope flared. "Then perhaps you can forgive me."

With a flick of a remote, the video on the TV continued. Listening to his own moans, Sebastian wished the ground would open and swallow him whole. Then he was punching in the code, opening the door. After he left to go back to the party, Steven quickly appeared again, punching in the code and slipping inside.

Then the video changed to a new camera angle, this one atop the wall safe in his father's room. Gone was the easy smile and rakish charm of the man Sebastian had met at the party. This Steven was all steely concentration as he fiddled with the safe just beyond range of the camera, seemingly able to crack it remarkably fast. He pulled out a small vial and then disappeared from frame as alarms sounded.

Arrigo turned off the TV. "The guard monitoring the cameras was apparently too busy watching football to do his job. He has been terminated."

Sebastian had a feeling the guard's status was permanent. "Father, please. I'll make it up to you. I'll do anything. *Papa*."

Arrigo sighed, a flicker of sadness crossing his hard features. Leaning over, he pressed a kiss to Sebastian's head before taking his face in his hands. "You have humiliated me for the last time. I have only one son now."

Panic flapped against Sebastian's rib cage. "Wait! No!" He stood but was shoved down by the guard. Arrigo left the room, and another man, one Sebastian didn't recognize, entered. This man was around forty, with salt-and-pepper hair and a calm, almost frighteningly serene expression.

They couldn't actually kill him. Could they?

Dazed, Sebastian walked, one foot in front of the other, as the guard and the new man—*an assassin?*—took him into the garage through a staircase from the basement. As he saw the car they were leading him to, a sedan with darkened windows, the daze shattered.

The trunk stood open and waiting.

"Ben! Ben!" he screamed as he tried to break free from the powerful hands now gripping him. "Ben!"

Kicking wildly, he struck one of the men and broke free for a moment. As he raced toward the opening garage door, his body slammed into the concrete. The air whooshed from his lungs, and he felt knees digging into his back. "Don't make this harder than it has to be," a smooth voice uttered.

The hit man hauled Sebastian up and shoved him face-first into the large trunk. God, no. No, no! Sebastian scrambled, knowing if the trunk closed over him, it was all over. He aimed his elbow backward and was rewarded with a grunt of pain as he hit solid flesh. On his knees, he fought with every ounce of energy he had, ramming his head back into the man's face.

But before he could get out of the trunk, pain exploded in the back of his skull, and his vision went double. The hit man shoved him down mercilessly. Sebastian fought to hold on to consciousness, pain and dizziness running riot through him.

He became aware of the sounds of a scuffle and popping noises followed by silence. With what felt like Herculean effort, he rolled onto his back. The lid of the trunk was still open. Ben. His brother had saved him. As Sebastian struggled to push himself up to sitting, a face appeared over him.

"You." Sebastian wanted to break the bastard's nose, but his arms refused to cooperate.

With a firm hand, Steven pushed him back down. "Lie still

and shut up."

Then the lid slammed down, and there was only darkness as the car roared to life and sped away.

CHAPTER THREE

As Como disappeared from the rearview mirror and the road became steeper, the thumping from the trunk started up again. After an initial burst of kicking and yelling as the sedan raced away from the Brambani estate, all had been quiet. He'd wondered if Sebastian had lost consciousness, but he was definitely awake now.

Although ominous clouds were rolling in, the lookout points on the road were clogged with tourists, and Kyle needed somewhere secluded to talk to Sebastian. He couldn't afford garnering any attention from local authorities, and judging by the muffled curses from the trunk, Sebastian was not in a pliable mood.

After another ten minutes, he spotted a private lane. Half a mile down, Kyle stopped the sedan, keeping the car running. He stepped out and peered through the trees with high-powered binoculars. The chalet nestled around the corner showed no signs of life. He scanned the area and saw only a small, furry marmot scampering through the brush.

It would do. He leaned back into the sedan and killed the engine. Immediately the thumping began anew. Kyle walked behind the car and contemplated the trunk for a moment before banging on the metal once. "Listen to me, Sebastian. I'm not going to hurt you. I'm going to let you out, and we're going to talk. Okay? So when I open the trunk, don't try anything. I don't want to hurt you, but I will."

His only response was silence, which Kyle hoped was acquiescence. With a press of the button on the key chain and a dull *thunk*, the trunk opened a few inches. Kyle waited a moment and then lifted the lid.

The blow staggered him, the tire iron striking the arm he threw up to protect his head. Sebastian fairly flew out of the trunk, dodging Kyle's grasp and taking off into the forest. With a frustrated sigh, Kyle pursued.

The kid was impressively quick, but Kyle was quicker. He tackled him to the ground, Sebastian crying out as he slammed into the dirt. With efficient movements, Kyle flipped him over and straddled him, Sebastian's wrists pinned over his head in one of Kyle's hands.

As Sebastian opened his mouth, Kyle slapped his other palm over it. "Shut up and listen. I said I'm not going to hurt you. But if you make me, there's no one around to save you. So don't waste your energy and my time with yelling." He squeezed his thighs around Sebastian's hips and tightened his grip on Sebastian's wrists to emphasize his point.

Breathing heavily through his nose, Sebastian's face flushed as he squirmed and bucked. After a few moments, he stilled and finally nodded. Kyle lifted his hand. Sebastian's voice cracked slightly. "What are you going to do with me?"

"Nothing. Provided you cooperate."

"What do you want with me? You already destroyed what was left of my life."

Kyle snorted. "In case you didn't notice, I just *saved* your life."

"Well if it wasn't for you, it wouldn't have needed saving!"

Kyle couldn't stop a smirk from lifting one corner of his mouth. Most people would be crying for God or anyone who would listen right about now, but the kid wasn't going to just fold. That fortitude would undoubtedly serve Sebastian well in the long run, but it wouldn't do him any good now. Kyle intended to get what he needed. "It was only a matter of time. You were never going to be able to live up to that man's expectations. Not being who you are."

"You don't know that."

"I do. You could have tried to hide it, tried to be the son he wanted. But you'd never be good enough."

"How the hell do you know anything about who I am?" He struggled in Kyle's grip.

"Feisty. I like that. In bed, that is." Sebastian's cheeks reddened even more, and Kyle continued, "In a hostage, not so much." He squeezed Sebastian's wrists hard. "Listen to me. I need to find something your father has. A lot of lives could depend on it."

Sebastian didn't give in, continuing to fight. "What? I don't know anything about what my father does." He swallowed hard. "Apparently I didn't know him at all." Wriggling, he tried to dislodge Kyle. "Let me go. I can't help you."

"Probably not, but you're all I've got right now. We worked for months to get the little information we had." Sebastian bucked, and Kyle held him harder, pressing his free hand down on Sebastian's chest as he leaned over him, their breath mingling. "Enough."

Sebastian exhaled raggedly as he turned his head and stopped moving. Utterly still, he seemed to be concentrating on deep breaths, and Kyle could feel Sebastian's arousal against his ass. Kyle nearly pushed back against the hardness, a surge of lust arching through him. He swallowed, eyes locked on Sebastian's full mouth, lips parted. *Just one more taste…*

Kyle shot to his feet, releasing Sebastian. He took a deep breath and ensured his voice was flat. "Now that we've calmed down, you're going to answer some questions."

Sitting up, Sebastian swiped his hand across his sweaty brow and wrapped his arms around his knees. He kept his gaze on his feet. "What did you try to steal?"

"I said *answer* questions, not ask them." Kyle leaned against a nearby tree, watching Sebastian's pulse flutter in his neck. He ran his gaze over Sebastian's dirt-smeared, tailored shirt hugging the curves of his shoulders, and cleared his throat. "But I'll tell you. A biological weapon called Chimera."

"K...what?"

"The name comes from Greek mythology. C-h-i-m-e-r-a, but pronounced with a hard *k*. A three-headed creature who breathed fire."

"Sounds...ominous."

"Indeed. It's a powder. When mixed with water, it creates a gas that makes napalm seem like Chanel No. 5. As the name suggests, it would be just like breathing fire, with comparably fatal results."

Sebastian took this in. "And you think my *father* has it?"

"We know he has it. He's planning on selling it to a South American terrorist group on Friday."

"What?" Sebastian sputtered. "But...why? My father wouldn't do that," he finished weakly.

"Wouldn't he? Look at what he was about to do to you. Look at what he did to your mother."

Suddenly Sebastian was on his feet, fists clenched. "What do you know about my mother?"

"Not much. That she grew up in Finale Liguria. Modeled in Milan, where she met your father. Spent much of her time fundraising for the San Paolo Hospital in Milan before he had her killed. The same way he was going to have you killed."

Sebastian turned away, shoulders slumping. He murmured something Kyle couldn't make out, but it sounded like a string of numbers. Kyle recalled a blog entry in which Sebastian had confessed to reciting pi to the twenty-sixth decimal when nervous or upset, joking that a lot of people had a favorite number but his just happened to be endlessly long.

Kyle couldn't imagine why on Earth anyone would have a favorite number. Even as a child he'd had more important things to worry about. Just like he did right now—so why did he find himself distracted by this spoiled rich kid with his messy emotions and charming idiosyncrasies? *He's only a tool. Use him.* "Listen, I know this can't be easy. But you need to help me. Or do I need to remind you that you're still in danger? There will be plenty more where those men in the garage came from."

With a deep breath, Sebastian faced him again. "How did you overpower them?"

Kyle reached into his black jacket and pulled out his gun. The silencer was still on the tip. It didn't kill all the noise of gunshots like in the movies, but suppressed it enough to get the job done.

Eyes wide, Sebastian jerked a step backward. "You killed them?"

"I sincerely hope so, because they'll try to finish the job."

Sebastian ran a hand through his disheveled hair. "And who are you anyway? Why should I help you? Who do you work for? You could be telling me nothing but lies. *Again.*"

Kyle smirked. "At least you're learning."

"Yeah, well, as they say in America, fool me once…"

"I'm the lesser of the evils you face right now, and you're just going to have to take my word for it."

"Terrific." Sebastian sighed.

Kyle relented. "I work for an organization that tries very hard to keep innocent people around the world safe. We need to get the Chimera before the terrorists."

Sebastian absorbed this. "So if I help you, then what? Do you just throw me to my father's men when my usefulness is over? Or do you expect me to believe you're going to be my bodyguard for the rest of my life?"

"I know people who can help."

"Who can help do what?"

"Give you a new life."

Sebastian frowned. "Like…witness protection?"

"Something like that. You help me, and I'll set you up with a new identity."

Hope flickered across Sebastian's face. "You could do that?" He shook his head. "Why would you?"

Good question. Kyle had to admit there was something about Sebastian that compelled him. He hadn't given it conscious thought at the time, but he'd looked forward to meeting Sebastian, and had examined surveillance photos repeatedly. Somehow Kyle didn't want him to end up as collateral damage. "Yes. You can get your life back. Well, not the one you had, but a new one. A better one."

"You'll really help me?"

"I'll do everything I can." *If he lives that long.* He needed Sebastian to stop fighting him; he'd figure out what to do with him later. It wasn't exactly a lie—he did have connections. But he needed to focus on one step at a time, and the first was getting Sebastian to trust him.

"I can't just walk away. What about my brother?"

"The one who works with your father?" Kyle scoffed. "Who was nowhere to be seen when you were getting hauled away by his assassins? You don't have a brother anymore. You have to leave all that behind, or you'll be dead."

It was Sebastian's turn to scoff. "Why will you care if I'm dead?"

"I won't. Get in the car. You have nowhere else to go." Despite his words, Kyle clenched his jaw against the niggling thought that Sebastian really would end up dead if he wasn't careful. He reminded himself sternly that it didn't bother him as long as he got the Chimera. *Just tell him what he wants to hear.*

"Of course you don't care. You just need me for information. That I don't have. So, what about you? How do I know you aren't going to kill me when you're done with me or when you realize I'm useless to you?"

Kyle watched Sebastian, the way he held his head high, trying to hide the tremors in his limbs. Trying to be brave. "You don't." He turned toward the car. "But I won't. Not unless you give me a reason," he added, but there was little conviction in the threat. The idea of Sebastian's piercing eyes going dead and cold troubled him. Shaking it off, Kyle said brusquely, "Come on. We have a plan to make."

He listened carefully as he walked casually to the car. After a moment Sebastian's footsteps crunched on the twigs and pine needles as he followed.

FAT RAINDROPS SPLATTERED on the windshield as Sebastian waited. Steven sat behind the wheel but hadn't turned the key. Finally Sebastian couldn't take the silence and the inaction any longer. "Steven? Where are we going?"

"Kyle."

"What? Oh. Okay." He doubted Kyle was his real name either, but it would do. "Where are we going, *Kyle*?"

"If he has it somewhere in the house, it's game over. There's no way we can get back in." Kyle stared off into the distance, talking more to himself than Sebastian, it seemed. "Our contact was a good one. Don't think he gave us bad intel. Brambani must have moved it."

"The powder?"

Kyle nodded absently, still peering out. The rain was coming down harder now, a sheet of water that obscured the landscape. Sebastian was keenly aware of how isolated they were, and how defenseless he was against this man. Would helping him even make a difference? Or would Kyle put a bullet in him anyway?

He'd be a loose end, and he had a feeling Kyle didn't leave many of those behind.

If he did manage to escape, where would he go? His own father wanted him dead. The pain sliced through him sharply as he thought of Ben. He couldn't trust his brother now either. The police? Would they even believe his story? Besides, given his father's many connections and long tentacles, Sebastian had a feeling the police would be of no help to him.

Then there were the people Kyle worked for. They could have the police in their pockets too. He gazed at Kyle's profile. Could he trust this man? His head said no, but for some reason his gut said yes. Either way he had no choice. At least if he helped Kyle find what he was looking for, Sebastian could buy himself some time. "He went up to his cabin a few days ago."

Turning to face him, Kyle's eyes narrowed with a laser focus. "There was no record of a cabin."

"It's an old place. Not fancy. I was only there once, many years ago. It was in his mother's family. I don't know why he kept it. He could buy a hundred cabins better than that one."

"How far from here?"

"I don't know. I have no idea where we are. I was locked in the trunk, remember?"

Reaching over, Steven—no, *Kyle*—opened the glove box and pulled out a map. As he brushed past Sebastian's thigh, Sebastian held his breath, trying to ignore the flare of heat in his belly. *Jesus, get it together. He's a killer.* He tugged at his collar, the shame prickling his skin. *He's a killer who gets me hard when I should be terrified.* What if he had reciprocated instead of releasing Sebastian?

Sebastian ran his sleeve over his forehead. He could tell himself that he would have resisted, but as he thought about Kyle's weight pinning him down, his iron grip on Sebastian's wrists and warm breath on Sebastian's slick skin, the desire ran thick in his veins. *Maybe Father's right—I am a dog in heat.*

"Well?"

Sebastian snapped back to attention. "What?"

Kyle scanned the map, which was unfolded across the dashboard. "If he was there this week, it's worth a look. Is he aware that you know he went?"

Sebastian pushed away his previous train of thought. *Focus. Staying alive is all that matters.* "No. I overheard him talking with Ben. I didn't hear much. Wasn't interested at the time. I was surprised Father was going up there, but I didn't ponder it. Do you think...does Ben know? About the weapon?"

"Doesn't matter." Kyle pointed to a spot in the Alps. "We're here. Roughly. Where's the cabin?"

"It matters to me." Sebastian swallowed thickly. Ben had been his hero. His savior.

Kyle watched him for a moment. Then he said, "I don't know. Safe to say he knows more than you do, but I'm not sure he knows quite how deadly your father's business has become." He pointed to the map again. "Where's the cabin?"

Sebastian forced thoughts of Ben from his mind and examined the map. "Not near here. A lot higher into the mountains, in the middle of nowhere, really. Near Courmayeur." He pointed to a faint line. "West. If we follow this road, we should get there. I'll have to try and remember."

The sedan came to life as Kyle turned the key in the ignition. "You'll remember."

Sebastian wasn't sure if it was encouragement or a threat.

As they traveled west into the Alps, the rain fell unrelentingly. The day became unnaturally dark, and while at first the break from the oppressive heat was welcome, soon gooseflesh dotted Sebastian's arms, even beneath his shirt. He rubbed his skin, shivering.

With a stab of his finger on the controls, Kyle turned off the air-conditioning. "Just say something if you're cold."

"Like you'd give a shit."

Kyle said nothing in response, keeping his eyes on the narrow, winding road. As they traveled deeper into the Alps and away from the tourist areas, they saw fewer and fewer cars. By late afternoon the rain had begun to crystallize into wet clumps of snow. Snow in the Alps certainly wasn't unheard of in summer, but considering the recent heat, it was surreal.

Sebastian couldn't take the silence anymore. "Weird weather, huh?"

Kyle frowned. "What?"

"This snow. It's weird."

"What's your point?"

Huffing, Sebastian looked out the window. "Never mind. Just trying to make conversation."

"Why?"

"Because that's what people do?" Sebastian rubbed his face. "I guess I just wanted things to be normal for, like, five minutes. But you're probably not used to making small talk with your victims."

He swore for a moment that Kyle was trying to suppress a *smile*, but he was surely imagining things. Kyle drove on silently, adjusting the windshield wipers as the wet snow intensified.

Sebastian was starving. He'd also needed to go to the bathroom for more than an hour but stubbornly refused to ask. As they neared a tiny village, Sebastian cleared his throat, unable to hold it any longer. "I need to stop."

Kyle glanced at him. "Are we there?"

"No, but I need to piss. If that's okay with you."

There was no response, but Kyle pulled off the road at a tiny café. "You're not going to try and run away or do anything stupid. Right? Because it'll be the last mistake you ever make. But if you do what I say, I'll make sure you stay safe. Your father's men are already looking for you, and believe me, you'll never survive on your own."

Sebastian wished he could argue, but sadly he had a feeling Kyle was right. He nodded, and they went inside. In the tiny, dingy bathroom, he relieved himself and considered his options. It was disheartening, to say the least. If he tried to escape, where would he go? He couldn't return home, that much was certain. He'd made some friends at Harvard, but none he could call in a crisis. Only Peter had been that close to him, and of course Peter was nowhere to be found.

The terrible feeling of betrayal rose up unbidden. It churned his stomach as he thought about Peter somewhere, living the high life with Arrigo's money. Far away from Sebastian and likely not thinking of him at all. While Sebastian had not a euro to his name. Not even a piece of ID.

He shook his head. *Focus.* What he needed was a weapon. But even if he had one, could he really hope to overpower Kyle? He'd experienced firsthand how strong Kyle was and how quick. Maybe if he had a gun. But where would he get one? He rubbed his forehead and choked on a bitter laugh. Even if he did have a gun—if he somehow took Kyle's—could he really use it on Kyle? *On anyone?*

He didn't know. He hadn't been able to bring himself to shoot the wide-eyed deer frozen in his sights when his father had forced him to go hunting once. What made him think he could pull the trigger on a human being? It would have to be an absolute last resort, which left him where he'd started. With no plan and no way out except to trust Kyle wasn't going to kill him just yet.

As he zipped his trousers, the bathroom door opened. Kyle surveyed him, and Sebastian realized he'd been lost in contemplation for longer than he thought. Kyle held up a paper bag. "Food. Come on."

They ate in the car as the snow began to accumulate on the ground. When he finished his sandwich, Kyle scrunched up his napkin and tossed it into the empty bag. "Tell me if you recognize anything. It'll be dark before too much longer. Especially in this weather."

"Okay."

It had been slow going, and as the snow continued, Sebastian became less certain he'd be able to see any landmarks, let alone recognize them. But before long he spotted a wooden signpost: MARIA TERESA. "There. Turn right."

"Maria Teresa?"

"It's the name of a chalet. The cabin is in the same vicinity."

Kyle slowed the car to make the turn. "You sure?" A moment later he added, "Right. Your mother's name."

Sebastian shifted in his seat. "Yes. I remember saying my father should name his cabin after her too." He had to swallow thickly over the thought of his mother. Her twinkling smile, her gentle touch. *How could he do it? How?*

Kyle said nothing and turned onto the road, which was even narrower. Pine trees shadowed the lane, and the tires slipped in the wet snow. They crawled along, passing the chalet, which appeared empty. The road was little more than a dirt path at this point, but Sebastian was certain the cabin was at the end of it.

The sun, completely obscured by the clouds and snow, was setting as the old building finally came into view. As Sebastian remembered, it was nothing fancy. His one visit as a youth had been his last, although his father brought Ben up each year to hunt.

As he stepped out of the car, Sebastian hugged his arms to his body tightly, shivering in the cold as the wet snow fell. He hurried toward the porch, but Kyle yanked him back. "Don't move."

Sebastian stayed put as Kyle circled the cabin, keen eyes searching. When he disappeared around the back, Sebastian peered at the thick forest surrounding them. His leather shoes weren't meant for running—let alone running in the Alps.

Besides, Kyle had proven he was faster.

A moment later Kyle reappeared. He dropped down and examined under the porch, shining a small but powerful flashlight into the murk. When he seemed satisfied, he climbed the creaky wooden stairs and landed a powerful kick to the front door. After another, it splintered and gave way.

Inside, it hadn't changed much from Sebastian's dim childhood memories. The utilitarian, wooden furniture was a marked difference from the opulence Arrigo usually favored. The cabin was a snapshot in time, with an ancient wood-burning stove and no electricity. Kyle lit the lantern sitting on the solid old table and began searching.

Sebastian watched as he methodically explored the room. There was no bedroom, and the bathroom was an outhouse. A double bed sat against the wall in one corner, and when Sebastian sat on it, the springs creaked.

It seemed as if Kyle forgot he was even there as he hunted, and Sebastian wondered if the keys were still in the sedan. Doubtful, and even if they were, he didn't think he'd be fast enough to get to the car before Kyle caught him. He thought again of Kyle's hard, strong body pressing him down into the ground. How his mouth had tasted the night before. The jolt of excitement and pleasure when he'd pushed his finger inside Sebastian.

Abruptly he stood and began pacing. Kyle's attention was now on the wood box beside the stove, where a few pieces of chopped wood remained inside. Sebastian couldn't imagine his father would have hidden a chemical weapon in there and was about to say as much when Kyle pulled firmly on the box and it slid out, revealing an old metal safe about three feet high.

Sitting back on his heels, Kyle inspected it. He leaned in closely, turning the knob this way and that.

"Can you crack it?" Sebastian asked. The sooner they got the powder, the sooner he could…what? What exactly was he going to do? Kyle had promised to help him, but, realistically, Sebastian knew Kyle was just as likely to put a bullet in his brain the minute he had what he wanted.

"Of course. It'll take some time. The older safes are actually harder. Fingerprint scanners and other modern gizmos make it much easier."

"How?" A deeply unpleasant thought occurred. "Do you…cut people's fingers off?"

At this Kyle smirked. "Only when I have to."

"That's really comforting."

"Most people don't wipe off the fingerprint scanner. You just need to lift the print from the scanner itself, and you're in."

"Good to know." Sebastian peered out the small front window. The wind had begun howling, and the pane shook slightly. Outside, visibility was poor and getting worse as night settled in. *Fantastic.*

"Get my bag from the car. Backseat." Kyle glanced over his shoulder. "I have the keys, so don't even think about it."

"If you have the keys, how am I supposed to get in?"

Kyle raised an eyebrow as he pulled the keys from his pocket and pressed a button. Sebastian could hear the faint *chirp* as the car unlocked. "Hurry up."

"*Yes, sir,*" Sebastian muttered under his breath.

Outside he gasped at how much colder it was now that night had fallen. Slipping in the wet snow and mud, he rushed to the car and flung open the back door. A brown duffel bag sat on the seat as promised. Sebastian grabbed it and hurried back to the cabin.

He dropped the bag by Kyle and eyed the stove. "Can we start a fire?"

"No. This won't take long."

Sebastian wrapped his arms around himself and grumbled as he resumed pacing. "At least you have a jacket."

Apparently ignoring him, Kyle pulled out a leather case from his duffel. He unzipped it and removed some kind of metal tool. "Any guesses as to what the combination might be?"

"How many numbers are there?"

"With this make and model, should be five."

Sebastian pondered. Should he really try to help Kyle break into the safe? Perhaps if his father's men showed up, he could reason with them. He thought of the cold, dark eyes of the man in the garage and sighed. *Just get this over with.* "Try fifty-two, sixteen, thirty-eight, seven, twenty-five."

Kyle turned the dial, alternating left and right. He turned the handle, but the safe remained locked. "Nope. Try again."

"I don't know. Maybe a different combination of those numbers. They're all to do with my *nonna*. This is her place, so he would probably have been thinking of her when he set the combination. Or he was thinking of something else entirely. I don't know."

Kyle tried a few more iterations of the numbers before reaching for another tool. He worked silently, head close to the metal door of the safe as he listened with something that looked like a modified stethoscope. After ten minutes of pacing, Sebastian felt like he had to break the unnerving quiet.

"So, how do I know you're really a spy and not just some mercenary?"

"I'm really a spy," Kyle said as he turned the dial on the safe.

Sebastian studied him. Kyle seemed like he was telling the truth, but then so had Steven. "You got lucky with the guard monitoring the cameras. Father said he was watching football. If he'd been doing his job, they would have caught you."

"It wasn't luck. The man's a huge AC Milan fan. Our contact made sure he was working the cameras that night. And I'm fast. It might have been closer, but they wouldn't have caught me."

A spy would have contacts who could arrange things like that, wouldn't he? At least that's how it worked in Bond films. "You're awfully sure of yourself." Sebastian shivered. "It's freezing. Hurry up."

"Well, shut up and let me concentrate. I only have one number left."

"They're always a lot faster in the movies." Sebastian stalked over to the stove and opened the door. As he tossed a log inside, Kyle was suddenly there, whipping him around, fingers digging into Sebastian's arm.

He towered over Sebastian. "I said *no fire*. I'm in charge, remember?"

"*Vaffanculo*. Fuck you." Sebastian tugged his arm free. He knew he was being childish, but he couldn't stop himself. "I don't take orders from you."

"Yes, you do. Now get a blanket, sit down, and shut up."

Sebastian stood his ground, toe-to-toe with Kyle. "No. Maybe I'll take my chances with my father and his men after all. Anything would be better than being with you."

Kyle's jaw clenched and his nostrils flared. "Sit. Down."

"Fuck. You." All the anger and fear and tension of the day boiled over, and Sebastian shoved against Kyle's chest.

A moment later he was tumbling backward, landing on the squeaky bed with Kyle on top of him. Kyle stared down, his gaze dangerous, Sebastian's wrists in his hands. "Are you done?"

They were both breathing heavily, and as Sebastian struggled to free himself, he only succeeded in rubbing against Kyle. "Go to hell." As punctuation he spit into Kyle's face, his saliva spraying Kyle's cheek.

For a long moment, Kyle was completely still, and a fresh, icy tendril of fear uncoiled in Sebastian's gut. *Too far.* Then Kyle dove at him, tongue driving inside as Sebastian gasped. His body responded immediately as Kyle mastered his mouth, leaving him breathless.

Suddenly Kyle tore away and rolled off the bed, shoving Sebastian to the floor. Sebastian kicked and punched at him. "Get off me!"

Kyle ignored him as he lunged at the table, dousing the lantern and plunging the cabin into darkness as the first bullets shattered the window.

CHAPTER FOUR

SWEARING UNDER HIS breath, Kyle drew his weapon as he reached for Sebastian, yanking him up and propelling him into the far corner of the cabin. There was only one window and one door, and both were currently being riddled with bullets.

He pushed Sebastian down behind him and crouched, pulse racing as he assessed the situation. He had no idea how many were outside, but they were clearly well armed. He should have had the safe open by now, but instead he'd let himself get distracted.

Now he had an unknown number of opponents covering the only exit, and he didn't even have the Chimera. The men outside could be on the trail of either him or Sebastian, but Kyle felt their presence could mean the Chimera was indeed inside the safe. He could send Sebastian out as a distraction, but he immediately dismissed the notion. He told himself if the Chimera wasn't in the cabin, Sebastian could still be useful. The fact that he didn't like the thought of Sebastian dead was irrelevant.

After the first initial burst of gunfire, silence settled as the gunmen assessed the situation. Kyle pulled out his gun and checked the clip. Almost full. He glanced between the door and the safe. He didn't know how many opponents were out there, and couldn't hold them off and crack the last number on the safe at the same time.

Sebastian frantically held out his hand. He whispered, "Give it to me. Hurry up and open the damn safe."

"So you can shoot me in the back? I don't think so."

"I wouldn't do that!" he insisted.

Another volley of bullets tore into the cabin. "I thought you wanted to take your chances with your father's men. Here's your opportunity."

Sebastian shook his head rapidly. "I changed my mind." He took a shaky breath. "I'll stick with you." He watched the door, eyes wide.

He knew he was a fool to trust the kid, but he didn't have a choice if he wanted to open the safe and get the Chimera. After removing the silencer and pocketing it, he handed the weapon to Sebastian, keeping his voice low. "Just point and shoot. They're waiting to see what we'll do. If anyone tries to come in, shoot. If you hear any movement on the porch, shoot. If you—"

"I'll shoot."

In the darkness, Kyle couldn't make out Sebastian's expression, but he admired the steel in the young man's tone. "And remember, those men out there will kill you and never think twice. You need me to survive. You put a bullet in me, and you might as well put one in yourself."

Sebastian nodded. Crouching, they made their way to the safe, and Kyle pressed his ear against the metal, listening for the telltale clicking. He'd already isolated the contact points, parked the wheels, and determined the first four numbers. Sebastian had been right about three of them, and now Kyle would try thirty-eight as the final number.

Of course, he'd need to be able to see. The light on his multi-device was handy in a tight spot. With a push of his finger, he illuminated the face, trying to shield the light as best he could as he twisted the dial on the safe.

As he pushed the handle, the safe remained stubbornly closed, and wood creaked outside. "They're coming. Get ready," he whispered.

Footsteps hammered the porch, and bullets rang out on

schedule as Kyle tried seven as the last number. He yanked on the handle, but it stood firm. Sebastian began shooting back, and Kyle glanced behind him to see if anyone had made it inside. Not yet. Pressing his ear to the safe, he tried one last spin of the dial.

Wood splintered amid the thunder of gunfire. A bullet whizzed overhead far too close for comfort, and Kyle gave up on the combination. Grabbing his duffel, he yanked the gun from Sebastian's shaking hands. The door was opening, and Kyle shot at a shadowed figure that disappeared, tumbling into the darkness of the porch. In the wind, the door slammed shut.

Sebastian tugged on Kyle's arm. "There's a crawl space. Hatch by the bed."

Kyle followed as they scuttled across the floor. Sebastian flung aside an ancient rug, and Kyle cursed himself for not looking under it to determine all possible points of exit. He'd been inexcusably sloppy—too distracted by Sebastian. The wood groaned as Sebastian pried open the hatch, and Kyle fired off a few rounds to disguise the noise.

After Sebastian dropped into the hole, Kyle rummaged in his bag for a small flash bomb. It wouldn't cause much damage but would distract their enemies. He pulled the pin and threw the canister out the window before following Sebastian. Under the cabin, there was barely room to move. Sebastian was already almost at the back of the structure when the explosive went off with a flash of light and a deafening *boom.*

Kyle quickly caught up with him and grabbed his leg before he could crawl out from underneath the building. "I have the gun. I go first." He shimmied past Sebastian and checked that it was clear. "We're going to run straight into the trees and then down. Go!"

They sprang out and raced to the forest's edge, and no bullets followed. The wet snow continued to fall, making the ground a mash of mud and slush. Sebastian slid wildly in his leather dress shoes and struggled to keep up with Kyle, who was better off in his sturdy black work boots.

Once they were quite a way down, Kyle stopped. The hillside had become rocky, and their path would be less visible than it was in the mud of the forest floor. It would have to do. With a tug on a panting Sebastian's arm, he turned and went back the way they came.

Sebastian resisted. "Wait! We can't—"

Laying his finger over Sebastian's lips, Kyle leaned in close. "Trust me."

He led the way back up the hill for a dozen yards before veering off to the right, away from the cabin. With his pocketknife, he wrenched a branch free and concealed their new tracks, the needles smoothing out where their feet sank into the snowy mess. Visibility was very low, and he hoped their opponents would miss this offshoot from their original path. By a rocky outcropping, he crouched down to wait and listen. Sebastian huddled at his side, fortunately keeping quiet.

The forest was still aside from the whistle of the wind and falling snow. Kyle could faintly smell the acrid remains of the explosion when the wind changed direction. Just when he was going to tell Sebastian the plan, the sounds of muffled footsteps reached his ears. Sebastian tensed beside him, and Kyle placed a hand on his shoulder. He squeezed lightly.

A number of men—four, he thought—came slip sliding down the hill. He couldn't see their faces through the dense pine trees and blowing snow. One swore in Italian as he stumbled. Then they disappeared into the whiteout, following Kyle and Sebastian's original path. Kyle waited, his muscles coiled and tense.

Five minutes passed, and then ten. After fifteen Kyle decided the ruse had worked. He turned to Sebastian, who was still crouched beside him, his lips pressed tightly together, arms wound around his body. "We're going back up. It's the last place they'll look."

"To the cabin?" It sounded as if that was the last place Sebastian wanted to go.

"No. We'll have to find shelter somewhere else. Come on." He paused before standing. "You're doing good."

He didn't wait for a response and propelled Sebastian in front of him as they climbed. The incline wasn't steep enough to use their hands, but it was still hard going in the thin mountain air. Kyle wiped out their tracks as best he could while keeping an eye out for any of their opponents.

With a soft cry, Sebastian tripped and sprawled on the ground. Kyle hauled him up immediately and pushed him onward. "You're all right. Keep going." He could barely feel his fingers, and he knew if they stopped in the snow, it could be deadly. Hypothermia was very near at hand.

Sebastian stumbled again but kept moving without complaint. As they neared the top of the ridge, Kyle guided them farther to the right. He'd briefly considered the Maria Teresa, but it was too obvious a choice if the men on their tail figured out that they'd come back up.

Finally they came across what appeared to be a tiny hunting shelter. There was no lock on the door, and inside were only a rickety chair and a thin pallet on the floor. An old blanket covered the pallet, but it didn't look as if anyone had used the lodge in some years. Still, the roof was sound, and with no windows they were protected from the elements once the door was closed.

The chair wouldn't hold up to an assault, but after his eyes adjusted to the dark, Kyle positioned it under the door handle as best he could. The noise of it breaking would at least serve as a warning. He turned to Sebastian, whose teeth chattered audibly. Blood dripped down Sebastian's cheek. "Sit."

Sebastian did as he was told and lowered himself to the musty pallet. He shook now more than shivered, and Kyle knelt down and gently took his head in his hands to examine the gash on Sebastian's forehead. He carried a small first-aid kit in his bag and pulled out a pad and bottle of disinfectant.

"This will sting." Yet as he dabbed the wound, Sebastian barely flinched, and he stared into space, seemingly dazed. Kyle brushed back Sebastian's hair, a completely unfamiliar feeling of tenderness welling up. "You'll be okay."

Sebastian met his gaze, and Kyle fought the urge to take him in his arms. He tore his eyes away and ripped open a bandage. Since when did he care what happened to a mark or how he or she was feeling? *Get the job done. This is business.*

Kyle quickly covered the gash with a small bandage and decided on the next course of action. His fingers were clumsy due to the cold, and he struggled to unbutton Sebastian's shirt. However, this seemed to slice through Sebastian's haze of shock and he pushed at Kyle's hands.

"What are you doing?"

"Our clothes are soaked. It's freezing, and we're going to die of hypothermia if we don't get warm. If we wait too long, we'll miss the window of opportunity. So stand up and get your clothes off." He didn't wait for a reply before pulling Sebastian to his feet.

As Sebastian worked on his shirt, Kyle picked up the old blanket. It was only a few strides to the other side of the shack and the dirt and dust would be thick in the air, but he couldn't risk going outside for the sake of their comfort. He shook out the blanket in the corner as best he could and turned back.

Sebastian had just peeled off his sodden pants, and stood in only his boxer briefs. He'd found a hook on the wall and went about hanging his clothing from it, leaving his shoes neatly by the pallet. In the dim light, Kyle could see the surprisingly muscular planes of Sebastian's chest, the roundness of his firm ass and his toned legs. For a math geek, Sebastian had the body of a champion swimmer.

Focus, goddamn it. Kyle hung his jacket carefully on another hook. He stripped off quickly, keeping his gun as he went to the pallet. Sebastian turned to him and gasped. "You're...you're..." He waved his hand to indicate Kyle's nakedness.

"Everything's wet. And body heat is the best way to warm up." His gaze traveled down Sebastian's body. "Are those wet?" He nodded at the underwear.

Sebastian nodded and, with a deep breath, yanked them off. Kyle couldn't see the blush stain Sebastian's cheeks, but he knew it was there. Forcing himself to go slowly, he approached Sebastian's shaking form. Unfurling the blanket, he wrapped it around them as he pressed against Sebastian and led him down to the pallet.

After apparently holding his breath as the seconds ticked by, Sebastian finally exhaled and lay back. Kyle covered his body, rubbing Sebastian's skin roughly with his hands. Although he had to admit he wanted Sebastian, he had no intention of having him. He needed to keep his head in the game. He'd let himself be dangerously distracted.

Yet the proximity of Sebastian's body and the sound and feel of his little breaths against Kyle's neck were intoxicating. Over time as an operative, Kyle had learned how to master his desires and his physical responses, but as he rubbed Sebastian to get his blood circulating, it took considerable effort to maintain his detachment.

Sebastian, however, began to respond after a few minutes as his body warmed. His cock filled and nudged Kyle's belly, and Sebastian turned his head away, clearly mortified.

"It's all right. It's normal." Kyle kept his tone calm. "It just means it's working. You're safe. I'm not going to do anything."

At this Sebastian met his gaze. "You're not?" He sounded decidedly disappointed.

"No. I'm not." Kyle reached around and rubbed Sebastian's back, keeping his touch rough and clinical.

Sebastian's voice was muffled against Kyle's neck. "I know you were acting last night. But back at the cabin...I thought..."

Kyle mentally kicked himself for letting his temper—and his desire—get the better of him. "Sleep. We need to move as soon as the weather clears."

Sebastian wormed out from beneath Kyle and curled away from him. "Pretty stupid," he muttered.

Despite himself, Kyle had to ask. "What's stupid, exactly? Waiting until the weather clears? Because it may be a summer blizzard, but it's a blizzard all the same, and if you'd like to get lost in it, that can be arranged."

"No. I just meant it was stupid of me to think for a moment that you actually wanted me for real. Never mind, okay? I'm just feeling a little sorry for myself."

Kyle watched Sebastian in the gloom, his body shivering as he curled into himself. "Well, freezing to death won't help." He pressed up behind Sebastian, dragging him back against his chest. After a moment he added, "It's been a hell of a day. Don't beat yourself up."

"Because you'll do it for me?" Sebastian joked.

Kyle found himself smiling. "Exactly."

"I can't believe I actually *shot* at someone today. I could have killed one of those guys."

Kyle snorted. "If you were lucky."

"Yeah, not as easy as it looks in the movies. Not that I want shooting anyone to be *easy*, but...well, you know what I mean."

Sebastian settled into his arms, the tremors subsiding. Kyle couldn't remember the last time he'd actually *slept* with someone. A countess a few months ago in Spain, but that had been part of the job. *This* is a job too, he reminded himself. He breathed deeply, but it only sent Sebastian's alluring scent right to his head. His cock was flush with Sebastian's round, firm ass, and Kyle fought to keep his desire in check.

It certainly didn't help that Sebastian was shifting back, rubbing against Kyle. He rotated his hips, and Kyle spoke sharply. "Go to sleep."

"Oh, sorry. Just trying to get comfortable."

He rubbed his ass against Kyle again, and Kyle's cock responded, despite his best efforts. He gripped Sebastian's hip. "Stop. You're not thinking clearly."

Sebastian took a shaky breath. "I want you. Since the first moment I saw you." Sebastian arched back, squeezing Kyle's swelling hardness between his cheeks. "You don't need to be a gentleman, or whatever it is you're trying to do. Please, I just want to feel…"

Sebastian had been through hell, yet he had a strength and resiliency Kyle admired. Most people would have lost it or given up after the day Sebastian had had. After a long moment, Kyle released his grip on Sebastian's hip and reached down to take his swelling cock in hand. "What?"

"Alive."

What could it hurt? It would warm them up. He rolled Sebastian onto his back as he leaned down to kiss him. He hovered over Sebastian's mouth. "It doesn't mean anything."

Sebastian nodded and wound his fingers into Kyle's hair as he kissed him, their tongues dueling for control. Kyle pressed him down onto the pallet and took both their cocks in his own hand. Sebastian moaned as their hard flesh rubbed together. He was already leaking and slick.

Moving down Sebastian's body, Kyle tasted him, squeezing and biting his nipples in turn, which made Sebastian gasp and shudder with pleasure. As Kyle moved lower, he lessened the pressure, and Sebastian raised his hips, trying to get more friction. As the head of Sebastian's dick hit Kyle's chin, Sebastian seemed to realize how low Kyle had gone.

His breathing hitched, and his voice was hoarse. "Yes. *Yes.*"

"What do you want?" Kyle couldn't resist teasing a little. He ran a fingertip down the length of Sebastian's straining shaft, tracing the vein on the underside.

"You know," he groaned, arching up.

"'Fraid not." Kyle ran his fingertips over Sebastian's sac next, eliciting another low moan. "You'll have to be more clear." Kyle rarely played like this, usually taking and giving pleasure quickly and with little to no conversation. He wasn't sure what had gotten into him, but he wanted to see Sebastian smile. *Must be the hypothermia.*

Laughing, Sebastian grabbed a fistful of Kyle's hair. "Come on."

Kyle flicked the slit of Sebastian's cock with his tongue.

With a growl, Sebastian tightened his grasp. "Suck me."

Desire hot in his veins, Kyle descended, taking Sebastian in deeply, swirling his tongue. Sebastian throbbed in Kyle's mouth as Kyle sucked him, his lips suctioned tightly. Little sharp breaths escaped Sebastian's lips as he writhed beneath Kyle's touch. When Kyle pushed the tip of a finger into his hole, Sebastian yanked out a few strands of Kyle's hair as he came, pulsing into Kyle's throat.

As Sebastian shuddered with pleasure, his head thrown back, eyes closed, Kyle swallowed, relishing the salty musk on his tongue. He milked Sebastian, teasing out as many aftershocks as he could.

"God. Kyle." Sebastian relaxed, utterly boneless.

The sound of his name from Sebastian's lips was unexpectedly arousing. He'd surprised himself earlier by telling the kid his real name, but it had just slipped out. Kyle stretched over him as he kissed him thoroughly, making sure Sebastian could taste himself. Sebastian smiled and mimicked Kyle's earlier question. "What do you want?"

What he wanted was to throw Sebastian's legs up and plow into him, lose himself in his tightness and heat. But if Kyle was right and it would be Sebastian's first time, he didn't want it to be because Sebastian was taking comfort where he could get it after his world had fallen apart. Sebastian said he knew what he wanted, but there was an unmistakable innocence mixed with Sebastian's aggression. For a reason he couldn't understand, Kyle wanted better for him.

But he still needed release. "Your mouth."

Sebastian's eyes widened, and his spent dick twitched against Kyle. He jerked out a nod and opened his jaw as Kyle straddled his chest and pushed inside. The wet, delicious warmth made Kyle moan, and he slid back and forth, keeping his movements shallow as Sebastian took him in.

Leaning forward and bracing his hands on the wall, Kyle rocked his hips and thrust into Sebastian's eager mouth. Sebastian's full lips stretched around him, and Kyle groaned as he watched his cock move in and out. As the pleasure started to build, he increased the tempo, and Sebastian took him enthusiastically, his fingers digging into Kyle's hips as he urged him on.

Then Sebastian pressed a finger to the sensitive skin behind Kyle's balls, and Kyle's whole body tightened as he emptied, biting his lip to stifle a gasp as the intense pleasure swept over him. Sebastian swallowed around him, and when Kyle pulled out, he spilled a last few drops over Sebastian's chin and cheeks. Sebastian's tongue darted out to snatch them, and Kyle felt a last spasm of pleasure as he spread out over Sebastian's body once more.

As they caught their breath, Sebastian wrapped his arms about Kyle, pulling him close. Kyle let him and spread the blanket out over them again. He listened for any sounds outside, silently cursing himself yet again for allowing such a monumental distraction. *Maybe the Association is right. I am off my game.*

But with a sated Sebastian warm in his arms, he couldn't quite regret it.

SEBASTIAN WOKE WITH a start, blinking in the unfamiliar darkness. He wasn't in his room and—

Everything flooded back as Kyle rubbed his arm slowly. "It's all right," he whispered. He didn't sound as if he'd been sleeping.

Exhaling, Sebastian processed the hard floor, the cold air, and the warm man wrapped around him. He had slept with his head on Kyle's chest, and he could hear the steady, reassuring *thump-thump-thump* of Kyle's heart. They were under the scratchy old blanket, but it was their bodies that generated the scant heat.

As he burrowed down into Kyle's arms, Sebastian tried to make sense of it all. His life had become unrecognizable in a mere day. His father and—all the more devastating—his brother, were involved in criminal dealings Sebastian couldn't even begin to fathom.

Then there was Kyle. Steven. Whatever his name was. Liar. Spy. Thief. Killer. Undoubtedly dangerous and not to be trusted. Yet Sebastian was drawn to him, to the man who now stroked Sebastian's skin with such a gentle, comforting touch. *Maybe this is what Stockholm Syndrome is like.*

He had to remember Kyle was responsible for ruining his life. He'd never be able to return to Harvard and his mathematics now. His father wanted him dead, and what Arrigo Brambani wanted, he got. There was no way out. For all he knew, the assassins on their trail were outside at this very minute, readying their guns.

Kyle spoke. "We should go now. Before the sun rises."

"Where? I mean, how? Is it safe to go back for the car?"

"We have to. It's too far to walk. If they're waiting, we'll deal with it. If they're not, we'll ditch the car in a town and find another way down. A bus would be good. We can blend in."

"Then what?"

There was a long moment of silence. "One step at a time."

Kyle extricated himself from Sebastian, flinging the blanket off without warning. "Get dressed."

Sebastian's clothes were damp, but he pulled them on quickly. Kyle's gun still sat by the pallet, and Sebastian looked at it from the corner of his eye. Kyle was bent over, lacing his boots. Maybe this was Sebastian's chance to get some control of the situation. He couldn't trust Kyle, no matter how attractive he was or how his kisses made Sebastian's head spin. *He couldn't.*

Slowly, as casually as possible, he took a step toward the gun. "Don't."

Sebastian froze. Kyle's head was still down. "What?"

Standing, Kyle walked to the pallet and picked up the gun. He stared at Sebastian, expression hard. "Just don't."

A denial was on Sebastian's lips, but Kyle had already turned away. Any understanding they may have found in each other's arms had evaporated. At the door, Kyle listened carefully, gun at the ready. With a hand motion, he beckoned Sebastian behind him. Then he eased the door open.

Breath caught in his throat, Sebastian waited for gunfire. But all was silent. Kyle slipped out first, and Sebastian stayed close. The snow had stopped, and the wind was gone. The forest was utterly still, and Sebastian scanned the trees for any signs of movement as he followed Kyle.

The air was still frigid, and he forced himself to breathe as they made their way back to the cabin. Sebastian was glad Kyle's sense of direction was better than his. He had to assume Kyle was going the right way, and sure enough, the cabin soon came into sight.

Kyle's breath was hot against Sebastian's ear. "Wait here. Keep your head down. I'll whistle when it's clear."

Sebastian was about to ask what he should do if it *wasn't* clear, but Kyle was already gone, somehow moving soundlessly through the trees despite his large frame. Crouching down, Sebastian waited. His pulse racing, he concentrated on breathing steadily.

Every few seconds he looked over his shoulders, but he could see no one approaching in the darkness.

After what felt like an eternity, a bird's whistle echoed in the air. It took Sebastian a few seconds to realize this was Kyle's signal. At least he hoped it was. Taking a breath, he moved, trying to keep quiet but likely failing utterly.

He rounded the cabin, but Kyle was nowhere in sight. Squinting, he could see the cabin porch was charred after the explosion, but the structure seemed mostly unaffected. For a moment Sebastian felt the urge to burn it to the ground just to spite his father.

Instead he carefully made his way over the charred wood and inside. Kyle knelt by the safe, his ear pressed against it once more. Sebastian wrapped a blanket around himself and perched on the edge of the bed, waiting quietly. He suggested some other numbers, but none matched. Finally Kyle tensed and carefully depressed the handle. The door opened, and he peered inside. Sebastian held his breath.

With a harsh exhale, Kyle stood, slammed the safe shut. "Either it was never here, or they took it."

He was clearly furious, and Sebastian wasn't sure exactly whom the anger was directed at. "So...what do we do now?"

Muttering to himself, Kyle pulled his gun from inside his coat, and Sebastian jumped to his feet, backing away. *God, please. Don't let me die like this!* He was almost to the door when Kyle grabbed him and yanked him back.

"Please!" Sebastian's voice was shrill with panic.

Kyle simply peered at him with furrowed brows, his free hand still gripping Sebastian's upper arm. Then he relaxed slightly, still holding on. "I'm not going to kill you. You can't go running outside until I check if it's clear."

"But...you already did."

"Fifteen minutes ago. Anyone could have arrived in the meantime." He released Sebastian. "Stay behind me. Remember, I've got the gun. I always go first."

"Right. Got it." Sebastian told himself firmly that he would never forget Kyle had a gun. *Never forget that he's a killer.*

Luckily the coast was still clear, and after Kyle examined the sedan's undercarriage and engine, they drove off down the slushy lane, the night still hanging on even as the sky began to brighten on the horizon. Sebastian fiddled with the heat controls, turning it up as far as he could. He felt like he'd never be warm again.

As they passed the ski chalet and turned onto the bigger road, Sebastian rubbed his hands over the vent. He was about to ask Kyle again what they'd do once they were off the mountain, when headlights flared to life behind them. Sebastian whipped around, adrenaline shooting through him as he watched the rapidly approaching vehicle.

Kyle simply said, "Seat belt," as he slammed on the accelerator and they roared forward into the dawn.

CHAPTER FIVE

I GNORING THE APPROACHING car, Kyle concentrated on the twisting road. He took the turns wide and fast, taking the chance that there were no cars climbing the old mountain road this early in the day. The freak snow that had fallen the night before was already melting, and Kyle suspected it would be hot as hell again by noon.

Beside him, he could sense Sebastian's terror as they whipped around slick turns. But Sebastian said nothing, not even when they skidded alarmingly close to the edge of the mountain as they flew off the forest road and onto the two-lane paved highway. There was a screech of brakes from an approaching car, but Kyle ducked in front of it and they were off down the mountain.

Glancing in the rearview mirror, Kyle couldn't see their pursuers. He hoped they hadn't made the turn, but a moment later he saw a flash of the car before rounding another curve. Now that the sun was rising, he could see the car following them was a black sedan much like the one he was driving.

The next bend in the road was not so much a curve as a *corner*, and they scraped along the barrier, the metal screeching. Sebastian let out a gasp as a car suddenly appeared in front of them, and Kyle jerked them back into their lane seconds before impact.

A small mountain town spread out below them, and Kyle considered their options as he sped around the next curve. They'd meet more traffic soon, with tourists clogging the alpine roads. Better to evade and take cover. A moment later more shots rang out, and the choice was made for them as the back right tire blew, sending the car reeling out of control.

Gripping the wheel, Kyle jerked them off the highway at the first side road. They exploded into the sleepy village, the remains of the tire shuddering and keeping the car off balance. Ahead Kyle spotted an alley between two small buildings.

"Get ready to get out."

"What? Where?" Sebastian shouted.

Wrenching the wheel, Kyle barreled into the narrow alley, which was fortunately empty. As the car scraped along the passenger side, Kyle pulled his seat belt off and pressed the button to release Sebastian's before throwing the car into park and killing the engine. As he leaped out, yanking Sebastian out behind him, the revving engine of the approaching car filled the air.

He shoved Sebastian to the muddy ground—"Under!"—and slithered after him, leaving the sedan door open. The other car roared into the alley before the brakes shrieked. For a long moment Kyle held his breath, his hand on the back of Sebastian's neck, ready to cover his mouth if need be. The car's undercarriage radiated heat only a few inches above them.

Then the enemy car roared forward again, taking off the open door of the sedan with a scream of metal on metal as they tore into the village after their prey. Kyle exhaled slowly. Their pursuers would think they were on foot somewhere in town, perhaps trying to acquire another vehicle. Instead they'd hole up and wait. It certainly wasn't Kyle's favorite method of evasion, and part of him wanted to just confront the men and finish it.

Beside him Sebastian moved, shaking just a tiny bit. Kyle smoothed his hand over Sebastian's head. "We're going to wait a minute and then find a place to hide."

Sebastian nodded. "Okay."

"You're doing good."

"Okay," Sebastian repeated.

"Keep low." He pointed up. "It's hot." They slithered out and onto their feet, encountering an elderly Italian man approaching the car, his bushy eyebrows disappearing into his hairline. Kyle propelled Sebastian down the alley. To the man, who was now asking questions in Italian, he called back, "*Scusa.*"

At the end of the alley, Kyle pulled his gun, keeping Sebastian safely behind him. There was no sign of their enemies, and despite the noise the sedan had surely made scraping into the alley, only the old man had come to investigate so far. That surely wouldn't last, and moving carefully, Kyle led Sebastian over a few streets, looking for an empty house. Halfway down the lane, a family climbed into their car. The mother was loading a cooler into the trunk.

Kyle angled over until they were behind the house, keeping low. He listened for the car leaving, and then crept to the back door. As he suspected, due to the trusting nature of small-town denizens, it was unlocked. A moment later they were safely inside the family's kitchen. The smell of bacon and eggs lingered, and Kyle's stomach growled in response.

"Stay," he whispered and quickly checked the small two-story house. Empty. Finally some good luck. Back in the rustic kitchen, Sebastian stood exactly where Kyle had left him by the stove. Opening the fridge, Kyle pulled out some cold meats. "Sit." He nodded to the rectangular wooden table.

"What are you doing? We can't *steal their food.*"

Kyle barely suppressed the urge to roll his eyes. "Yes, we can. We can't exactly go for a stroll down to the local café, and we need to eat." He glanced down at his filthy clothing. "We also need to clean up. We'll stick out like sore thumbs covered in mud."

Something flickered across Sebastian's face. "Yeah, I guess *we* will."

"What's that supposed to mean?"

"Nothing." Sebastian shrugged. "You're just talking about us like we're a team or something."

The kid was right. He narrowed his eyes. "*You and I* have a common goal. Don't get carried away." He opened the bread box and tossed a loaf to Sebastian. "I'll find clothes. You make sandwiches. Stay."

"Okay, okay. But would you stop talking to me like I'm a dog? I'm not fetching if that's next on your list of commands."

Kyle locked the door and pulled the blinds on the kitchen window. "Back in a minute. Stay down, and stay quiet." As he left the kitchen, he turned back and added, "Good boy."

Sebastian couldn't hide his laugh and gave Kyle the finger. Upstairs, smiling stupidly to himself, Kyle quickly found suitable T-shirts. Unfortunately none of the jeans or pants would fit either of them, so he hoped there were a washer and dryer. It would take an hour, but they needed to kill a bit of time anyway.

As Kyle entered the kitchen, Sebastian glanced up from the slice of thick bread he was buttering. He nodded to several sandwiches neatly sliced in half and stacked on a plate. "I wasn't sure what kind you liked. There's ham and chicken."

"Thanks." Kyle picked up the sandwich on top, not caring what it was. The ham was salty and rich, and he relaxed against the fridge as he chewed. Chases always worked up a hell of an appetite in him. He washed down the sandwich with a cold soda and passed one to Sebastian, who picked at his sandwich.

On the far end of the kitchen was a pantry, and inside it, a door to the basement. Kyle was pleased to find a small washer but no dryer. They'd passed laundry lines at the back of the house, so he wasn't surprised. It would have to do. They just needed clothes that wouldn't attract attention; whether they were damp or not was simply a matter of comfort.

He walked back upstairs. "Take off your pants."

Sebastian coughed and struggled to swallow the bite of sandwich in his mouth. "What?"

"That dirt will never come out of your silk shirt, but the pants should be fine. Besides, there's nothing the right size." Kyle nodded to the selection of T-shirts he'd draped over one of the kitchen chairs. "Pick one of those." He held out his hand for the pants. Sebastian seemed hesitant, and Kyle sighed as he pulled off his own grimy jeans. "Suit yourself."

"No, no. Clean would be good." Sebastian stood and kicked off his slacks. He looked down at himself in his muddy shirt and dress shoes and chuckled. "I look pretty stupid, huh?" He took off his shoes and tossed Kyle his socks before unbuttoning his shirt.

Stupid. Kyle didn't answer as he removed his boots and peeled off his own socks for the wash. Sebastian's black boxer briefs showed off the firm roundness of his ass, and as he bared his toned upper body, *stupid* was the last thing in the world Kyle was thinking. *Control. Get control.* Before he could be disastrously distracted again, Kyle escaped to the dank basement.

As the washer filled, he shoved the clothes in roughly and poured detergent over them. He had to concentrate on the mission. He needed to find the Chimera. And Sebastian had no idea where it was. Logically Kyle knew what he should do. Leave Sebastian to his own devices and find out where the Chimera was.

Sebastian would only slow him down. Besides, Kyle had saved his life. What more was he supposed to do? He wasn't a bodyguard. He had his own life to think of. Sebastian would have to make it on his own. If his father was determined to see him dead, Kyle couldn't save him. *This isn't the job.*

But he'd promised Sebastian he'd help him escape. *You've told a million lies to any number of marks. It's just one more.* Yet the guilt ate at him, and he knew he'd have to keep his word. He had the connections to make it happen. He could get Sebastian on his way to a safe new life and never see him again.

Unbidden, the memory of Sebastian in his arms filled Kyle's mind. Sleeping so soundly against him, breath warm, lips parted.

His mind went back further, and it was as if Kyle could taste him on his tongue again, hear Sebastian's cries of pleasure, feel the heat and connection between them.

Groaning, Kyle rubbed a hand over his face. He needed to stop that train of thought before he went upstairs and took Sebastian on the kitchen table. He'd met his fair share of men over the years. Men he'd been attracted to, men he'd shared time with. Not much time and rarely more than once, but that was a consequence of his work. He'd accepted it long ago.

He shouldn't have gone back to the Brambani estate at all, and now here he was, hiding out in a stranger's home, saddled with Sebastian. Slamming down the washer lid, Kyle swore. *This should be an easy decision.*

"Kyle?" Sebastian called softly from the top of the stairs.

For a moment Kyle's options seemed to crystallize in his mind: door number one and door number two. He hesitated, telling himself to go through the first, familiar door, to do his job as he'd been trained for so many years.

"Everything okay down there?"

Sighing, Kyle shook his head at his own foolishness as he made his choice. "Fine."

He wished it were true.

SITTING IN A strange kitchen in the Alps, wearing only his underwear and a borrowed black T-shirt that was a little too big for him, Sebastian had to marvel at how truly bizarre his life had become. It already seemed so long ago that he'd been at home, bored at his father's party and thinking of ways to avoid his brother's matchmaking attempts.

He took a little bite of his sandwich, still feeling guilty about being in someone's home uninvited. Yet he couldn't deny his hunger, so he ate more as Kyle returned from the basement. At the sink, Kyle placed his gun on the counter and shrugged out of his black jacket and mud-smeared T-shirt, which he tossed into the garbage.

As Kyle rinsed his jacket and wiped it clean, Sebastian watched from the corner of his eye. Kyle wore simple white briefs that left nothing to the imagination. Although they'd touched each other the night before, Sebastian still felt a thrill of excitement examining Kyle's long, lean body.

"See anything you like?" Kyle asked, not taking his eyes from the sink.

Sebastian turned his head and fought the blush, but it was no use. "No. Maybe." He glanced up to find a tiny, teasing smile lifting Kyle's lips, and his stomach flip-flopped with desire. "Yes."

Kyle seemed about to say something, but then the smile faded and he turned back to his jacket, dabbing it dry with a towel. "We need to figure out where your father is hiding the Chimera."

Sebastian went back to his sandwich, feeling…well, he wasn't sure what. Definitely confused. If Kyle was telling the truth about the Chimera—and if Sebastian finding it could mean saving a lot of lives—then he should be focusing on that. Instead, here he was lusting after Kyle. Sex should be the last thing on his mind considering the circumstances. "What about the men after us? You think they work for my father? Or maybe it's you they're after."

Kyle hung his jacket over the back of a chair and sat. He hadn't put on a fresh T-shirt yet, and his muscled chest was extremely distracting. Sebastian tried not to stare at the sprinkling of hair across Kyle's pecs and surrounding his nipples.

"Could be. More likely it's your father's men finishing the job. Even if I managed to kill these two, there are plenty more where they came from." Kyle picked up a second sandwich and bit into it with gusto.

"This doesn't bother you at all, does it?"

Kyle swallowed. "No." After a moment he added, "I'm used to it."

"How do you get used to *this?* Don't you want a normal life?"

"Normal's overrated. I like my life. I like my job. I'd eat my gun if I had to have a *normal* job, sitting in some cubicle, watching the clock."

"There is some middle ground, you know. Between a cubicle and…what are you? A spy? Agent? Operative?"

"Yes." Kyle took another mouthful of his sandwich.

Chuckling, Sebastian shook his head. "Top secret, huh?"

That wry smile graced Kyle's lips again. "Eyes only."

Sebastian found himself smiling back, but it faded as his thoughts returned to his predicament. "Those men who work for my father…they won't stop until I'm dead, will they?"

"Probably not."

"Thanks. That's reassuring."

"Pretty lies aren't going to help you. It depends on how badly your father wants you dead. He might reconsider and call them off. But it seems unlikely." Kyle certainly didn't appear too concerned about it.

"I always knew Papa liked Ben better. It's not as if he hid it. But I still…I still thought he loved me. That's what fathers are supposed to do, right?"

Kyle's expression was unreadable. Finally he nodded and pushed back his chair. "Laundry should be almost done." He disappeared back to the basement, and Sebastian tried to banish thoughts of Arrigo from his mind. It would do him no good to brood on his father's betrayal.

A minute later Kyle returned and hung their clothes over chairs to dry. Sebastian ran his hand through his hair, which was crusted with dried mud. "Ugh. Do you think I can take a shower? Do we have time?"

Kyle pulled on a white T-shirt and checked his watch. "Yes.

Still have another half an hour before we should attempt a move."

"Do you want one too? I mean, not at the same time. Unless you want to." As the words left his mouth, Sebastian wanted to call them back, but he forced himself to meet Kyle's eyes. If he was going to die any minute, he might as well take what he wanted.

Kyle shook his head. "I have to keep watch. Go on." He handed Sebastian his damp trousers. "Take your time, but be ready to run."

Upstairs, Sebastian tipped his head back under the small stream of hot water. Eyes closed, he washed his hair and soaped his body. He couldn't remember ever feeling this tired yet wound up at the same time. He wished he could open his eyes and have this all be a dream. *But you'd have never met Kyle if this wasn't real. Sure, you'd be safe and sound—but miserable and lonely. And safe for how long? Your father was never going to accept you.*

As he remembered Kyle's touch and the taste of his kisses, a thrill shot up his spine. Despite his best intentions, his cock came to life as he thought about the wet heat of Kyle's mouth wrapped around him. He skimmed his hand down his belly as he rinsed the soap from his body and—

Thunk.

Sebastian's eyes flew open. He strained, listening. Had it been the pipes? Or something else? Leaving the water running, he stepped out, quickly toweling himself off and throwing on his clothes. He'd left the bathroom door ajar, and he eased it open, listening.

The house was silent but for a low murmuring. As Sebastian crept down the stairs, he realized it was Kyle on the phone. Exhaling, Sebastian was about to go back upstairs when he heard his name. He inched down the stairs, his bare feet quiet on the carpet. He couldn't see Kyle, who was still in the kitchen at the other end of the small house, but at the bottom of the stairs, he could hear him.

"Don't worry about him."

A pause. "I guarantee he won't talk."

A longer pause. Then, "Understood. I'll neutralize the problem."

Heart pounding, Sebastian sucked in a breath. *Oh, Jesus.* Kyle was still talking, but Sebastian couldn't hear him over the blood rushing in his ears. For a long moment he was frozen. Kyle had brought him this far. *Would he really kill me?*

Along with the terror, Sebastian felt foolishly wounded. Somewhere between lying naked in Kyle's arms and escaping his father's men, he really had started to think of them as being in this mess together. Being a team. Despite his best judgment, he realized he'd started to rely on Kyle. To trust him.

Reality set in with a jolt, and Sebastian went into action. Glancing around, he saw several pairs of shoes on a mat by the front door. Moving as quietly as possible, Sebastian stuffed his feet into a pair of sneakers, knotting them tightly.

He examined the front door. He didn't think he could get it open without Kyle hearing, and tiptoed back up the stairs. He crept into a bedroom at the front of the house and eased the window up. There were large bushes beneath the window, and if he lowered himself out, perhaps it wouldn't be too far to fall. At the mere thought of falling, his palms prickled and his head spun.

It was certainly better than the alternative.

He peered out again. The home was small, and the drop wasn't as far as it could have been. He swallowed thickly. *Do it! Man up!* There was no way he could best Kyle. The man was simply too strong and too skilled. Even without the gun, Sebastian was no match for him.

Resolved, he threw one leg over the sill, but he froze as memories of the tree churned his gut. There had to be another way. Ben wasn't here to climb up and help him down this time. Giving up on the window, he crept back downstairs and listened. Kyle seemed to have gone back to the basement for some reason, so Sebastian edged the front door open and slipped out.

Go, go, go!

He didn't look back as he raced toward the main street. He knew the other men who wanted him dead were still out there, but his first priority was getting away from Kyle. He stayed close to buildings, running as fast as he could. The sneakers pinched his toes painfully and his lungs burned, but he kept moving. When he reached the center of town, Sebastian stopped in the shadow of a church. Breathing harshly, he looked back.

He was alone. Perhaps Kyle hadn't heard him. Maybe he'd gotten lucky. Turning back to the street, Sebastian examined his options. A police car sat by the alley where he and Kyle had left the crippled sedan. Maybe he was wrong, and the police could help him. Surely his father's reach couldn't come this far up the mountains? He had no idea who Kyle's employers were and how many connections they had. Perhaps he could give a false name. *And tell the police what, exactly?*

Too risky. That direction was out. To his left, two tour buses were parked on opposite sides of the street by the town's café. As parents and children wandered off the buses, snapping pictures and venturing into the café, Sebastian left the shadow of the church and walked calmly toward one of the vehicles.

His pulse thrummed, heart thudding against his rib cage. The driver was smoking on the sidewalk, and Sebastian climbed on board. A few people had remained on the bus, including an older woman near the back. Blowing out a long breath, Sebastian made his way down the aisle. When he reached the woman, he leaned down, smiling his best, most charming smile. "Is this seat taken?" he asked in English since he wasn't sure where the tourists were from and assumed they wouldn't understand Italian.

The woman blinked in surprise. In a heavy French accent, she replied, "No." She picked up her cardigan, giving him a quizzical look, eyes flicking over his wet hair.

Sebastian's French was quite good, so he spoke to her in her own language, asking her about herself. The woman was only too happy to talk to him, and as the passengers returned to the bus, Sebastian forced himself to nod and smile and act normal. From the corner of his eye, he watched the street and saw no sign of Kyle or the other men.

The driver returned, asking if all were aboard. After a chorus of replies, the engine rumbled to life and the bus headed up the street. Sebastian leaned over the woman, keeping his head low as he gazed out. He muttered an excuse about forgetting to look at the church, and scanned the street.

As they turned on to the main highway, Sebastian thought he saw movement in the shadows of the church where he had been minutes before. He couldn't be sure, and a moment later they were on the highway. As the bus climbed the mountain and into Switzerland, Sebastian waited to be pulled over. Waited for gunshots.

Yet none came, and after a few hours, he allowed himself to relax. He was safe.

For now.

CHAPTER SIX

A S HE SPED down the mountain, careful not to go too fast and attract the attention of the *carabinieri* or civilian police, Kyle kept an eye on the white roof of the bus several hundred yards in front of him. It disappeared from sight around bends but reappeared below as the road twisted and turned.

It had only taken Kyle twenty seconds to breach a car parked around the corner from the café and hot-wire it, but a dozen cars were between him and his quarry now. Still, it was nothing to worry about. He began passing one car at a time, quick and careful. The bus drove on ahead, and Kyle guessed it would stop at the next lookout.

As he waited out a line of traffic heading north, he replayed the conversation with Marie in his mind. He hadn't been surprised that she called; it would be easy for her to check if he'd left Italy as instructed. The reception was spotty, but Marie's anger at being disobeyed came in loud and clear.

"Where are you?" Her voice was tinny.

Kyle chuckled. "I'm sure you're tracking my phone as I speak."

"Yes, and I'm sure you're using the blocking chip you were not *supposed to have in your company phone."* She exhaled sharply. *"You're off the reservation, as you Americans say. Mr. Grant, don't be foolish."*

"I'm finishing the job, Marie. I'm finding the Chimera. That's all."

"I told you to go home. The director himself is getting involved.

He's very displeased. I haven't told him yet that you aren't back in New York. I can't delay much longer, or it'll be my head on the block."

"All I want is to do my job. I'm going to find it. I won't fail."

There were a few moments of static, and when Marie spoke again, Kyle had to strain to hear her. "Do you really think you can?"

"Yes."

"What?"

"Yes!"

The phone went dead, and Kyle wasn't sure if she'd gotten the message. He went to the bottom of the stairs and listened to the running water. Sebastian had been upstairs for—he glanced at his watch—six and a half minutes. Would probably be ten more at least. Let him enjoy his shower.

Ninety-two seconds later, his phone rang again. Marie started talking as soon as he picked up. "You have forty-eight hours. Get it done. And we heard about your heroics. Where did you leave the boy?"

"He's with me. He can help." Kyle didn't think that was true, but it was in Sebastian's best interests to be helpful to the Association.

"He knows too much. Take him out of the equation."

"Don't worry about him."

"This is not negotiable, Mr. Grant. It comes from the director."

Kyle blinked in surprise. The director. "I guarantee he won't talk."

"Take him out and go find the Chimera." Marie's voice faded, and the line crackled. "There's no room for error. Kill him."

"Understood. I'll neutralize the problem." If he didn't agree, the Association would send someone else. He and Sebastian had enough problems to deal with.

"See that you do, and find that goddamned powder."

"I will. I have a lead." A complete lie, but it would reassure her.

"Then stop talking." The line went dead.

As he pocketed his phone, Kyle was already going through a list of options, none of which appealed. All he knew was that he didn't want *to kill Sebastian. He needed an alternate solution.*

Two vehicles remained between him and the bus. As it turned off the highway at a lookout point, Kyle followed. He pulled up and stopped fifteen feet from the bus door. Watching the tourists pile out, he readied himself, his door an inch ajar.

Yet Sebastian didn't leave the bus. Perhaps he'd realized he was safer on board. Kyle didn't blame him for running—trusting anyone with your life was reckless at best, fatal at worst. The problem was Sebastian didn't stand a chance against his father's men—or the Association's other operatives.

The portly driver heaved himself down the stairs and stood in the shadow of the vehicle. In sharp contrast to the snow they'd suffered through at higher altitude the night before, the day was indeed growing very warm, the sun bright in a cloudless sky over the white peaks and green valleys.

Smiling, Kyle approached. When the driver gave him a quizzical glance, Kyle said, "Gonna wake my friend up. Can't let him miss this amazing view!"

The driver spoke with a German accent. "Do you have the right coach?"

"Of course." Kyle smiled again. "Glad to have you driving me around all these treacherous curves."

The driver seemed to relax at the compliment. "But everyone is off the vehicle. Your friend must be hiding from you." He chuckled.

"I bet he's in the bathroom!" Kyle laughed as he climbed on board and scanned the bus. Holding his gun inside his coat, he started down the aisle, checking all the seats. Empty. The toilet door stood closed, the indicator reading *FREI*. Unoccupied.

Drawing his gun, Kyle reached out for the door handle. Then in one quick movement, he wrenched it open and propelled himself forward to take Sebastian off balance and get him under control.

Instead, he slammed into the far wall of the empty toilet. Had he guessed wrong? Was Sebastian still hiding in the town? After he'd realized Sebastian had been upstairs too long, he'd analyzed the possibilities. Sebastian couldn't hot-wire a car. Likely would leave stealing one as a last resort.

He could hide elsewhere in the town, knowing his father's men could still be there.

He could blend in and try to sneak away. A bus. Right away Kyle had known this would be Sebastian's choice. It was instinct—just as it was when he'd realized he couldn't put his gun to Sebastian's head and pull the trigger. He'd learned long ago not to second-guess it.

Hiding his gun, Kyle strode back down the aisle and outside. Dispensing with the ruse, he cut off whatever the driver was about to say. "Did you pass another bus when you stopped this morning near Courmayeur? One ahead of you, or going the other way?"

The driver blinked, and the wariness returned. "Yes. A bus going to Courmayeur left just before we did."

Damn it.

It must have left moments before Kyle made it to the main street. He slammed the door as he climbed back into the car. He needed to ditch it soon or risk the plates coming up as stolen. He needed to get out of the Alps and find the Chimera. *And* Sebastian, who was now likely well on his way to Switzerland.

He should concentrate on the Chimera. It was clearly the more important goal. Go back down to Como and find it. If Brambani's men located Sebastian in the meantime, it would be out of his hands. Sebastian would be dead, and Kyle wouldn't have to disobey another direct order. Things could go back to normal.

For a moment, as children giggled and shouted, their parents snapping photos of the alpine vista, the possibility that he could let Sebastian die hung in the air as it had earlier in the dank basement. It stretched out and filled Kyle's field of vision, blurring the edges.

Sebastian was nothing to him. His usefulness was at an end. Even if Kyle couldn't kill Sebastian himself, if the job was done for him…it should be a favorable outcome. *He shouldn't care.*

This was not protocol.

Blinking, Kyle twisted the key in the ignition and turned onto the highway, roaring back up the mountain.

IT WAS MIDAFTERNOON when Sebastian reached Geneva. To keep Kyle guessing, he'd left the tourist coach at a rest stop and caught a regular bus that traveled through the Mont Blanc Tunnel into Switzerland. He'd had to lift some euros and a credit card from an older man on the coach who'd left his wallet sticking out of his fanny pack as he dozed. There had been at least five credit cards, and Sebastian hoped this one wouldn't be missed and that the man wouldn't have to pay any of the charges.

It had been a few years since Sebastian had visited Geneva, but he knew the shops on Rue du Rhone and Rue du Marche in the city center were far too expensive for his currently meager budget. Instead he hopped on a city bus to Rue des Paquis.

Along the shady street was an eclectic collection of vintage shops, antiques, and bookstores. Sebastian's toes had gone numb from his pilfered sneakers, and he picked up a slightly worn pair of low-top black sneakers along with a baseball cap, T-shirt, and light jacket.

As the clerk ran the stolen credit card, Sebastian examined a counter display of lighters, his heart in his throat as he waited. A few moments later the bill was printed, and Sebastian exhaled as he scribbled an approximation of the man's signature. Fortunately the young girl with green-streaked hair didn't check the back of the card before returning it to him.

In a busy café beside a sex shop, Sebastian squeezed into a tiny bathroom and changed out of the too-big T-shirt he was wearing. He pulled the cap down low over his forehead. Examining himself in the mirror, he wondered if he should dye his hair. That's what people in movies always did when they were on the run.

On the run.

He barked out a laugh, which echoed loudly off the tile. Changing his hair wouldn't do a thing. Hell, changing his *face* wouldn't help. If Kyle and the other men wanted to find him, they would. He hoped with a desperate flutter of his stomach that they'd lose interest in pursuing him.

Then what?

He went over his options again. He had a few euros and a stolen credit card to his name. No close friends. His classmates from high school were all sons of men who knew his father. He'd been friendly with a few of the boys growing up, but he had no confidence that they'd risk their own lives to help him. Why would they? Sebastian had always been quiet and a bit of a loner.

At Harvard, he'd come out of his shell, but then Peter... At the thought, he had to close his eyes and breathe deeply. *First Peter, now Kyle.* Shaking his head at his own foolishness, he left the bathroom and ordered a coffee at the counter.

He knew it was ridiculous to compare Peter and Kyle at all. At least Peter had cared a little. Peter had liked him, and how could Sebastian blame him for taking Arrigo's money? Few people could resist such an offer. Even if he could talk to Peter or another classmate, what would he say? Besides, it would only put them in danger, and he couldn't let anyone get hurt.

Sipping his coffee, Sebastian sat at a corner table. He stared at the jazz festival posters on the walls and kept his head down when anyone pushed open the door. A bell tinkled every time, and Sebastian watched from the corner of his eye to make sure there was no threat.

He played with a packet of sugar as he pondered his options. First he needed money. The stolen credit card would not be unreported for long. He didn't have his wallet, so although he had thousands of euros in his account, he couldn't access them. Besides, any transactions would undoubtedly be flagged.

Sebastian hated stealing, but he didn't see any other options. He'd gotten lucky on the bus, snagging the sleeping man's wallet on the way to the toilet and then slipping it back on his way when he returned. Glancing around the café, he looked for any wallets or purses sitting unprotected.

He stared at an open purse on the floor beside a chair a few tables over. Its owner, a young woman, was laughing and chatting with a friend. Perhaps he could bump into her chair and drop something, and in the commotion snatch her wallet...

Sebastian glanced up to find the woman's companion watching him, her gaze narrowed. Before he could think, he was up and practically running from the café, guilt warming his cheeks as he hurried away. After a few turns on the clean streets, he spotted the train station. He found a bench outside and tried to think of a good place to go. It would probably be good to get some more miles under his belt.

He thought of Ben. In the past he would have called his brother and had him pick him up. He'd relied on Ben to fix everything. But no more. He rubbed his face. With hit men and God knows who chasing him, he had no one to rely on but himself. It was time to step up and show just what kind of man he could be. Was he the weakling his father had always believed?

No. He'd already escaped a professional spy. He steeled himself. There were depths of strength in him if he could access it. He wasn't going to be anybody's victim. Taking a deep breath, he decided the first step was to figure out where to hide.

A block away stood a shabby hotel, appearing enticingly anonymous. Leaving the train station behind, Sebastian shuffled down the street, hat pulled low. He needed to get off the street and come up with a plan.

KYLE STARED OUT at the passing scenery as the train rumbled past a valley lush with flowers and greenery. A loud British couple sat across from him, exclaiming at every new vista. When the woman had introduced herself, Kyle answered in German with an apologetic smile, which had effectively curtailed any further discussion attempts.

Glancing at the screen of his smartphone—which was a good deal smarter than most civilian versions thanks to some tweaks from the Association's technicians—Kyle frowned. Still nothing.

After ditching the car in Chamonix, he'd caught the train to Geneva. Kyle's instincts told him Sebastian would try to lose himself in a city. Most people would, and Geneva was the logical place to go in the area. However, Kyle still hadn't been able to receive confirmation, and he didn't want to waste precious hours.

The train chugged along, and Kyle wished he'd stolen another car and driven himself, even though he knew the safest course of action was to take transit. Stealing cars was something he tried to avoid, since attracting the attention of local authorities was always to be prevented whenever possible.

Still, he hated not being behind the wheel. As they traveled through the mountainside, all he could do was wait. Wait for information, and wait to get to Geneva. If Sebastian wasn't there, then he'd be back at square one. It was possible Sebastian had gone somewhere else in Italy, but Kyle doubted it. His instincts rarely failed him.

The British woman stood up to take a picture and stumbled slightly as the train rounded a curve. She stepped on Kyle's duffel, which he kept between his feet, one hand gripping the handles. As she rattled out a string of apologies, Kyle smiled through gritted teeth, willing her to stop talking to him.

Dismissing his irritation, he stared out the window as the train passed a village carved into the mountainside. *Damn it, Sebastian.* He should be back in New York, following orders. Waiting for his next job—assuming he wasn't being terminated himself. But he hated home for the same reason he hated waiting on this train: too much time to think.

Home. He mentally scoffed. New York wasn't home to him any more than the countless cities he'd visited around the world. It was just the place he went to more often. He'd chosen a one-room studio apartment over a laundromat that had no nosy neighbors to wonder where he disappeared to. He had no friends there, and in New York it was easy to become another face in the crowd.

He didn't have room in his life for friends. *Yet here you are, chasing Sebastian across the Alps, and he's more than just a friend.* Kyle swore under his breath, garnering a curious look from the British couple. Ignoring them, he tried to clear his mind and stop thinking about all the things he shouldn't. He'd simplified his life when he joined the Association, and he'd gotten dangerously off track on this mission thanks to Sebastian Brambani. He should have learned his lesson by now.

Without warning his father's voice echoed through his mind: *"That boy's always been a bit slow."* Stomach clenching, he closed his eyes as images of the house on South Street flickered through his mind. The room he'd shared with his three brothers, with the faded cowboy wallpaper and battered bunk beds. His two older sisters in the kitchen peeling potatoes and arguing with their mother about going to school dances—a discussion they didn't dare have with their father.

Archibald Grant—Archie to everyone but Kyle's grandmother—ruled their little house with an iron fist, and they all struggled to live up to his expectations. Kyle had been the youngest, a chubby boy who wasn't the natural athlete his brothers were. He'd been born two weeks late, and it was a lasting first impression as far as Archie was concerned. But Kyle had shot up in his teens and worked hard getting in shape to prove he wasn't the slow, underachieving runt of the litter.

Kyle's thoughts returned to the last time he'd seen his family or had a real home. The memory of that night was punctuated by his mother's sobs, the blood streaming out of his nose as he—

"Excuse me?" The British woman touched Kyle's arm tentatively, and he barely resisted the urge to pull out his gun.

He fixed her with a glare.

She leaned back in her seat, eyes wide. "Your phone." She held it in her hand. "It slipped onto the floor."

He grabbed it from her. "*Danke*," he grunted.

The screen suddenly came to life, and he read the message eagerly, pushing memories of the past from his mind.

Geneva. 4:26 p.m. Train station perimeter.

A picture appeared, Sebastian's face clear under the brim of a cap as he looked up. Relief soothed Kyle's tense muscles, and he exhaled. At least he knew Sebastian was still alive, or had been not long ago. He just needed to find him before their opponents did. There were cameras everywhere now, and if you knew the right people with the right face recognition software, finding a target was child's play.

Typing quickly, Kyle responded. *Blue: I owe you. K.*

"Blue" was the only name he knew this contact by, which was fine by Kyle. Over the years he'd obtained some helpful acquaintances—people unconnected to the Association. He'd learned that at times it was wise to have separate channels to gather intel.

He examined the picture again, and memories flickered through his mind: *the taste of Sebastian's lips, his hard, lean body pressed close as they moved together, the heat of his mouth as Kyle slipped inside...*

Clearing his throat, Kyle sat up straighter and checked his watch. If he'd been able to ascertain Sebastian's location, it was likely the others had as well. In all probability, Kyle was closer. As he glanced out the window, the glittering water of Lake Geneva came into view.

Leaving the annoying tourists behind as the train entered the city, he made his way to the front of the carriage, duffel in hand.

SEBASTIAN'S EYES FOLLOWED a faint crack in the ceiling that ran diagonally across the small, musty room. Checking in hadn't been a problem, despite his lack of luggage. He'd stopped himself from launching into an explanation of being robbed, choosing instead to say as little as possible. The clerk had seemed utterly uninterested as long as the credit card cleared.

He shifted on the lumpy mattress. He still wore his clothes and shoes in case he needed to make a quick escape, and he told himself sternly to go to sleep for a couple of hours. Although he was utterly exhausted, his mind stubbornly whirled whether his eyes were opened or closed. He hadn't slept in days aside from the few stolen hours in Kyle's arms in the shack, yet he couldn't relax enough to drift under.

Kyle.

He was too smart to trust a spy, yet he had. A *killer*. But when Kyle had touched him, Sebastian had felt an undeniable connection between them. *All lies. Get as far away from him as you can.* Turning onto his side, Sebastian resolutely closed his eyes. He'd gotten a train schedule from the front-desk clerk and had decided on the latest departure going to Paris. In the meantime he could recharge.

After another five minutes, he flopped onto his back. *Just go to sleep!* But his stomach churned, and then a noise in the hallway had him holding his breath. He crept to the door, peeking through the peephole. An old man shuffled by, shoulders stooped. Exhaling, Sebastian wondered when he'd ever be able to truly relax again.

Kicking off his shoes, he shimmied out of his clothing, hoping it would make him more apt to drop off. He padded to the bathroom and washed his face, wishing he had thought to buy a toothbrush and paste. The curtains were drawn, with only small cracks of light finding their way in.

He'd been through so much and had slept so little that he should have been out like a light, but his brain remained stubbornly engaged. There was one thing that usually never failed to put him under, so he took his cock in hand, squeezing lightly as he began the familiar strokes.

Yet when he closed his eyes, it wasn't Peter's face he saw or Peter's slight hands he remembered caressing him. In his mind, Kyle loomed over him, all coiled tension and power, his hands rough and strong as they claimed him.

Giving in, Sebastian spread his legs, planting his feet on the bed with knees bent. After wetting his finger, he reached down underneath himself and pushed inside the tight ring of muscle around his hole. He thought about the length and thickness of Kyle's cock and how it had felt in his mouth, and imagined it thrusting inside him, opening him up.

With a twist of his wrist, he worked a second finger inside, fucking himself as he jerked his cock with his other hand. Sebastian heard Kyle's voice saying his name in his ear, felt his warm breath on his neck. His own moan was loud in the stillness of the room, and it spurred him on and he moaned again, panting as he brought himself racing to the edge.

Increasing the pressure on his dick, he stroked faster as his balls tightened, tingling with simmering pleasure that licked out to the end of his cock and deep inside his hole where he rubbed his fingers against his prostate.

Shaking, he erupted, spraying his stomach in thick spurts as his body was awash in pure bliss. He emptied, squeezing onto his fingers as he twitched. Then the pleasure receded, and he splayed out, limbs spread, his sticky chest heaving. He closed his eyes and finally fell into a fitful doze.

He awoke two hours later from a nightmare of being chased yet unable to make his legs function, straining in place as if mired in quicksand. As he took in his surroundings, coming back to a reality that was little better than his nightmare, he wiped the sweat from his brow, more determined than ever to get himself out of this mess.

He cleaned himself up from earlier and dressed, trying to ignore the nagging guilt over getting off on thoughts of the two-faced man who was trying to kill him. He shrugged into his jacket and pulled the cap on. Perhaps food would help him focus.

The elevator groaned as it ascended to the fifth floor. As it neared, Sebastian patted the pocket of his jeans and realized his cash and credit card must have fallen out when he kicked them off onto the floor. Grumbling—and feeling like possibly the most unqualified person in the world to be on the lam—Sebastian retreated down the short hallway joining the two longer sides of the hotel, telling himself he had to be more vigilant.

The elevator doors creaked open, and Sebastian glanced back as he rounded the corner, catching a glimpse of Kyle's gun as he emerged.

CHAPTER SEVEN

FROM THE CORNER of his eye, Kyle caught a blur of movement and a flash of golden hair. He stuck close to the wall and peeked around the corner. At the end of the hall, the door to the stairwell was swinging shut. Kyle raced forward, diving into the stairwell after Sebastian.

One flight down, an instinct told him to stop. He listened for Sebastian's footsteps but heard only silence. Kyle smiled to himself. *He's learning.*

Kyle retraced his steps and listened at the stairwell door before edging it open. Sebastian was just slipping out of a utility closet, and he dashed across the hall to a room, jamming a key card into the lock. Kyle was there moments later, and he toppled Sebastian to the floor inside, kicking the door shut.

Sebastian bucked and struggled, but he was no match for Kyle, who pinned him to the floor facedown. "Stop." Holding his gun in his right hand, Kyle jammed his knee into Sebastian's lower back. "I said *stop.*"

After a growl of frustration, Sebastian went still, his body tense as a wire. Kyle loosened his grasp just slightly. "Are you going to listen to me?"

Sebastian nodded jerkily.

Kyle moved to stand, and with a *crack*, Sebastian's elbow flew back and caught Kyle's jaw. He ignored the explosion of pain and struggled to maintain his balance as Sebastian kicked at his legs. *Since when do you trust anyone's word? Maybe you are slow after all.*

He kept Sebastian down but a moment later felt intense burning in his wrist. Inexplicably Sebastian knew just where to pinch, and Kyle's fingers opened helplessly, the gun clattering to the floor. They both dove for it, but Sebastian managed to grasp the weapon first. He turned and scuttled away from Kyle, the gun outstretched. "Stay back!"

Cursing under his breath, Kyle raised his hands as if placating a wild animal. He modulated his voice and spoke in an even tone. "It's okay. Everything is okay."

Sebastian's laugh was high-pitched. "Everything is as far from okay as it can get."

"Put the gun down and we'll talk."

"Right. I put the gun down and then you kill me."

"I'm not going to kill you. Although the more you fight me, the more tempted I am. Calm down and listen to me."

"Calm down? The life I knew is ruined, and I'm on the run with no money and several people trying to kill me, including you."

"If I wanted to kill you, you'd be dead."

"I heard you on the phone. You said you'd eliminate me. Don't lie. I know what I heard."

"I said what they wanted to hear. If I'd said no, they'd have sent someone else to do the job. I was buying time."

Sebastian took this in and then shook his head. "Why should I believe you?"

"Because if I could find you here, that means your father's men can too. We need to get out of here. *Now.*"

Sebastian glanced at the door as if expecting it to burst open. "I can't trust you. Not now."

"We've been through this already. Listen to me, Sebastian. If you cooperate with me, I'll get you out of this alive. Or you can take your chances with the trained killers closing in. If I wanted you dead, we would not be having this conversation. And I won't have it again."

As Sebastian opened his mouth to answer, there was a muffled sound from the hallway. Kyle dove toward Sebastian, rolling with him to the safety of the other side of the bed as bullets tore through the door. Above them, the old window was heaved up.

Sebastian didn't resist as Kyle grabbed the gun and fired. They were caught in a tangle of limbs, but soon Kyle hauled Sebastian against the wall by the window, which opened to a fire escape. As their opponent outside edged in for a look, Kyle yanked the man's head and smashed his knee up into his face.

The man staggered, and Kyle burst onto the fire escape, the momentum helping as he shoved the man over the railing. Spinning, he fired into the room as he grabbed Sebastian and propelled him down the wrought-iron stairs.

The fire escape shuddered as the thunder of feet sounded overhead. A woman stood by the body of the fallen man, and Kyle tugged on Sebastian as he slowed, staring at the splattered mess with mouth agape. The woman regarded them with a similar expression as they raced by.

Ducking into an alley, Kyle went around the long way to the train station, their pursuers not far behind. In daylight and with the police surely on their way, no more shots were fired for the time being.

Barreling into the station, Kyle was glad to see the crowd of people and suitcases. Suddenly slowing to a calm walk, Sebastian panting beside him, Kyle led the way to a bank of lockers where he'd stored his duffel.

"They're here!" Sebastian practically vibrated with fear and tension.

Kyle knelt down, and Sebastian followed. Reaching into his bag Kyle pulled out a cap and slapped it on Sebastian's head as he shrugged into a blue jacket. "We're going to get lost in the crowd. Look at the departures board. When's the next train?"

Peering up, Sebastian squinted. "Five minutes. Paris."

"Good. Now when's the next train after that?"

"Um… Ten minutes. Rome."

"We're going to stand up and walk to the bookstore right there. Blend in with the people reading magazines."

Sebastian licked his lips and nodded. As the minutes ticked by, Kyle watched for their opponents—there were two left at this point—in the security mirror high in the corner of the store. The men were easy to spot, running around with a frantic air. Arrigo Brambani needed to hire more competent hit men.

As they disappeared in the direction of the tracks, Kyle put down his magazine and nodded toward the ticket machine. He paid for their tickets with cash and they made their way to the platform, three over from the Paris train, which was preparing to pull out. There was a commotion on the platform, and as other passengers turned to watch, Kyle and Sebastian boarded the Rome train.

It was the night train, and Kyle had bought a two-berth sleeper cabin. They slipped inside the small room. The two bunks were to their left, with a few feet of space on the right to stand and store suitcases. A small basin was tucked just inside the door.

Kyle pulled the shade and sat on the edge of the lower bunk as Sebastian shut the door. Through an inch of space at the bottom of the window, Kyle watched. As the whistle blew, the train lumbered forward. Beyond another train, Kyle caught a glimpse of their pursuers, now surrounded by several security guards. They gestured toward the departing Paris train, shouting.

Sitting back, Kyle allowed himself to unclench. He glanced up to where Sebastian stood rigid, clutching the wall for balance as the carriage swayed. "It's okay, we lost them. Sit down. Relax."

"Relax?" Sebastian asked, eyebrows raised. "Sure, sure. I'll just have a nap."

"Not a bad idea." Kyle yawned.

"It doesn't bother you at all, does it?"

"What?"

"That man at the hotel. You killed him."

"He was trying to kill you. At this point I'm sure I've been added to the hit list."

"So you don't care that he's dead."

Kyle shrugged. "I don't *like* it, but it is what it is. Part of the job." His curiosity got the better of him, and he asked, "How did you know where to press? The pressure points in the wrist to make me drop the gun?"

"It was a trick my brother taught me. We used to play around a lot. It was just kids' stuff, but I guess it still works."

Sebastian really was full of surprises. "Clearly."

There was a knock at the door. Kyle put his finger to his lips as he squeezed past Sebastian and presented their tickets to the conductor. When they were alone again, Kyle extended his hand. "I get the Chimera. You get a new identity. No more running away from me."

Sebastian regarded Kyle's hand for a moment before reaching for it, nodding. Kyle ignored the spark of desire that skittered through him as their palms clasped. "Let's eat. I'm starving."

SWISHING THE MERLOT around in his mouth before swallowing, Sebastian savored it as it slid down his throat. He'd devoured his steak, and now he leaned back in his chair, sated. Across from him, Kyle chewed a roasted potato as he stared out the window at the dark mountains.

"How did you start?" Sebastian asked.

Kyle met his gaze. "Start what?"

"Being a spy, or whatever job title you people have these days. Espionage technician?"

Kyle's lips twitched. "I was recruited when I was nineteen."

"Were you in college?"

"No."

It was like getting blood from a stone. "What were you doing?"

"If you're going to play twenty questions, I'm moving to another table."

"Come on," Sebastian cajoled. "We're going to be on this train all night; we might as well talk."

Kyle grumbled, but his heart didn't seem to be in it. "Fine. I was enrolled at the academy, but it didn't work out."

"Academy of what?"

"The police academy."

"You were going to be a cop?" Sebastian chuckled. "Well, I can definitely imagine you handcuffing people." A moment after the words left his mouth he realized the implication. "I mean...you know what I mean."

An eyebrow raised, Kyle took a long pull from his bottle of beer.

Sebastian hurried on. "So why didn't it work out?"

"It just didn't."

"What made you want to be a cop?"

"I just did."

From the way Kyle's eyes flicked away, Sebastian knew he was onto something. He took a guess. "Was your father a cop?"

Kyle sliced into an asparagus spear forcefully. "This is all irrelevant."

"He was, wasn't he? Come on, spill."

Nostrils flaring, Kyle answered. "Yes. My two older brothers as well. I wanted to join the force my whole life, but life doesn't always turn out the way we plan. You know that. So when the Association came calling, I answered. Left Pittsburgh for training camp overseas and haven't looked back since."

"You're from Pittsburgh? I've never been. Is it nice?"

Kyle took a swig of his beer. "No."

"What did your parents say? When you left?"

"There was nothing to say."

"Oh." Sebastian felt a flush of guilt for prying. "I didn't mean to upset you."

"I'm not upset."

"You seem a little upset." At Kyle's withering expression, Sebastian took another sip of wine. "All right, then tell me more about you."

"No."

"Why not? It's only fair. You know everything about me." Kyle said nothing. "Right? You know about my mom, and I bet you know about Peter."

Kyle didn't answer, eyes on his plate. Sebastian threw back the rest of his wine and signaled the waiter for another.

"Take it easy." Kyle glanced up. "I need you sharp. You slow me down enough already without being drunk."

Sebastian scoffed. "*Please*, two glasses of wine will not get me drunk. I'm Italian, remember? I was weaned on Chianti." He picked up his napkin, smoothing out the creases in the linen. "So do you know? About Peter?"

"Yes."

"I bet you've seen the picture."

"Of course."

"He deleted it after I freaked out, but you can't really delete anything these days, can you?"

"No." Kyle took another bite. "He left school a few days later. Dropped out after a transaction with your father."

Sebastian grimaced. "Yep, he paid Peter off to get out of my life." He laughed wryly. "As if that would fix the problem. Fix me."

"There was no one before Peter?"

"You tell me. What did your research turn up?"

"Nothing. From what I could tell, you never even kissed anyone until you went to Harvard and fooled around with your roommate."

"Does it say that in my file? 'Twenty-year-old virgin'?"

Kyle smirked. "No."

"But you knew just how to approach me. How to make me do what you wanted."

"It's my job. It's not…" Kyle frowned and sipped his beer.

"Personal? That's what you were going to say. It's not personal."

"It can't be."

"Of course not." Sebastian cleared his throat in the awkward silence. "So why didn't you just stay put and kill the rest of those guys?"

"Which guys?"

"Right, I have to narrow it down. In Geneva, at the hotel. For a superspy, you seem to do a lot of running away."

Kyle snorted. "It's not quite like it is in the movies. Evasion is always the best tactic. Avoid engagement except when there is no alternative. You'll stay alive a lot longer."

"Can't argue with the logic. So how are you going to find this powder? What's so special about it? Aren't there a ton of chemical weapons out there?"

Kyle finished his meal and placed his knife and fork side by side on the plate. "Yes, but the Chimera is special. It's virtually undetectable. It can be disguised as anything. Coffee grounds. Sugar. Sand. It only takes a tiny amount mixed with water to kill everyone in the vicinity. Kill them horribly. The affected area will be toxic for a long time afterward. Perhaps years."

"How can my father put this out into the world? It doesn't make any sense."

"Neither do nuclear weapons. But for the right price, people like your father sell them to madmen. Odds are the terrorists would only use the Chimera once. But their power is in the world knowing they have more and could attack at any time. It's all about fear."

"Do you think my brother knows?" *God, Ben. Please don't sell your soul for our father.*

Kyle shook his head. "I don't know. I wish I could tell you."

Sebastian squared his shoulders. "Okay, how are we going to find it? I really have no idea where he might have hidden it."

"I'm waiting for fresh intel. I've made some inquiries. We might as well get a good night's sleep tonight and start fresh in the morning. Your father's company has an office in Rome, correct?"

"Yes. I think so. I never paid much attention." He thought again of Ben and missed him with a powerful pang.

"What's wrong? Aside from the obvious."

"Nothing." Sebastian forced a smile. "Just tired. And everything. You know."

Kyle nodded and went back to staring out the window. The waiter brought dessert, a flaky French pastry that Sebastian picked at with his fork. Kyle cut his into neat squares, eating them one at a time. Sebastian wondered what it would take to affect his appetite.

When they returned to their cabin after Kyle performed a search of the train for "any unexpected issues," as he put it, Sebastian stood by the window. He shoved his suddenly sweaty hands into his pockets.

Kyle, on the other hand, seemed utterly calm. He stripped off his jacket and T-shirt, placing his gun on the lower bunk. The muscles in his back flexed as he leaned over the small basin and splashed water onto his face and chest. Sebastian watched in the reflection in the window, his throat gone dry. He held his breath as Kyle's hands dipped lower, and waited for him to shuck his jeans.

Instead Kyle turned, his eyes meeting Sebastian's in the glass. Sebastian averted his face and bent over to unlace his sneakers.

"Don't. Stay ready. Shoes and pants on. Shirt can come off."

"Right. I forgot." Sebastian straightened up. He pulled his shirt over his head and edged past Kyle in the narrow space. Their skin grazed, and Sebastian's heart thumped as he resisted the urge to let his hands splay over Kyle's broad chest. He kept his face down, as he was sure his cheeks were flaming. *Snap out of it!*

When he was safely at the sink, Sebastian turned on the tap and tried to ignore Kyle, who stretched out on the lower bed, his booted feet crossed at the ankle, his gun tucked in beside him. Sebastian flipped off the overhead light before opening the shade a bit to let in some moonlight.

An hour later he stared at the ceiling, which was all too close to him from the vantage of the top berth. Below him, Kyle breathed deeply and evenly. Sebastian kept telling himself to go to sleep, but his brain whirled overtime. It was all still like a dream he'd soon wake from and find himself back in his room in Como. Or better yet, his dorm room in Cambridge. Even without Peter, it was still the place he felt most at home. Most himself. But there'd be no going back there now.

After a few more minutes, he leaned over to see if Kyle was really asleep. In the dim half-light of the moon, he could see Kyle's still form. The train jostled him as it swayed, and he gripped the edges of the bunk as he leaned a bit farther, squinting into the shadows of Kyle's berth.

Sebastian wanted to go for a walk through the train, but Kyle would surely object. The men hadn't followed them on board, so what harm would it do? Perhaps if he burned off some restless energy, he could sleep.

Holding his breath, he inched over a bit farther. And then the train wasn't swaying but slowing, and Sebastian grappled with air, trying to balance himself as gravity and momentum conspired against him.

As he tumbled off the bunk, there was a flash of motion and he was in Kyle's powerful grip, landing on top of him as they crashed to the floor. Sebastian sat up, his legs straddling Kyle's hips. "Sorry. Thank you. I thought you were asleep."

Kyle's hands still clutched Sebastian's arms. "Have to sleep light in my line of work."

"Oh. Right."

Kyle loosened his grip and dropped his hands to Sebastian thighs. "You should try to rest."

"Uh-huh." Sebastian shifted slightly, and his cock twitched in the confines of his jeans. Straddling Kyle, desire burst to life with a rush of heat.

Their eyes locked for a long moment, and then Sebastian dove at Kyle's mouth. Their tongues met as Sebastian moaned. When they parted to gulp in air, Sebastian barely recognized his own voice, thick with need. "Fuck me."

With a low groan, Kyle pushed on Sebastian's shoulders, keeping him at arm's length. "Not a good idea."

"Why?" Sebastian ground down with his hips, rubbing their hardening cocks together.

"Have to stay focused."

"Because this will make it harder to kill me."

Something Sebastian couldn't name flickered across Kyle's face as the moment of silence stretched out. Then his fingers were in Sebastian's hair, yanking his head down in a fierce kiss.

They were lost after that, hands roaming and bodies rutting as their mouths met. Sebastian's head was light with the rush of lust, and he struggled to tug down his jeans, needing more contact. They banged elbows and knees in the narrow space, and Kyle growled with frustration as he sat up, Sebastian still straddling his lap.

They both eyed the bunks, which had little headroom. Kyle

reached for his pillow, and after some maneuvering, they knelt on it as Sebastian leaned over the bunk facedown, Kyle behind him. Resting on his elbows, Sebastian shivered in anticipation as Kyle pressed kisses down his spine. The knowledge of who Kyle was and what he did should have terrified him, yet it only seemed to make Sebastian want him more.

Sebastian was certain Kyle wouldn't hurt him. Maybe it didn't make any sense—maybe he was a fool—but he trusted him. "Do you have something?" Sebastian asked.

"Of course." Kyle deftly had Sebastian's jeans and underwear around his knees in no time. He reached for his duffel, and Sebastian watched over his shoulder as Kyle removed a condom and packet of lube. He wondered just how many men Kyle slept with on his missions.

He suddenly felt very exposed, bent over and naked. Vulnerable. He shivered again, his body tensing as he looked over his shoulder. Kyle's hands stilled on the zipper of his own jeans. He smoothed a warm palm over Sebastian's hip. "Okay?"

Sebastian jerked out a nod, and Kyle leaned over and kissed him lightly as he massaged Sebastian's back. The tension melted away as desire rushed back, flooding Sebastian's limbs. He broke their kiss. "Yes," he breathed. "Please."

He lowered his forehead to the thin mattress as Kyle kissed and sucked his neck, his lips finding sensitive spots Sebastian didn't even know were there. He heard a tearing sound, and Kyle's slick finger teased Sebastian's hole, coaxing him open. A moan escaped Sebastian's lips as Kyle entered him, pushing his finger past the tight ring of muscle.

Kyle continued kissing Sebastian's neck and shoulders as he opened him, sliding another finger inside and stretching him until Sebastian pushed back, eager for more. The crinkle of foil seemed very loud in the darkness, and Sebastian's pulse raced as he spread his knees.

His breath lodged in his throat as the head of Kyle's cock inched inside him. It burned, and a warm puff of air fluttered across Sebastian's ear. "Breathe."

Sebastian forced his lungs into action, shuddering as Kyle filled him slowly. When he could feel Kyle's hip bones against his ass, Sebastian squeezed his inner muscles, reveling in the incredible sensation of fullness. He'd fantasized about it so many times, and it was more intense than he'd ever imagined to feel another man throbbing inside him.

Kyle seemed to bite back a moan, and when he leaned over, Sebastian could feel Kyle's heart pounding against his back. "Need to move," Kyle ground out.

Sebastian squeezed again, ignoring the pain as he pushed back against Kyle. "Fuck me," Sebastian repeated, and Kyle grasped his hips, sliding halfway out and then back in. As he rocked in and out at a steady pace, each thrust became easier for Sebastian until he was moving with Kyle, spreading his legs even wider.

Sparks of pleasure ignited his body as Kyle rubbed against his prostate, and Sebastian cried out. Their harsh breathing filled the air as they strained together. Kyle twisted his fingers in Sebastian's hair, turning his head and kissing him, their mouths open as they panted.

Sebastian had gone soft when Kyle entered him, but now his cock leaked, rock hard beneath him. The sparks blazed into flames as Kyle reached around and took hold of him, jerking him roughly.

"God, Kyle. *God.*"

Kyle groaned low in his throat, speeding up his thrusts, his balls slapping against Sebastian's ass. He drove into him, and Sebastian could only moan and gasp as the ecstasy built, Kyle's cock inside him and hand around his shaft working in perfect unison. The wave crashed over Sebastian as he came, splashing his stomach.

Kyle laid his forehead on Sebastian's back, gripping Sebastian's hips as he thrust wildly, until he shook and moaned a few moments later as he found his release. Sebastian pressed his cheek to the mattress, Kyle boneless on top of him. They struggled for breath, skin slick with sweat.

When Kyle pulled out, Sebastian winced. Kyle was still resting over him, his lips soft on the back of Sebastian's neck. When he spoke, it was only a whisper. "I won't kill you."

Then he was gone, returning with a small wet towel. He eased Sebastian onto the bottom bunk and washed him clean. As Sebastian tried to formulate a thought, Kyle tossed the towel into the basin and disappeared up the ladder to the top berth. "Go to sleep."

This time Sebastian drifted off within minutes.

CHAPTER EIGHT

AS THEY NEARED Rome, Kyle finished dressing and watched Sebastian. Fast asleep on the bottom bunk, Sebastian's lips were slightly parted, his face relaxed. Kyle bit back the ridiculous impulse to smooth down Sebastian's hair where it stuck up wildly.

A voice reminded him how foolish it was to keep Sebastian with him. In more than nine years in the field, he'd never compromised his mission like this. He'd made mistakes—he winced just thinking about Singapore—but to disobey direct orders and become...*attached* was unheard of. Certainly for him.

He'd known another operative, Petersen, who'd gotten mixed up with a woman during a mission. She'd seemed an innocent, the assistant of an arms dealer who'd been in the wrong place at the wrong time. Petersen should have brought her in or eliminated her, but instead he'd kept her hidden.

It was Kyle who'd been sent to assess the situation. He'd convinced Petersen to give him their location, but by the time he arrived it was too late. Of all the bodies he'd seen over the years, Petersen's glassy eyes and mouth open in surprise stayed with him. The woman was KGB, but they'd never been able to track her down.

He gazed at Sebastian again. While it was possible, Kyle didn't suspect Sebastian of being anything but what he seemed, and his instinct had never been wrong yet. But even though Sebastian wasn't a spy on his own mission, it didn't make him any less dangerous.

He was possibly the most dangerous person Kyle had ever met.

Leave. He'd never be able to track you or keep up on his own. He's not your responsibility. Do the job. Get your head back in the game. Stop breaking the rules. Rules keep you alive.

The train slowed, and Sebastian stirred. He blinked sleepily at Kyle, a smile forming on his lips. Kyle turned away sharply, busying himself with his gun, checking the chamber. "Get up," he barked.

"Sorry." Sebastian's voice was small.

Kyle stopped himself from saying it was all right. Sitting up, Sebastian tensed, sucking in a quick breath. "Okay?" Kyle asked before he could tell himself to shut up.

Sebastian nodded and pulled on his T-shirt. After the sex they'd had, Kyle wasn't surprised Sebastian was sore. It had been incredible; Kyle was in danger of getting hard just thinking about it. Sebastian had been so tight and hot and eager, and Kyle wanted to push him back onto the bunk and have him again. Taste him and drive inside him and—

Shaking his head, Kyle focused on an equipment check, methodically going through the built-in compartments in his duffel that held weapons and various devices he might need on any given mission. He went through his mental checklist, counting bullets and double-checking triggers.

As the train pulled into the station, Kyle led the way through the car to the doors, where they joined the line of people eager to disembark. It was just past nine o'clock, and Kyle could see that Termini station was bustling. It would make for good cover if anyone was meeting their train.

As they made their way briskly through the crowds, Kyle scanned for threats. There were none he could identify. Perhaps Brambani's incompetent men had gone to intercept the Paris train. As they left the station, blinking in the bright sunlight, Kyle's phone vibrated in his coat. He steered Sebastian over to the edge of the sidewalk in the shade of the stone building and scanned the message.

"What is it?"

"Floor plans to your father's office here in Rome."

"We're going there?" Sebastian sounded surprised. "But they'll recognize me. Ben and I had to go to all the Christmas parties here and in Milano."

Kyle scrolled through the additional information his contact had included. "We're not going to just walk in."

"Oh. Then how—"

"You'll see."

SHIFTING SLIGHTLY, SEBASTIAN lifted his foot and circled his ankle, trying to banish the pins and needles. He didn't have to see Kyle's face in the dark closet to know he was glaring. "How much longer?" Sebastian whispered.

"As long as it takes," Kyle hissed.

A broom handle dug mercilessly into Sebastian's back. "Couldn't you find a better place to hide?"

"Support thinks it's just me. This space is sufficient for one operative."

"Why didn't you tell them I'm here?"

Kyle didn't answer. Sebastian was pressed into his side in the tiny confines of the closet, and along with his extreme discomfort, Sebastian struggled to ignore the heat of Kyle's body and the desire it stirred in him. After the night before, he wanted more. He wanted...*everything.*

Sebastian wasn't sure what he'd expected when he woke up after having sex more incredible than he'd ever imagined. It was much more than he thought it could be after his fumbling with Peter in their dorm room. Sex with Kyle was in a different stratosphere.

He certainly hadn't expected romance or declarations of eternal love, but…a kiss in the morning would've been nice. But in the light of day, the gentle and passionate man had disappeared. Kyle was all business, stone-faced and impatient.

Getting into the office tower itself had been easy; the lobby and entrance bustled with workers. Kyle led the way down several hallways until they'd reached the janitor's closet. Glancing about, Kyle had slipped a thin metal tool into the lock and pushed Sebastian inside in the blink of an eye.

Now they'd been crammed in the closet for what seemed like an eternity but was probably twenty minutes. "Why can't you just go into the office and make up a story? You're good at that."

"Because the receptionist received a fax yesterday with my picture on it, saying I'm a disgruntled former employee of the Milan office and that security guards will be on duty until further notice. I want to avoid any confrontations. They're messy. Too many variables."

"What if we take the stairs from another floor?"

"These floors are all secure. Again, too many variables. Too many people we could encounter."

Sebastian was about to ask again what the plan was when the light around the cracks of the door vanished and the electricity audibly powered down. Then they were moving, Kyle in the lead as the low emergency lights blinked on. They were at the back of the building, and Kyle stopped when they reached the service elevator, pressing the call button.

"But the power's out," Sebastian whispered.

"The service elevator runs on a different power source."

Sure enough, the doors slid open. The floors ticked by as they traveled up to fifteen. Sebastian wondered what they were going to do when they got there, since it wasn't as if it would be dark enough to sneak in with the emergency lights on. As they passed fourteen and the elevator slowed, Kyle pressed the emergency stop, and they jolted to a halt.

"Now what?"

Kyle didn't answer and seemed to be waiting for something. A moment later the fire alarm echoed in the elevator shaft. Kyle glanced at his watch. "Floor should be clear within four minutes. We'll give them five."

"Who's doing this? Turning off the power and making the alarm go off? Who's 'support'?"

"Ground support from the Association. Someone in a cubicle in Frankfurt. Maybe Vienna. Doesn't matter. With today's technology they could be on the moon and flip the fire alarm."

As the minutes ticked by, Kyle removed a small, thin metal bar from his duffel. He pulled on one end, and the bar extended and locked into place. He checked his watch again and stood at the ready.

"Don't you hate it?"

Kyle raised an eyebrow, his eyes on his watch again.

"All the waiting."

"You get used to it." He inserted the bar into the tiny space between the elevator door and the side of the car. With a heave, he levered the door opened a few inches and then changed positions so he could push it with his full body weight.

When there was enough room to squeeze through, Kyle disassembled the crowbar and lifted his duffel up onto the floor. The elevator had stopped before fully reaching the fifteenth floor, so Kyle had to boost himself up over his head. Kneeling, he wheeled around and extended his hand to Sebastian.

"Come on."

The fire alarm still screeched, setting Sebastian's nerves on edge. "What if it moves?"

"Then I'm about to lose an arm, so get up here."

Grasping Kyle's hand, Sebastian was half lifted as he tried to boost himself up. He was shorter than Kyle and struggled to pull himself over the threshold. Kyle hooked his other hand under Sebastian's armpit and hoisted him up.

Sebastian couldn't remember the last time he'd been in his father's Rome office—parties were always held at restaurants or local attractions—but Kyle strode unerringly to Arrigo's office. It must have been the biggest one on the floor plan.

Kyle shut and locked the door behind them. He quickly peered behind the paintings in the room but found nothing. Gaze narrowed in concentration, he knocked on the walls, ear against the light paint. The alarm still wailed, and Sebastian wished they'd just turn it off.

As Kyle searched for what Sebastian assumed would be a safe, Sebastian glanced around his father's office, looking back at the door frequently, his heart pounding in time with the bleats of the fire alarm. On the large, polished desk sat a framed photo of Arrigo and Ben, taken on one of their hunting trips. Sebastian missed his brother acutely in that moment. *Did I really ever know him?*

With a deep breath, he turned away from the desk. Kyle was now on his hands and knees, examining the marble floor. Under one of the large windows, he paused. Sebastian watched as Kyle carefully pried up a piece of marble that covered the safe inset into the recess of the floor.

Kyle tapped something into his watch, which looked like something James Bond would wear, and a few moments later with a chorus of beeps from throughout the floor, the power came back on. The number pad and display glowed on the face of the safe, which was about two feet square. "Should I try to guess?" Sebastian asked. "He might use some of the same numbers."

"Let's see what we have." Taking out a small brush and container of white powder, Kyle dusted the keyboard. Fingerprints appeared on six of the keys. "That eliminates a few. Do these other numbers look familiar?" Sebastian studied the numbers, imagining them lined up before him. "Here, write them down." Kyle reached for pen and paper.

"No. I don't need to. Just wait."

He rearranged the numbers in different permutations. Then the lightbulb went off, and he jolted with excitement. "It's a pi sequence."

"You sure? We only have one chance—a wrong entry will trigger an alarm somewhere, and we're going to have company very soon as it is."

"Positive, I…"

"What?"

"It's just weird. He never liked math. I'd talk about it when I was a kid and he'd tell me I needed to be more like Ben. Play more sports and have more friends. Not be such a *secchione*." At Kyle's confused expression, he added, "Like a nerd. My father never even graduated high school, didn't think it was much use in the real world. He built an empire, so maybe he's right."

"Fathers can be wrong."

Although Kyle's tone was flat, Sebastian could sense the emotion behind it. "Like your father was?"

Kyle shook his head, exhaling sharply. "It doesn't matter. Look, I guess your father had a soft spot for you after all. Or he just thought it would be a good code." The fire alarm was suddenly silenced. Kyle drew his gun and nodded at the keypad. "Punch it in."

Breathing deeply, Sebastian put in the sequence. With a beep, the door released, and he sat back on his heels. Kyle pulled out the only item inside—a large manila envelope. After stuffing the envelope in his bag, he closed the safe and shoved the slab of marble flooring back into place. Sebastian followed as Kyle edged the office door open. He listened for a long moment, and then they crept down the corridor.

There was a distant *ping*, and suddenly a clamor of voices and footsteps as the workers returned to their office. Kyle continued on, ducking into a small office and shutting the door behind them. Before Sebastian could ask what exactly the plan was, Kyle was standing on the desk, unscrewing the grate over an air vent in the ceiling.

He gestured sharply to Sebastian, and Sebastian clambered up onto the desk beside him. Kyle interlaced his fingers, palms up, and Sebastian placed his foot there for a boost. Once he was up in the narrow shaft, he heard the *thunk* of Kyle's duffel and then Kyle himself joining him in the tight space.

On his stomach, Sebastian pulled himself forward, slithering as fast as he could. Kyle whispered for him to turn right down an intersecting shaft, and Sebastian continued on, moving as quickly and quietly as he could. When he reached a wall, he peered out through another grate into what he feared was an elevator shaft.

He couldn't see down, but he couldn't imagine what else the space was. When he glanced back at Kyle, Kyle was typing into his phone. "What are you doing?" Sebastian asked, voice low.

"Ground support is bringing up the elevator." He reached into his bag and passed Sebastian something that looked like a laser gun. "The grate is screwed in from the other side. Melt it around the edges and pull it off."

Sebastian discovered the tool *was* some kind of laser gun, except this laser burned through metal like a knife through warm butter. The elevator rumbled toward them. When Sebastian had the grate off, he leaned out into the shaft cautiously. The elevator roof had stopped about ten feet below. "How are we supposed to get on?"

"Just jump down and we'll get through the access panel."

"Jump?" Sebastian's voice raised an octave. "I can't."

"Yes, you can. Shimmy around and go feet first. I'll hold on to you."

"I...I don't like heights."

"Turn around. *Now.*"

Since there was nowhere else to go, Sebastian did as he was told, scooting backward until his legs dangled in the air, the edge of the vent digging into his hips. He gripped the metal bottom of the air duct, fingernails white.

Kyle pried Sebastian's hands up, clasping them. "The elevator's right there. You can't fall."

"There's some space around it. I could slip in between the elevator and the shaft and we're fifteen stories up and—"

"I won't let you fall." Kyle squeezed Sebastian's hands.

Heart thumping painfully, Sebastian swallowed, his mouth bone-dry. He inched out until his armpits were on the edge of the shaft, his body dangling as panic flapped against his rib cage. "I can't."

Kyle didn't respond, and the next thing Sebastian knew, he was falling. A scream lodged in his throat as he jolted to a stop. Above him, Kyle hung halfway out of the vent, his arms fully extended, holding on to Sebastian. "Let go. It's only a few feet."

Struggling to force air into his lungs, Sebastian shook his head.

"It's okay, Sebastian. Let go." Kyle's tone was soothing, in direct contrast to the orders he'd barked earlier.

There's no other way. Screwing his eyes shut, Sebastian released his grip.

He landed with a thud on the elevator roof a second later. It really had been only a few feet, and he felt silly for his panic. The duffel landed beside him, and when he looked up, Kyle was somersaulting out of the duct. He landed gracefully beside Sebastian without comment and knelt to open the service hatch.

Dropping into the service elevator was much easier, and Sebastian was breathing normally again as they traveled down to the ground floor. "I'm sorry. It's a phobia."

Kyle was typing on his phone again. "It's all right." He sent the message and reached out, rubbing Sebastian's arm almost unconsciously. Then, as if he realized what he was doing, he jammed his hand in his pocket.

"I know it's stupid, the whole heights thing. Thanks for…" He waved his hand around.

Kyle gazed at Sebastian evenly for a long moment. "You're stronger than you think."

Then the elevator opened, and they were off.

THE CAR HE'D requested waited on a side street two blocks away, the keys resting on the front driver's side tire. Kyle tossed them to Sebastian. "Drive."

"Where to?"

"Out of Rome. Somewhere quiet. Isolated."

Sebastian froze, clearly uneasy. "Why?"

Tell him to shut up and get in the goddamned car. Instead he took a step closer, reaching for Sebastian's hand and squeezing it. "I told you not to worry about that." Kyle remembered the heat of Sebastian's body beneath his, his throaty cries as Kyle moved inside him, his fierce kisses…

He dropped Sebastian's hand and strode around the car. *For the last time, focus.* "Come on."

As Sebastian navigated traffic, Kyle scanned the document from Arrigo's safe, which was a single page.

"Sucks that it wasn't in there. The Chimera, I mean," Sebastian said. He seemed uneasy, likely because Kyle had been hot and cold with him all day. Hell, since they'd met.

"I didn't expect it to be. Wherever it is now, it's under very heavy guard. I doubt your father's letting it out of his sight." Kyle flipped the page over.

"Then why did we risk going there?"

"For this." Kyle tapped the paper. "We need to find out who his buyer is."

Sebastian merged onto the freeway. "I thought you said it was terrorists."

"It is. Unfortunately there are plenty of groups to choose from. This narrows it down."

Glancing over, Sebastian's brow furrowed. "It's all numbers."

"It's encoded, of course." He pulled out his phone and tapped away. "I'll get one of the computer techs started on it."

"But if they haven't made the exchange yet…"

"No way would your father hand anything over without a sizable deposit. This is likely the contract. With banking information would be nice."

"You guys can just trace transactions and find out who made them? Even on Swiss accounts? I'm sure my father uses them."

"Not instantly, but yes. It can take a few hours or a few days. It depends. First they have to crack the code. They'll give me an estimate in a couple of hours."

"What are we going to do in the meantime?"

"Get us into the country and you'll find out."

Sebastian glanced over, wary.

Kyle smirked. "It's important. Trust me."

"Like I have a choice?"

"We all have choices."

Sebastian kept his eyes on the road.

"Why are you afraid of heights?" The question slipped out before Kyle could stop it. *You shouldn't care. It's irrelevant.*

Sebastian paused before answering. "It's stupid. When I was a kid—eight or nine—I climbed a tree at my grandparents' place in Sicily. It was a huge Banyan tree, with all these twisty branches. I'd always been fascinated by it." He paused again, eyes on the road. "I climbed up really high. I remember feeling like I was climbing to heaven. I didn't look down until it was too late."

"You were stuck."

"Yeah." He smiled ruefully. "I started crying and calling for my mother. My father came instead, absolutely furious. Told me to stop being a little girl and climb down. But it was like I was frozen up on this branch, my fingernails dug into in the bark."

Kyle waited for him to continue, anger beginning to simmer in his gut.

"My brother told me he'd climb up and get me, but my father wouldn't let him. He yanked Ben back down by his collar. My father's face was beet red. I remember thinking it was like he was going to explode. He told me I had to come down on my own. But I couldn't move."

"How did you get down?"

"Ben snuck out in the middle of the night and climbed up to get me."

"Your father left you up there in the dark? Alone?" He regretted that he hadn't had the opportunity to make Arrigo Brambani bleed.

"Said he'd make a man of me yet. In the morning my mom had a big bruise on her cheek. Said she tripped."

Kyle clenched his jaw. "Father of the year."

"Yeah. For so many reasons. I never thought he'd want to kill me, though. I still thought…" He shook his head. "Well, now I know." He glanced over. "What about your father?"

Kyle's body tensed. "What about him?"

"What was he like?"

Memories of his father flickered through his mind: *the booming laugh; spinning Kyle's mother around the kitchen for an impromptu dance; cheering in the bleachers as Kyle rounded the Little League bases; the spit and polish of his uniform.* He cleared his throat. "Just your average father." The recollection of the spittle on his face and the slam of the front door behind him as Kyle was shoved out of the house rang in his ears.

"So why don't you talk to him anymore? Or your mom?"

"The job," Kyle lied.

"On the train you said there was nothing to say to them."

He shifted and drummed his fingers on his thigh. "Are we almost there?"

Sebastian let him off the hook. "Yeah. Anyway, that's why I'm afraid of heights. Of falling, really. I have trouble even climbing a ladder. It's stupid, I know."

"It's not stupid." He wondered how many times Arrigo had called Sebastian names growing up.

"I bet you don't have any irrational phobias."

"Not really." Kyle shrugged. "But I'm a superspy, remember?"

Sebastian laughed. "Was that a *joke*?"

He couldn't help but smile in return.

"So where do you live? Do you have a home somewhere?" Sebastian exited the highway.

Kyle thought of his lifeless apartment. "I have a place in New York. I'm not there much, though. I'd rather be working."

"New York? I love it there. When I was a kid we got to stay in the Waldorf Astoria and see *Cats*. Do you live in Manhattan?"

"Yes. Hell's Kitchen."

Sebastian made a turn onto a country road. "Is it as scary as it sounds?"

"No." Kyle chuckled. "It's changed a lot over the years. Lots of good restaurants and it's close to the theater district. I can walk to Central Park. It's convenient."

"Wait, you go to the *theater*? Like, you get home from a long day of spying and you see *The Lion King* or something?"

"I'm not exactly the Disney type. But yes, I like the theater. Saw a few good plays last year."

Sebastian didn't answer, and when Kyle looked over, Sebastian was watching him with an incredulous smile. Kyle was suddenly self-conscious—an emotion he was unfamiliar with. "What?"

Turning his eyes back to the road, Sebastian shook his head. "Nothing. You're just…surprising."

"When I'm not working, I need to stay busy. Keep my mind occupied."

"I just didn't peg you for a Broadway fan." Sebastian grinned. "Guess you're gay after all."

"I haven't convinced you yet?" Seemingly of its own accord, Kyle's voice had dropped an octave, and he cursed himself. *Stop it! No more flirting. No more talking about your life.* He cleared his throat and looked out the window, sitting up straighter. "Do you know where we're going? We shouldn't waste time."

"Yeah. We're almost there."

When Kyle glanced back, Sebastian was watching him with a gaze that was far too knowing. The kid had gotten under his skin, and he had to put a stop to it. He shouldn't have told him anything personal. But it had been so long since anyone had asked, and he found himself saying and doing things he normally never would.

They stopped in a small village to pick up lunch, and Sebastian drove them out into swaths of farmland. They finally stopped by a field that didn't seem to have anything around it for miles. Sebastian killed the engine. "Does this work?"

"It works."

Kyle went around and opened the trunk. He'd requested the car "fully loaded," and sure enough there was a cache of weapons and ammunition under the false bottom of the trunk. As he pulled out a pistol, Sebastian appeared. He stared at the gun, then up at Kyle. Apprehensive but not afraid.

"If you want to survive, you'd better learn how to shoot." He held out the pistol, handle toward Sebastian.

After a moment's hesitation, Sebastian took hold of it. "I don't want to shoot anyone."

"Sometimes you have to. There are plenty of people out there who won't hesitate to shoot. If *you* do, you're dead. It's a simple equation."

Using rocks and their soda cans from lunch, Kyle set up targets. Sebastian missed wildly at first and then started getting closer. Kyle stood behind him, coaching. "Use both hands. Keep steady, and squeeze the trigger with as little movement as possible."

"I'm never going to be able to hit anything. Not at this distance."

"Accuracy is difficult with handguns, but when you're being chased, you can't stop to assemble a rifle. Try again."

Sebastian planted his feet and went through all the steps Kyle had shown him. Kyle stepped to the side, watching the concentration and determination on Sebastian's face. Sebastian squeezed off another shot that hit the base of one of the rock targets.

After a deep breath, Sebastian reset and took another shot. The soda can went flying with a metallic clang, and Sebastian whooped with joy. "Did you see that?"

In that moment, with the sun streaming down and a smile of pride lighting up his face, Sebastian was irresistible. One hand threading through his golden hair, Kyle drew him close and pressed their lips together.

Just one kiss.

Sebastian melted into him, his arms circling Kyle's waist. Their mouths opened, and they stroked softly with their tongues. Kyle breathed Sebastian in, pulling him closer. This time there was no great sense of urgency, and they both seemed content to explore each other's mouths. He knew this was reckless, but Kyle couldn't resist.

He wasn't sure how long they'd been standing there when the dart pierced the back of his neck. He took a sharp breath, breaking the kiss and reaching for the gun in his jacket—which he'd left in the car. He shoved at Sebastian. "Run."

Sebastian squinted in concern, arms still locked around Kyle. "What?"

As his head spun, he stumbled and sank to his knees. *You let your guard down.*

"Kyle?" Sebastian followed him to the ground, clutching him with eyes wide. "What's happening? What's wrong?"

As the blackness rushed in, Kyle heard the approaching opponents. He ordered his hands and limbs to work, but toppled over onto the warm grass. Sebastian gasped, and a shot rang out.

Then it was over.

CHAPTER NINE

A PERSISTENT ACHE penetrated Kyle's consciousness. His shoulders felt as if they might dislocate, his arms wrenched behind the back of the hard wooden chair he sat in. Metal handcuffs enclosed his wrists, and each ankle was bound to the chair legs with heavy rope.

He hadn't opened his eyes yet or given any indication he was awake. He breathed steadily. There was at least one other person in the room. Kyle listened intently. His head was still foggy from the drug, and he struggled to concentrate and not drift back into a fog. Whoever was in the room was conscious, as he—Kyle was certain it was a man—coughed approximately every ten seconds.

It wasn't Sebastian; of that much Kyle was sure. The door opened, and footsteps sounded on a concrete or stone floor. Some kind of warehouse, Kyle guessed. The air was damp and dank. Surely their location was suitably isolated. He had no idea how long he'd been under.

Pain exploded in his jaw as a fist struck him. "Wake up, Mr. Grant."

Kyle opened his eyes to find a middle-aged man with blond, wiry hair looming over him. The man wore a neatly pressed suit. He bared his teeth in an approximation of a smile. "Nice of you to join us. Now let's make this easy on everyone, shall we?"

Kyle had known the moment the dart hit him that it wasn't Brambani's men. Hit men had no use for prisoners. The man's Danish accent confirmed it; Brambani's men had all been Italian.

Of course it was possible Brambani had looked elsewhere to find someone competent, but Kyle doubted it.

As Kyle's fuzzy mind put the pieces together, he peered around the empty concrete room. Fluorescent lights flickered somewhere behind him, and the walls and floor were stained with blood. A disused slaughterhouse, perhaps.

Turning his head took Herculean effort, but Kyle glanced behind him. Another ten feet of concrete. Empty. Sebastian wasn't here, and if he wasn't here he was—

The grief struck like a snakebite, and Kyle's chest burned. He dug his fingernails into his palms as he fought to remain impassive.

Dead.

Sebastian would have been of no use to these men. As the drug overtook Kyle, they'd have executed Sebastian. A bullet in the skull, less than a second. He was likely still in that field, the sun streaming down as the flies gathered, and—

The sharp clap of the blond man's flat hand across Kyle's other cheek echoed in the abattoir. The memory of Sebastian's face filled Kyle's vision, and a terrible sadness and inexplicable sense of loss flooded him, as though he'd been hit by another poisoned dart.

You barely knew him.

"Tell me where it is, and we can all be on our way." The Dane smiled, his teeth gleaming in the gray, dingy room.

Swallowing, Kyle could still taste Sebastian on his tongue, and he tamped down the howl that threatened to rip from his throat. *You shouldn't care. You can't care. Focus!* Keeping his face blank, he allowed himself a deep, slow breath.

The incomprehensible sorrow coalesced into a soundless fury, and Kyle met the Dane's gaze evenly as he examined his options.

The Dane pulled over another chair close to Kyle's, crossing his legs elegantly as he unbuttoned his suit jacket and sat back.

"Your reputation precedes you, of course. I must say I was surprised to find you with the young man."

Kyle stared straight ahead.

"Thing is, your reputation has been a bit tarnished of late. Unsuccessful missions. More than one. Now this. I've begun to think that perhaps there's something else going on."

Clearing his throat, Kyle evenly asked, "And what would that be?"

"You tell me."

Kyle lifted a shoulder in a careless shrug.

The Dane uncrossed his legs and leaned his elbows on his knees. "Now, we both have a problem here. Perhaps we can work together. Help each other." He waited for a response, but Kyle didn't give him one. "I think we can come to some sort of arrangement, don't you?"

"Perhaps." The only arrangement Kyle would make with this man was the terms of his painful death at Kyle's hands.

"You obviously haven't gotten the location out of him yet."

"Location?"

The Dane huffed impatiently. "The Chimera, of course. Clever of you to try and romance it out of him. Of course if you'd been successful, he'd be disposed of."

Kyle's stomach flip-flopped as he ran the Dane's words over in his mind. *"You obviously haven't gotten the location out of him yet."* Yet. He kept his tone even. "Where is he now?"

"Nearby."

Pulse racing, Kyle glanced around casually. "I don't see him." *Was he really alive? Was he hurt?* Elation jumbled with worry.

"All in good time." The Dane's lips quirked up. "Now, you Americans have a term that I quite like. I believe it's 'good cop/bad cop.' Did I get that right?"

Kyle waited for him to get to the point.

"So my cohorts and I are obviously primed to play the role of the bad cops in this scenario. If our methods don't yield results, then I thought you could step in. The young man looked quite…pliable when we found you earlier. I think we can help each other convince him to give us the information. Time is of the essence, after all."

Kyle pretended to consider it. "And if I agree, and he tells us the location. Then what?"

"I'm sure there's a sum we can agree on. Something that will allow you to make a clean break. Start anew."

"Why should I trust you?"

The Dane laughed. "Well, you haven't much choice, have you? I give you my word."

"The boy?"

"We'll take care of it." He waved his hand dismissively. "Unless you'd prefer to?"

"Either way." *Either way I'm going to rip your lungs out.* "What if he won't talk? He's…surprising."

"If we can't get it out of him, we move to plan B. But I think it would be mutually beneficial to give plan A a try. Don't you agree?"

Adjusting his arms behind him, Kyle nodded.

HE WAS IN the tree.

It was just as Sebastian remembered it from that awful day as a child. He was high in the air, almost as if he could reach out and touch the clouds—if he could only open his eyes. The bark of the branch was rough and damp beneath his cheek.

He was on his stomach, one leg somehow bent beneath him painfully. He tried to open his eyes once more, but it was as if they were fused shut. The pain in his body intensified as he tried to move, so he gave up and drifted away.

The next time he opened his eyes, he was in his room in Como. The bed dipped beside him, and Kyle was there, dressed in a tuxedo as he had been the night they met. Smiling, Kyle—Steven?—leaned down and kissed him.

"I shouldn't." Sebastian was breathless, excited. "If my father found out..."

But he felt totally safe with Kyle and certain they wouldn't be discovered. He felt as if he was flying. Yet as he arched into Kyle's hands, a sharp pain throbbed in Sebastian's stomach. He was back in the tree and it was cold and damp, and then he was falling—

"Up!"

Sebastian blinked at the hulk of a man glowering over him. The man bared his teeth. "About time. Need you conscious, don't we?"

He was on a concrete floor, hard and gritty. All Sebastian could see was dank gray. His ribs ached from where he'd just been kicked. His head was a lead weight he could lift only a few centimeters before collapsing back down to the floor.

A hand fisted in his hair, and Sebastian was dragged to a sitting position. The man, sporting a bandage over a fresh wound in his shoulder, tightened his grip and leaned in close, his foul breath invading Sebastian's senses. This time the man spoke in broken Italian. "I'm gonna enjoy making you scream, faggot."

Sebastian's mind felt like pieces of a puzzle scattered across the room. He'd been with Kyle—*Oh God, Kyle!* Wincing, Sebastian looked for him in the dark room, but he was alone with his captor. Gazing at the man, he had a flash of memory—firing a gun. The field. Target practice.

Kyle had suddenly staggered against him and gone limp. Had told him to run, and then... The gun had been in Sebastian's hand, and he fired at the men charging toward them. Then blackness and concrete. "Where is he?" Sebastian's throat was like sandpaper. *Please let him be all right. Please.*

The man sneered. "You'll be reunited soon, don't worry."

Sebastian struggled to make sense of it all. "Who are you? What do you want?"

His captor's laugh echoed off the dank walls. "What do you think?"

"I don't know. Do you work for my father?"

Someone approached, and the metal door groaned on its hinges. Another man appeared. "He's ready."

They hauled Sebastian to his feet, dragging him by one arm. Sebastian struggled futilely for a few moments before accepting it was useless. He was badly outmatched. As they shoved him into another large room in the old warehouse or wherever the hell they were, Sebastian's heart leaped at the sight of Kyle bound to a chair.

For a split second, their eyes met, and Kyle gazed at him with an intent expression of relief and concern and something Sebastian didn't dare name. Then Kyle blinked, and it was gone, a look of boredom taking its place.

The men dumped Sebastian on his knees, which cracked painfully on the floor. A blond man in a suit approached slowly, hands clasped behind him. "Well, hello, Mr. Brambani. I must say you are…unexpected." He addressed Kyle. "Shot one of my men as we came to collect you. Had to put a dart in him too."

Kyle's blank expression was unchanging.

"Now, Mr. Brambani, tell us where the Chimera is."

Sebastian blinked, surprised. "I don't know."

The man chuckled. "Of course you do. That is why Mr. Grant went after you. Why you're still alive." He stepped closer. "You know where the powder is, or you'd be in your grave. Mr. Grant doesn't bring along toys on his missions."

"I have no idea where it is." All Sebastian could do was tell the truth.

His interrogator adjusted his jeweled cuff links and went on as if Sebastian hadn't spoken. "Not that you are without charms, of course." He ran a fingertip down Sebastian's cheek, and Sebastian squirmed away. "Boy or girl, with a mouth like that, who cares? Of course you prefer him the way he is, Mr. Grant. So sorry to have interrupted you earlier, but time marches on."

Kyle stared at the man, face still utterly blank.

The man clapped his hands together sharply. On cue, one of the three other men tugged over a large hook hanging from the ceiling on a rail. Sebastian realized with a sinking sensation that the dark stains on the floor and walls were blood. The meat hook dangled above him, creaking as it swayed. The man he'd shot bound Sebastian's wrists in front of him with rope and tore the T-shirt from his body.

Sebastian's heart thumped as he was hung from his wrists on the hook, the toes of his sneakers barely skimming the floor. The rough rope dug into his wrists, his arms protesting as he wiggled, trying to take some more weight on his feet. "I don't know where it is. I swear, I don't!"

Grinning, the man he shot held up a taser gun and reached toward him. Before Sebastian could say anything else, a spark of pain in his side ignited and screamed through his body as he shook helplessly, every nerve on fire. It stopped as suddenly as it began, and he hung limply from his wrists.

The leader brushed his thumb over Sebastian's lower lip. "Now tell me where it is."

With the man in front of him, Sebastian couldn't see Kyle, and he found himself murmuring his name.

The leader smiled. "You're wondering why we don't simply ask Mr. Grant? Well, we did, of course, but the fact of the matter is we could torture him from now until Christmas and he wouldn't tell us the time. You, on the other hand…"

Sebastian screamed as another jolt of electricity seared his body. It was a pain so intense he thought his heart would explode.

Gasping, he dangled, sure his arms would tear from their sockets.

"Tell me where it is, and it will all be over."

"I don't fucking know." Sebastian gritted out every word, anger surging in his gut. "Even if I did, I wouldn't tell you."

The smile vanished from the blond man's face. Grabbing the taser, he jammed it into Sebastian's stomach and another scream tore from Sebastian's throat, blood flooding his mouth as he bit his tongue. He shuddered in agony.

Through it all, Kyle wore the same bored expression. Sebastian wanted to shout at him to do something, but he could only whimper pitifully. Did Kyle really not care at all? Had Sebastian imagined the connection between them? The fleeting moments of tenderness? Affection, even? The way Kyle had kissed him earlier, Sebastian had felt as though the wall around Kyle was crumbling…

Suddenly he fell, cut down from the hook. He groaned as he hit the concrete, his limbs jelly. Metal scraped over the floor, and a tub of water a few feet deep appeared before him. His wrists were freed, but before he could even rub them, he was swallowing water, choking as powerful hands thrust him over the side of the basin.

Thrashing, he fought to free himself, the panic taking hold as his lungs burned, his head completely underwater. *No no no!* His mind screamed, and he clawed at the hands holding him down.

Then he was yanked back, and he gasped for air, hyperventilating.

His captor crouched on the other side of the tub. "Where is it? Just tell me and this will all be over."

Sebastian tried frantically to think of a lie. Anything they might believe. The cabin, perhaps? Anything to make them stop. But before he could get the words past his lips he was under again. He kicked at the air behind him, scrabbling at the man holding him down, digging in his fingernails. Lungs burning, he saw stars as his vision went dark around the edges, the blackness creeping in and taking over. Screaming, he swallowed water—

With a jolt, he was back on his knees, gasping and coughing, his chest on fire. "Wait," he croaked. "I'll tell you."

He looked at Kyle, who did the strangest thing. He *smiled.* Then Kyle was somehow moving, one arm free as he burst forward onto the crouching blond, chair and all.

Sound and movement exploded all around, and Sebastian was kicked to the floor, his head smacking the hard surface. He fought to stay conscious as his vision went double. There was the sound of splintering wood, interspersed with grunts and moans, and then gunshots that blared in Sebastian's eardrums.

His eyelids were fifty-ton weights he couldn't lift. Somewhere nearby, men grappled with each other, flesh striking flesh. Another shot rang out, and all was still. Someone moved toward him, and Sebastian inched away on his stomach, willing life into his useless limbs.

He tensed and tried to kick as strong hands touched him, one on his back, the other lifting his head. "It's all right. I've got you."

At the sound of Kyle's voice, Sebastian slumped to the floor, exhaling. He tried to answer but could only moan. He was somehow moving through the air, and then he was safe in Kyle's arms, pressed against his warm, powerful body. "I've got you," Kyle repeated, his lips brushing Sebastian's forehead.

CHAPTER TEN

A S KYLE SCROLLED through the Dane's cell phone contacts, Sebastian murmured in his sleep beside him on the bed. Kyle reached over and brushed Sebastian's hair off his face before grazing his throat. His pulse was strong and steady beneath Kyle's fingertips.

The narrow face of the manager of the little run-down hotel in the outskirts of Milan had pinched comically as Kyle half carried Sebastian into the lobby. Five hundred euros slid across the counter had done the trick, and the manager hadn't commented on the bloody and bedraggled state of their clothing.

Kyle leaned back against the headboard, left hand resting in a bucket of ice beside him. He thumbed through the numbers dialed on the cell phone. All had perfectly innocent and generic names such as "Mom" and "Dave" and "Uncle John." Everything about the Dane and his men had been strikingly familiar, from the make of their weapons to their operating procedures to the codes in their phones.

Now there were four bodies in an old abattoir with Kyle's fingerprints everywhere. Yet he couldn't call for a cleaning crew, because the Dane and his men had been sent by the Association. Kyle's stomach twisted at the thought that it could have been Marie. She'd been his handler for nine years. His *friend*.

Pushing thoughts of Marie from his mind, Kyle checked his watch: *7:18*. Twenty-eight hours and twelve minutes until Arrigo Brambani was scheduled to meet his buyers, location unknown.

Of course he could simply follow Sebastian's father to the rendezvous point, but it was a last resort. Too many uncontrolled variables. He needed to get there first and control the area.

Kyle picked up the letter-sized envelope he'd found in Arrigo's Rome office. It had been with the Dane's other belongings in the man's vehicle, and Kyle had no way of knowing if his opponent had read the information or passed the series of coded numbers on to anyone.

Sebastian moaned softly as he rolled onto his side, blinking. Tensing, he looked up, eyes wide as he took a shuddering breath. "Kyle?"

"It's all right. You're safe." Kyle touched Sebastian's hair lightly. He wanted to pull Sebastian into his arms until the trembling stopped, but he didn't want to alarm him. "How are you feeling?"

Sebastian rubbed his eyes. "Like I was hit by a truck. And dragged a mile."

"That's normal. It'll pass. You can take some painkillers. Sleep more."

"Normal." Sebastian laughed ruefully.

"It's all relative."

"Where are they? Are they…?"

"You don't have to worry about them."

"What does that mean?"

"You know what that means. They're dead."

Sebastian rolled onto his back. After a few moments of silence, he looked down at himself. Kyle had stripped off his jeans and left Sebastian in his underwear. "How did I get here? How did you get loose?"

Kyle held up his swollen left hand. "Dislocated my thumb."

Sebastian's eyes widened. "How the hell do you dislocate your own thumb?"

"Years of practice."

"Don't you need to see a doctor?"

"Popped it back in myself." He flexed his fingers gingerly. "It'll feel better tomorrow."

"Just like that? Fixed overnight?"

"All relative." Kyle shrugged.

"You did that while you were sitting there looking bored? I thought you were about to take a nap. I thought…" He flushed. "Never mind."

Kyle found himself caressing Sebastian's cheek with his knuckles. "If they thought I cared, it would've been worse."

Sebastian met his gaze. "So you do? Care?"

When they'd dragged Sebastian in, weak but *alive*, the relief and joy Kyle experienced was extraordinary. Watching them torture Sebastian had been an agony he never knew existed, and the satisfaction in spilling their blood was great. "Sebastian…" His heart beat faster, he cupped Sebastian's face. "I—"

A shrill ring pierced the air, and they both jumped. Kyle reached for his duffel, which he'd recovered intact from the Dane's vehicle. It was his private, untraceable phone. *Unknown caller.* He picked up but said nothing.

"Kyle?" Marie's voice, pitched higher than usual, rang in his ear.

"Yes, I'm alive. Sorry to disappoint you, *chéri*."

"Shut up and listen. I need your help, and I bet you need mine. Where are you?"

Kyle laughed hollowly. "So you can send another team? Afraid not."

She huffed. "Mr. Grant, I'm on your side. Listen to me."

"Not this time. *Au revoir*." He hung up.

"What's going on?" Sebastian asked quietly.

"Doesn't matter. Just rest."

"It matters to me." Sebastian tried to push himself up with his arm, but it wavered before he flopped back down. He clenched his teeth, clearly frustrated. "I thought tasers only affected people for a few minutes."

"You'll feel better in a couple more hours. That wasn't exactly your run-of-the-mill taser gun."

"Who were those men? Tell me what's happening."

Kyle debated for a moment before acquiescing. "They were sent by the Association. Which means I'm on my own. I can't trust any of them." Marie's betrayal hurt more than it should have, and his jaw clenched.

Sebastian rested his palm on Kyle's denim-clad thigh. "You're not alone."

Enough of this. Make it a clean break. Kyle removed Sebastian's hand. "I reached my contact, the one who arranges new identities. I'm taking you to him first thing tomorrow. He's arranging transport now."

"What? I'm not going anywhere." Sebastian heaved himself up to a sitting position.

"There's no other option. Forget the hit your father put on you—you've got the Association after you now. They wanted you dead, but now it's worse. If they think you have information, they will pursue every avenue available. Baseball caps and keeping your head down won't put them off."

"But my father's deal is supposed to happen tomorrow night, right?"

"Yes, as far as we know."

"Then one way or another it'll be settled. Someone will have the Chimera, and anything I might have known will be moot."

"They'll still want you dead. You're too big of a loose end after what happened today. This is for the best. I should have taken you straight to my contact after I found you in Geneva." *You shouldn't have gotten hurt today.*

"So you'll just drop me off, and what? That's it? I never see you again?"

"Right." Kyle kept his gaze averted from Sebastian. "They'll do the surgery somewhere in Russia. Ukraine, maybe. Then you'll have a new passport, and you can go anywhere."

"*Surgery?*"

"Of course. You need a new face. Hair color. Everything. A fake name isn't enough."

"I…" Sebastian's face creased, and he laid back down, eyes on the ceiling. "I can't believe this is my life."

"It's the best way to keep you safe. You can start over again. You'll be fine. I've made the arrangements."

"Why?"

"To save your life, whether you like it or not."

"No, I mean…that can't be cheap. You don't need to do this."

Kyle could feel Sebastian's intent gaze, and he took another chug of beer. "I said I would." He'd told Sebastian what he'd needed to hear to ensure his cooperation, but now he couldn't imagine not delivering on his promise.

"Why don't you just leave me by the side of the road? Why do you keep looking out for me?"

Shrugging, Kyle got up and walked to a small table in the corner of the room. He started a weapons check. "You should eat. I'll order something."

"This afternoon you were kissing me, and now you can't even look at me."

"No more kissing." Kyle opened the chamber of one of his guns, eyeing it before sliding it shut. His head was strangely light. He'd never felt this way about anyone. It was disorienting in the extreme. He concentrated on speaking with conviction. "We got off a few times. It's not going to happen again."

"But you want it to."

Kyle picked up the next gun. "You could be anyone. It didn't mean anything. You'll understand."

"When? When I'm all grown up? Stop patronizing me."

"When you're away from all this. When you have some per-

126

spective."

Sebastian scoffed. "Right. Then I'll see there was nothing between us. That it was just sex."

Kyle kept his head down, focusing on his task. "Exactly."

"Liar."

Sebastian's voice was suddenly closer, and Kyle turned in time to catch him as his knees wobbled. "I told you to stay off your feet."

His arms wrapped around Kyle, Sebastian wavered, but his tone was firm. "It *is* more, and you know it. You're just too afraid to admit it."

Taking a few steps, Kyle gently pushed Sebastian down onto the end of the bed, where he sat looking up at Kyle with an unnerving gaze. Kyle exhaled slowly. "I'm not afraid. It's just not practical. You've seen what I do."

"I don't care. I want to be with you."

Kyle laughed incredulously. "*Be* with me? It's impossible. Even if I wanted—"

"But you do, don't you? Admit it."

"It's irrelevant." Kyle turned back to his equipment. He checked the chamber of his pistol.

"You did that already."

Jamming the gun into the back of his jeans, Kyle grabbed his coat. "I'm hungry. Don't open the door for anyone. Don't touch anything. Don't…"

Sebastian arched an eyebrow.

"Just *don't*." Kyle slammed the door behind him.

SEBASTIAN SWALLOWED HIS last spoonful of minestrone soup and sat back, exhausted. He hurt down to his bones, and he just wanted to go to sleep. He and Kyle had barely spoken since Kyle

KEIRA ANDREWS

returned, and the awkward silence was taking its toll. But before he went to sleep, he needed a shower.

However, when he tried to stand, he took a shaky step and then tumbled back onto the sagging mattress. Kyle was around the bed in a flash. "Careful."

Sebastian rubbed his face. "I need to get clean." It was as if he could still feel the hands of the men pulling him down while his lungs filled with water.

"Okay." Without another word, Kyle wrapped a firm arm around Sebastian's back, and they walked a few steps to the tiny bathroom.

Sebastian eyed the ancient bathtub, and his chest tightened. *Water all around, swallowing it, can't breathe, can't get up, can't breathe—*

Kyle gently took Sebastian's chin between his thumb and finger, turning his face. "You're okay."

Focusing on Kyle, Sebastian nodded. Kyle turned on the water, and it sputtered from the rusted showerhead. Sebastian peeled off his underwear and, with Kyle's grip firm on his arm, climbed into the bathtub. To his surprise, Kyle followed a moment later, his clothes in a pile on the floor.

After pulling the ratty shower curtain, Kyle held Sebastian close. He unwrapped the cheap bar of soap and smoothed it over Sebastian's body. Any remaining tension between them seemed to dissipate in the steam of the shower.

Kyle shampooed Sebastian's hair, his hands gentle. By the time they were both clean, Sebastian felt utterly boneless and wavered on his feet. He wanted so badly to touch Kyle, to drop to his knees and suck him. But he was a rag doll in Kyle's hands as Kyle turned off the water and wrapped a towel around Sebastian's waist and then his own.

He laid Sebastian facedown on the bed and straddled his thighs, keeping his weight off. His right hand kneaded Sebastian's

128

shoulder, the left skimming lightly over Sebastian's skin. "This'll help your muscles." Kyle's earlier bad humor seemed to have dissipated in the shower.

Sebastian nodded against his pillow. "How's your thumb?"

"A little sore."

Sebastian guessed that was an understatement. His body ached, but as Kyle rubbed him, he began to relax. The light touch of Kyle's left hand sent shivers up Sebastian's spine. Beneath him, his cock stirred. He rotated his hips, the friction sending pleasure to his sore muscles.

Kyle said nothing as he worked his way down Sebastian's back and arms. When he reached the towel at Sebastian's waist, Sebastian arched up into his touch, wanting more. His exhaustion had been replaced by growing desire.

But instead of giving Sebastian what he wanted, Kyle shifted down the bed to his feet. He was all business, and Sebastian couldn't help but whine in protest. As Kyle massaged Sebastian's calves, Sebastian spread his legs, moaning softly as he relaxed into the mattress. His cock grew harder with every caress, and Kyle's hands moved upward, his fingers dipping to caress Sebastian's sensitive inner thighs.

When Kyle stopped touching him, Sebastian glanced back over his shoulder. Kyle's hands were tight fists, and his eyes were closed. The towel couldn't hide Kyle's erection, and Sebastian felt a moment of triumph that Kyle was as turned on as he was. He spoke quietly. "I know it doesn't mean anything."

Kyle's eyelids popped open. "We shouldn't. We never should have."

"But we did. We both want this. Don't deny it."

With a quick movement, Kyle peeled off Sebastian's towel. He kneaded Sebastian's ass with strong hands, diving down to kiss the bared flesh. Sebastian groaned, the pleasure overtaking any remaining pain in his body. Kyle's breath was warm against him, and he parted Sebastian's cheeks, skimming his fingertips along Sebastian's crack. "Feeling better?"

Sebastian could only mutter yes, and then he gasped as Kyle's tongue followed his fingers. He'd read about rimming and seen it on the Internet, but Peter had thought it was gross and refused to try it. Now Kyle was licking Sebastian's ass from top to bottom, and Sebastian was on fire in a way he never wanted to end.

Kyle spread him wider and circled Sebastian's hole, licking and nibbling it, thrusting his tongue inside. The pleasure radiated outward, sweeping Sebastian's body as he moaned. Kyle spit into him, his tongue going deeper.

Sebastian rutted against the coarse towel, his cock almost unbearably hard as Kyle opened him up and did things with his mouth and tongue Sebastian had only dreamed of. As Kyle licked inside him even deeper, Sebastian came, mouth open in a silent cry as the ecstasy washed over him.

Breathing in deeply, he rode the aftershocks and tried to speak. All he could do was murmur unintelligibly. Kyle rolled him onto his back, a smile playing on his lips as he smoothed his hand over Sebastian's chest. His hard cock jutted out from his body, and Sebastian reached for it feebly. Still smiling in a way that made Sebastian's heart swell, Kyle playfully batted his hand away. "You're in no condition."

Kneeling over him, sitting back on his heels, Kyle was the most beautiful thing Sebastian had ever seen. Although he'd just spent, Sebastian's dick twitched, and he licked his lips. Kyle's voice was husky. "You want to watch?"

Sebastian nodded, swallowing hard. "Come on me."

Kyle's nostrils flared, and he took hold of his cock with his right hand. He tugged a few times before stroking roughly, eyes locked with Sebastian's. He spit into his palm and jerked himself with sharp strokes from base to tip, his thighs flexing as he thrust up into his fist, his breath coming in a staccato rhythm.

When he came, it splashed up onto Sebastian's face and chest, and Kyle groaned loudly. Sebastian swiped at a salty dollop on his chin, savoring the taste before Kyle leaned over and kissed him, his tongue caressing Sebastian's.

Then he was gone, up off the mattress and into the bathroom. He returned with a damp washcloth and cleaned Sebastian, tossing the towel onto the floor. Sebastian waited for him to get dressed and go back to business as usual. But instead Kyle snapped off the light and climbed into bed, pulling the covers over them.

He drew Sebastian close against his chest, fingers playing in his hair. "Just for tonight," Kyle murmured.

Sebastian nodded and held on.

KYLE ROLLED OVER and peered at the bathroom door. Light shone around the edges, and he couldn't hear any sounds of activity or illness. He checked his watch: *4:17.* Creeping silently out of bed, he stepped into his underwear. At the door, he listened. For a moment all was still, but then he heard a scratching. He leaned in closer. A pencil on paper.

He rapped his knuckles on the door sharply. "Sebastian?"

"Um, yeah? I'm fine."

"You've been in there for twenty-three minutes. Are you sick?"

"No. I'm just...I couldn't sleep. I'm reading. I didn't want to wake you." The pitch of his voice was all wrong.

"Open the door."

The scratching of the pencil intensified. "Just one minute."

"Why?" The hair on the back of Kyle's neck stood up, and his fists curled. *What's he hiding?* "Sebastian. Open it."

"Hold on, I'm almost done."

Kyle stepped back to kick the lock, but as the toilet flushed, Sebastian opened the door. Naked, he held a piece of paper and a pencil, his eyes bright. A grin bloomed on his face. "I cracked it."

Kyle realized which piece of paper Sebastian was holding, and couldn't help but be impressed Sebastian had lifted the envelope without Kyle hearing. "What does it say? Where's the meeting?" Kyle snatched the paper from Sebastian's hand, pulse racing. But the sheet of numbers was unchanged. Kyle looked up, brow furrowing. "Where is it?" A pad of hotel paper sat on the counter, and he flipped through the sheets. Blank.

Sebastian simply smiled and tapped his head.

Realization set in. "You flushed it."

"Don't worry. I have a really good memory. Take me with you, and I'll tell you. I want to help you. I don't want to run and hide."

"Goddamn it, tell me what it said." Kyle menacingly stepped closer, dropping his voice to the level he used to deliver threats. "Tell me now."

Sebastian actually leaned in. "Or what?"

Kyle exhaled sharply. "Or I'll make you very fucking sorry." He vibrated with tension. *It's for the best. Stop putting him in danger. Give him a new life.*

Sebastian shook his head slowly. "No, you won't."

For a long moment they stared at each other, the dare hovering in the air between them.

With a muttered curse, Kyle hauled Sebastian against him, kissing him long and hard. He plunged his tongue inside Sebastian's mouth, and Sebastian moaned into him as they stumbled toward the bed. Kyle was on fire, his blood singing in his veins as they surged together.

They fell onto the mattress, Sebastian on his back. He tugged at Kyle's underwear. "God, hurry. Fuck me."

Kyle was already reaching for his bag as he kicked his briefs off. They rutted against each other, both growing hard, kissing each other desperately. Kyle had never wanted another man like this. *Ever.* Sure, Sebastian had a tight ass and pretty face, but so did countless other men. Yes, Kyle wanted to fuck Sebastian senseless, but he also wanted to make him smile. Hear him laugh. Keep him safe.

Sebastian took hold of Kyle's cock, rubbing him roughly. "Need you."

Kyle kissed him, thrusting his tongue inside Sebastian's mouth. Maybe it was Sebastian's resilience or sense of humor or that he had more nerve and grit than some of the spies Kyle knew. He had no idea if it was chemical or emotional; all he knew was that he never expected this. The job was his life, and Sebastian Brambani wasn't in the training manual.

They were both bruised and battered, but they urged each other on, Sebastian moving onto his hands and knees as Kyle tore open the condom. He slapped on some lube and thrust into Sebastian, who cried out. "Yes! More. *More.*"

Gripping his hips, Kyle plowed Sebastian's ass. He knew there must be pain mixed with the pleasure, but Sebastian never hesitated, urging him on with breathy moans and pleas as Kyle rammed into him. "God, Sebastian," Kyle muttered.

He was so hot and tight, but it wasn't enough. Kyle wanted to see Sebastian's face when he came. *Needed* to see him. He pulled out and turned Sebastian over, lifting his legs up. Their eyes locked as they moved together, and Kyle groaned as Sebastian squeezed around his cock. "So good, Sebastian. You're so good."

He couldn't remember a lover who'd ever felt as good as this. He'd been with plenty over the years, but this *boy* was inexplicably the best by far. Sebastian was rock hard between them, and Kyle wrapped his palm around him, stroking in time with the thrust of his hips. He slapped against him, and Sebastian panted, lips parted, clear green eyes focused on Kyle.

Driving deep, Kyle reached up and brushed Sebastian's hair from his bruised face. "You shouldn't be here," he muttered. Still pumping into him, Kyle kissed a mark marring Sebastian's collarbone, soothing it with his lips and tongue. He should be safe somewhere far away from Kyle's world of death and deception.

Sebastian only clung to him harder, grasping Kyle's hand and threading their fingers together as he met Kyle's thrusts. Kyle rubbed against Sebastian's prostate, making Sebastian gasp. "Again. Yes, *yes*." Repeating the motion, Kyle flicked the head of Sebastian's cock with his thumb as well, and Sebastian came, moaning. He shuddered as Kyle milked him, his head tipped back, eyes shut. Kyle slowed his pace, holding himself still as he watched Sebastian's ecstasy.

He clamped down on Kyle's cock inside him, and Kyle groaned at the scorching heat. Kyle moved again, slamming in and out as his balls tightened. When he flew over the edge, the bliss radiated out to his fingers and toes as he emptied.

Chest heaving, he pulled out carefully and tossed the condom in the direction of the bathroom. He lowered Sebastian's legs, flopping down on top of him. They kissed softly, and Sebastian nipped Kyle's lower lip. "If this is your method for making people talk, you must be the most popular superspy in the world. At this rate I'll never tell you."

Kyle shook with laughter, slapping Sebastian's ass playfully. He should be furious. He should be putting a gun to Sebastian's head and demanding the information. He should be more than ready to say good-bye to Sebastian, do the job, and get his life in order. He should be worried about the Association turning on him and what that meant for his career. For his life expectancy.

But the lure of spending one last day with him was too strong to resist. He kissed the hollow of Sebastian's neck. "You win—for now."

He should be doing *anything* but falling in love.

CHAPTER ELEVEN

"**W**HAT AM I going to wear?"

Sebastian was still naked and in no rush to get out of bed. To his delight, Kyle had woken him with his mouth wrapped around Sebastian's cock, and as the room brightened, they laid with heads close together, the sheet tangled around their feet. "I think I'll get a bit of attention running around shirtless."

Kyle caressed Sebastian's chest. "Mmm. Definitely." He pressed a kiss to one of Sebastian's nipples and got out of bed. "Don't worry; room service should have delivered by now."

"Room service? In *this* place?"

Kyle picked up a gun and opened the door cautiously before bending out of view. When he straightened, he had a plastic bag. He locked the door and dumped out the bag on the bed. "Underwear, socks, shirts, jeans. Told the manager not to cheap out or his tip would be affected."

It was just past dawn, and the curtains were still drawn for safety. Kyle flipped on the light, and Sebastian gasped softly as the bruises and scrapes on Kyle's body came into view. He kicked off the sheet and went to Kyle, skimming his back with his fingertips. "Aren't you in pain? Why didn't you say something?"

Kyle glanced over his shoulder and stepped into his jeans. "It doesn't tickle. But it's fine."

"Years of experience?"

Kyle's smile was wry. "Exactly." He turned and reached for Sebastian's ass, stroking it lightly. "We went pretty hard last night."

Sebastian smiled just thinking about it. "Uh-huh. We're not planning on any horseback riding today, right?"

As Kyle laughed, Sebastian felt a little thrill. Kyle wasn't simply smirking as usual—he was smiling and laughing with a new lightness, as though an invisible wall had come down. Sebastian's heart skipped a beat.

It was insane to think he'd known this man less than a week. He still didn't really know what to make of him or which Kyle he was going to get in any given moment, but he found himself hoping his father's meeting tonight was postponed so he could spend as many days or hours with Kyle as possible.

"I don't know where we're going, remember? I sincerely hope there won't be any horseback riding involved."

"Speaking of going, we should get to the train station in about forty-five minutes." Sebastian kissed Kyle lightly and pulled on his new clothes.

"It's not far. So how did you break the code without a computer?" Kyle asked.

"It was easy once I figured out the language key was German. The numbers represented certain letters, and of course they weren't in order, so then I had to figure out the columnar transposition and—"

"Okay, okay, I'll leave the codes to you." Kyle raised his hands.

"And I'll leave the killing people to you. See? We're a perfect team."

Kyle's smile faded, and he zipped his duffel. "Only for today. Don't start daydreaming. You realize how dangerous this is? You can still change your mind and get out. Start a new life now."

"No. I'm not finished with this one yet. So don't think about ditching me for my own good once we get where we're going."

Kyle regarded him evenly. "Still considering it."

"I'm seeing this through, Kyle." He extended his hand as Kyle had to him on the train. "Promise me. We're a team."

A few seconds ticked by, and Sebastian held his breath. Kyle took his hand, shaking it firmly. Not letting go, he tugged Sebastian toward him, kissing him hard.

THE TRAIN TO Naples had barely left the station when there was a knock on the door of their private compartment. Kyle had a number of credit cards under aliases the Association was unaware of, and for the first time he'd had to use one to buy their train tickets. His stomach knotted as he thought of his now former employers. He'd trusted them. He'd been a fool.

Sebastian was by the sink, and he put his eye to the peephole. Before Kyle could tell him to stop, he was opening the door. "It's okay; it's a woman."

As Marie stepped into the room, Kyle whipped his gun from his belt. After a moment of clear surprise, Sebastian quickly closed the door and flicked the lock. Marie raised her hands. "I'm not the enemy, Mr. Grant. I just want to talk."

Kyle's arm didn't waver as he aimed the gun at her chest. "Not going to happen."

"I think you owe me that much. Five minutes."

Kyle simply shook his head.

"Please." Her eyes implored him.

He barked out a laugh. "Your feminine wiles won't work on me. You set me up. Sent that team after us."

"No. It was the director. He wants the Chimera for himself so he can sell it to another buyer. I had no idea. But one of the section chiefs grew suspicious. He alerted me yesterday."

"Likely story."

"It's the truth. I'm glad you're all right." She glanced back at

Sebastian, who hovered by the door anxiously. "Both of you."

"Really? Because two days ago you instructed me to kill him."

"I was simply following orders."

"Good thing I didn't."

Sebastian spoke up. "I have to agree."

"Kyle, I'm here to help." Marie's face shone with sincerity. "We both want the same thing. Hear me out."

Sebastian stepped forward. "I can leave you two alone. Go get breakfast."

"No. You stay here." Kyle lowered his gun and tucked it into his jacket. "Do *not* open the door for anyone but me. Not her and not any other woman. A woman can kill you just as easily as any man."

Sebastian nodded, and Kyle motioned for Marie to go first into the hall. He listened to hear the *click* of the lock after the door closed behind him. The dining car was adjacent, and Marie led the way. She walked by the first table, which was empty, but Kyle stopped her. "This'll do." He sat in the far chair, giving him a clear view of the aisle and the door to their room twenty feet away.

As a waiter took their breakfast orders, Kyle watched the hallway. A man walked by but didn't pause or seem to give the door to the cabin any notice. Focusing on Marie, Kyle kept one hand in his lap, in easy striking distance of his weapon. "Talk."

"He set you up. The director. He knew the Chimera wasn't in that safe. I think he also knew you wouldn't stop looking for it. He's going to be there tonight—from a distance, I assume—and he's counting on you being there to take the fall. Going to let you get the weapon and kill you."

"Why me?"

"You're good at your job. I think he hoped you'd find the Chimera before tonight. You'd turn it in like a good little boy, and he'd take it. Replace it with a fake."

The waiter returned with a steaming carafe of coffee and filled their cups. Kyle sipped his and pondered what Marie had told him. "Why the charade with breaking into Brambani's room?"

"He knew you'd want to prove yourself. Especially after Singapore. Which wasn't your fault, by the way."

Kyle sat back in his chair. "Explain."

"We went back and checked the transmissions. The final information you were sent was bogus. Sent you to the wrong house, right next door to the target. Of course he, or whatever minion did his dirty work, covered it up. But the lab tech found a layer in the transmission. Underneath was the original message to you with the incorrect location." She stirred milk into her coffee. "He made us doubt you. Planted the seeds in case he'd need to pin this on you down the line."

"What about Rio?"

She smiled. "No, that was all you. But everyone gets to make a stupid mistake sometimes."

He raised an eyebrow, his lips twitching up. "Even you?"

She nodded, her smile disappearing. "I should have known better. I'm sorry."

"So if I believe you, what's the next step?"

"Go to the meet in Positano. Get the Chimera. Kill or capture the director."

"Positano?" Small town. Built into a cliff. The rendezvous location would likely be a challenge to access.

Marie's brow furrowed. "You're on your way there, *non*?"

He paused before replying. "Sebastian broke the code. He wants to come along and help."

"And you've agreed to this?" Marie asked incredulously. "Why didn't you get rid of him days ago?"

A man appeared in the corridor beyond the dining car, and Kyle tensed. The man—average build, brown hair, fanny pack around his waist—examined his cell phone as he slowly approached the cabin door. Kyle reached for his gun, flicking off the safety with his thumb as he held it under the table.

Marie turned to look as well. "Not one of ours. I think he's nothing to worry about."

Kyle didn't answer, staring intently and inching to the edge of his chair as the man came abreast of the cabin. His pulse thrumming in his veins, Kyle exhaled deeply as he prepared to intercept.

But the man didn't even glance at the door as he continued toward the dining car, his attention focused on whatever message he was tapping on his phone. He walked by their table and joined a family halfway down the car. Kyle heard a few snippets of Swedish as the man spoke to a young boy.

Sitting back, Kyle slipped his gun back into his jacket. Marie stared, blinking. "What?" Kyle barked. Despite himself, he felt his face heat.

Marie peered over her shoulder again in the direction of the cabin. When she looked back, she wore an expression of wonderment. "You've fallen for him." It wasn't a question.

A denial sprang automatically to Kyle's lips, but he couldn't quite force it out. He hitched his shoulder in a shrug.

"I never thought I'd see the day, Mr. Grant." Marie smiled, shaking her head. "And I thought I'd seen everything. You've barely ever fucked the same man twice."

"And how would you know?"

"I know everything, darling. Or at least I thought I did. The closest you've ever been to a relationship is that fellow in London you had sex with three times. Shame he was working for the opposition."

Kyle's smile held no humor. "Hazard of the profession."

The waiter brought their omelets, and they ate quietly for a few minutes. Marie wiped her mouth daintily with her napkin. "You're sure this boy isn't something other than he seems? Those big, innocent eyes might be hiding something."

"I'm sure." He knew he shouldn't be—he hadn't suspected

Lee of being a double agent until it was almost too late—but he was. He felt it in his bones. He could trust Sebastian.

Marie grinned. "Mr. Grant, I never knew you were a romantic." Her smile faded. "You know they'll kill him, even if the director is ousted. He knows too much."

"I'm taking care of it. They won't be able to find him. And you'll ensure they don't look too hard." This wasn't a question either.

"All right."

"All right? That was easy." *Far too easy.*

She glanced back at the cabin door. "It goes against every procedure, but yes. I'll do everything I can to help you. To help your young man."

"He's not...I'm never going to see him again after this."

"But you wish you could."

Kyle wanted to deny it, but somehow he couldn't. It was alarming. He'd never felt so off balance in his life. "What I want is irrelevant."

"Very true."

"Why are you helping me? You should be reporting me. Arranging for another operative to take out Sebastian."

"I should." She sipped her coffee. "Yet here we sit."

"You still haven't answered the question."

"Which one?"

"*Why?*"

"Because we've been friends for a long time, Mr. Grant. Because I owe you one."

He wanted to believe her so badly. "If this is a ruse, if you're..."

"You have my word. Whatever that's worth to you." She reached across the table, and Kyle allowed her to take his hand. "I'm on your side. I always have been. I'm not perfect. I made an error in judgment. Let me make it up to you."

After a long moment, Kyle nodded and hoped he wasn't making a mistake of his own.

THE KNOCK WAS followed immediately by Kyle's voice. "It's me."

Sebastian hurried to the door and took the plate of food Kyle handed him as he entered. Stomach growling, Sebastian settled on the bottom berth to eat as Kyle paced the length of the cabin in slow, measured steps.

After swallowing a bite of buttered toast, Sebastian asked, "So? What did she say?"

"Several things." Kyle continued his steady pace.

"About?"

"Several topics."

Sebastian tapped his fork on the side of his plate. "Anything about tonight, perhaps?"

Kyle stopped by the window, eyes on the horizon. "Yes. She has the location. We developed an approach strategy."

"Oh." So much for the advantage he'd gained by knowing where they were going. "I'm still coming."

"That might prove to be a problem."

Sebastian put his plate aside with a clatter and shot to his feet. "What? No, I'm coming, Kyle."

"I don't think you can."

"You promised." He realized he sounded like a petulant child and took a breath. "Kyle, I want to do this."

"It's extremely unwise given your limitations."

"What *limitations?* Fine, I'm not a trained killer like you, but I can do this. Look at what I've already done!"

"You've done more than most people could. But we only have one possible point of entry." Kyle turned from the window to face him. "The meeting is at a villa atop one of the highest cliffs just outside Positano. By land it will be too heavily guarded. Chance of success is too low."

"So how…" Sebastian's stomach clenched. "But you can't. That cliff is too high. I've been to Positano. That would be insane." His heart rate increased just thinking about it.

"I can handle it."

"Then so can I." The defiant words were out before he could stop them.

Kyle's expression softened, and he stepped close, cupping Sebastian's cheek with his palm. "You don't have to prove anything. It's too dangerous."

"But…" Sebastian sighed. He knew Kyle was right. "I guess I liked the idea of doing something, of being on the attack. Not just running and hiding. You know what I mean?"

"Yeah. But even without the cliff, it's too dangerous. I need to be able to focus and get the job done. I can't do that if I'm—" He broke off suddenly.

Sebastian inched closer. "Worrying about me?"

Kyle kissed him then, Sebastian's face in his hands as his tongue opened Sebastian's mouth. Sebastian moaned into him, wrapping his arms around Kyle's back. Kyle broke away and brushed his thumb across Sebastian's lips. "I should have left you behind days ago."

"Are you sorry you didn't?" Sebastian realized he was holding his breath waiting for the answer.

After a long moment, Kyle shook his head and rested their foreheads together. "Are you sorry you met me?" His voice was barely a whisper.

"I should be." Sebastian smiled, kissing Kyle deeply. No matter how upside down his life had become, he could never regret what they'd shared. "But with you it's…"

"What?"

"How I always imagined it could be. With a man."

KEIRA ANDREWS

Reaching down, Kyle stroked Sebastian through his jeans. "What did you imagine?"

There was sudden heat between them, and he thrust into Kyle's hand. Sebastian had fantasized many things over the years. Meeting someone he could spend the rest of his life with. Someone he loved, who loved him back. But as Kyle touched him, his mind went straight into the gutter. "Getting fucked. Having a big cock inside me. Opening me up."

"Where did you learn about it?" Kyle's voice was husky.

"My cousins had horses, and I'd hide in the barn sometimes, watching. I'd sneak away for hours, hoping to see something. There was this one stallion; he couldn't get enough."

Kyle's breath was hot against Sebastian's neck. "Did you get off?" He opened Sebastian's fly and pulled his cock free, stroking roughly.

"Yes," Sebastian breathed. "I'd be so hard, hiding in the hay-loft."

"How did you touch yourself? Like this?" Kyle squeezed his palm around Sebastian's shaft.

"Uh-huh. But first I'd start with my nipples." He snaked his hands under his T-shirt. "I'd squeeze them like this. Get them hard."

"Then your cock?" Kyle flicked his thumb over the head, sending a tremor through Sebastian.

"Not yet. I liked to make it last. I'd get on my hands and knees."

"Show me."

His jeans sliding down his thighs, Sebastian crawled onto the lower bunk. Glancing back at Kyle, who stood stock-still, his hardness bulging in his pants, Sebastian slipped two of his fingers into his mouth. Eyes locked with Kyle's, he sucked and licked, making them slippery with his saliva.

"Then I'd fuck myself." He reached back and pushed one

finger inside as Kyle groaned. "I'd open myself up and wish it was a cock." He squeezed another finger in, shoving back with his hips.

"Did you make any noise?" Kyle asked, his voice a growl.

Sebastian shook his head as he pistoned his fingers into his hole. "Had to be quiet. I'd whimper like this"—he moaned as he brushed his gland—"and it was so hard not to shout." He sat back on his heels for a moment and yanked his belt out of its loops, fingers still inside him. "Sometimes I'd bite down on something." He put the leather between his teeth.

With a muttered curse, Kyle was on him, yanking at his jeans as he covered Sebastian's body, flattening him on the mattress, his own fingers joining Sebastian's deep inside him, filling him. Sebastian could feel Kyle's hot cock against his ass, already dripping.

It took him a moment to register the knock at the door. Kyle's curse was louder this time. Breathing heavily, he continued pressing his fingers rhythmically against Sebastian's prostate, sending sparks of electricity through his body as his balls tightened. He reached for Sebastian's cock, stroking it roughly as the pressure built.

Kyle cleared his throat. "Yes?"

"Am I interrupting?" Marie asked, laughter in her tone.

"Five minutes." Kyle's voice sounded utterly normal and relaxed. He batted Sebastian's hand away and teased the slit, making him moan over the belt in his mouth.

Marie answered, laughing softly. "Of course, Mr. Grant. I'll give you ten."

Sebastian was so close, his whole body on fire as Kyle brought him to the edge with his hands. "Come for me," he murmured, and Sebastian did, falling apart as his orgasm erupted. "Next time it'll be my cock," Kyle whispered in his ear, and Sebastian shook as another load spilled from him.

Panting, he collapsed to his stomach. Kyle was still hot and hard against him, and Sebastian closed his legs and captured his flesh. Kyle rutted between his thighs, and Sebastian turned his head so they could kiss wildly, teeth clashing, tongues thrusting.

They groaned in unison as Kyle came, hot and sticky on Sebastian's skin.

Ten minutes later, Sebastian sat on the bed, dressed and wiped clean, cheeks still flushed, body still humming from the fierceness of his climax. He'd never told anyone about the barn before. Peter probably would have thought he was weird.

But with Kyle, Sebastian felt he could say anything. He wondered if Kyle would go with him to a farm some day and fuck him blind in the barn. The mere thought stirred him, and he banished the idea from his mind as Marie entered the cabin. *It's not going to happen anyway. There's not going to be a "someday" with Kyle.*

"Hello, Sebastian." A smile played at Marie's lips, and her eyes twinkled.

"All right, all right. Back to business." Kyle held out his hand.

Still smiling, Marie pulled a folder from her satchel and handed it to him. "As you wish."

Sebastian fidgeted. "Do you want me to go? I can wait outside if you want to talk about…secret stuff or whatever."

Kyle and Marie shared a glance, and Kyle sat down on the end of the bunk, keeping a few feet between him and Sebastian. "No, you can stay." He opened the folder and read silently.

Folding her legs gracefully under herself, Marie sat across from them, leaning against the wall. Sebastian stood. "Would you like to sit here?" He indicated the bunk with his hand.

"Ah, a gentleman! What a pleasant change of pace." She arched an eyebrow at Kyle, who ignored her. "*Merci*, but I'm fine here." She watched Sebastian with a curious gaze. "You really are good with numbers, hmm?"

Before Sebastian could answer, Kyle snapped, "We're here to

talk about tonight. That's all. Focus."

"Yes, of course. So sorry to interrupt your...*focusing* earlier."

"*Marie.*"

"Well, get the map and blueprints out then, Mr. Grant."

As Kyle unfolded the documents, Sebastian attempted to will the blood from his cheeks. The fact that Marie knew what they'd been doing and probably *heard* them was mortifying. She clearly delighted in teasing Kyle, and Sebastian found himself fascinated by watching their interaction as they studied the map on the floor. They communicated with a kind of shorthand that came from time and trust. Sebastian hoped she was worthy of that trust.

Lifting his hand below his T-shirt, Sebastian ran his fingertips over a bit of dried semen he'd missed during their hasty cleanup. This remnant on his skin made him tingle, and he thought again of the barn and being there with Kyle. Being mounted as he'd fantasized about so many times.

Shaking his head slightly, he focused his attention on the villa blueprints Kyle now pored over. *Enough daydreaming.* Even if they made it through the night, there'd be no excursions to the countryside in their future. Kyle would be off on a new mission, and Sebastian would be God knows where.

His new life.

He shivered. Where would he go? What would he look like? Who would he *be?*

"Sebastian?"

He looked up to find Kyle and Marie gazing at him as if awaiting a response. "Pardon?"

Kyle asked, "Did you ever meet this associate of your father's?"

"Sorry, what was the name again?"

"Bruno."

"As in the mobster?"

Marie answered. "That's him. Do you know him?"

"No. But my brother knows his daughter."

She nodded. "Not surprised. All the better to keep control over your father. They've been in business together for years, but a connection by marriage would be extremely beneficial to Bruno."

Sebastian ran a hand through his hair. *Oh, Ben. What are you mixed up in?* He tried to put his brother from his mind. As Kyle and Marie began discussing someone called the director, Sebastian's thoughts returned to what tomorrow—and the days and months after—would bring.

All he knew was that he'd be alone.

CHAPTER TWELVE

THE SUN GLEAMED off the water as they neared Positano. On one side, buildings hugged the cliffs, the sea spreading out on the other. In the backseat of Marie's rental, Sebastian listened as she and Kyle mulled over strategy.

"It would help if I knew what the director looked like. He could jump in this car at the next stoplight, and I wouldn't know it," Kyle said.

Marie laughed. "Well, you'd shoot him either way, so what does it matter?"

Kyle wasn't laughing. "It matters."

"I haven't met him either. But the section chief is sending a team to locate him tonight. It's believed he won't be at the actual rendezvous, but he'll be close by in Positano. The team leader is contacting me at seventeen-hundred."

Sebastian couldn't see Kyle's face but knew he was clenching his jaw. "How do you know the section chief isn't in on it? What if they're setting us both up?"

"I don't. We can never be certain of anything in life, can we?"

"*Marie.*" Kyle huffed, exasperated.

Marie reached over and pinched his cheek affectionately. "We do what we can in our line of work. If the section chief wanted to take us out, there are much easier ways than leading us on this merry chase."

"True," Kyle admitted.

A siren wailed behind them, and Marie glanced in the mirror.

"*Merde.*" To Kyle she added, "Carabinieri."

"You weren't speeding." Kyle sounded grim. He glanced back at Sebastian. "Don't say anything. Follow our lead."

Sebastian nodded as Marie pulled over on the narrow shoulder. She lowered her window. "Hello, Officer," she said, speaking flawless Italian. "I must apologize if I was speeding."

The officer regarded her silently for a moment. Finally he asked for her license and papers. Kyle handed her the rental agreement as she slid her license from her wallet. Sebastian wondered what name appeared there.

From his vantage point in the backseat, he could see only the policeman's nose and mouth, the lips slack and conveying no emotion. Sebastian shifted, his pulse increasing as the cop silently surveyed the rental papers. What if the carabinieri were in his father's pocket? Or the director's? He felt strangely guilty although they hadn't technically done anything wrong. At least not on the drive.

Crossing his legs restlessly, he kicked a cup holder and sent a soda can spinning with a metallic clang. The officer bent down and observed Sebastian, his eyes hidden behind mirrored sunglasses.

"Careful!" Marie laughed, shaking her head. "My clumsy brother. My husband and I are stuck with him for a week. A whole week! Can you imagine?"

Sebastian smiled weakly. "Shut up." It was a lame retort, but all he could think of and the type of thing he would say to Ben. At any moment he expected the cop to pull his gun and arrest them. Or maybe shoot them dead on the side of the road.

Fortunately he did neither. He handed Marie back her license and intoned, "This is a construction zone. Slow down."

"Yes, of course. My sincere apologies." Marie did sound genuine. Sebastian wondered how Kyle knew when she was telling the truth.

No one spoke until they were back under way, Marie driving at a sedate pace. They passed a bright sign declaring the construction zone, and she sighed. "Possible he really was enforcing regulations."

"Possibly," Kyle replied. "Possibly they know we're coming."

"They who? My father? Or the director?" Sebastian asked.

Kyle shrugged. "Take your pick."

"Plan stays the same." Marie checked the rearview mirror. "The director was already expecting you anyway, and this might be nothing. No way to know."

Sebastian spoke up. "Isn't that kind of like going into a trap?"

"*Oui*." Marie met his gaze in the mirror. "Welcome to the wonderful world of espionage."

Outside Positano, Marie pulled into a gas station. Kyle leaned over and checked the gas gauge. "You've only used a quarter tank."

"Correct, Mr. Grant. But I like to keep a full tank on a mission. Always be prepared." She nodded her head toward the pumps. "I'll let you do the honors."

"So generous." Kyle shook his head, but Sebastian could see his small smile as he got out of the car.

As Kyle filled the gas tank, Sebastian said, "So you've known Kyle a long time."

Marie caught his gaze in the mirror. "I have. And what do you make of our Mr. Grant?"

"I…" Sebastian floundered, searching for something to say. "I don't know if I can sum it up in a sentence."

Marie laughed gaily. "You can use two if you like. Three, even."

"He's…" *Sexy. Dangerous. Brave. Strong. Amazing.* "Confusing."

"Ah. Well, you certainly have *him* confused."

"I do?"

KEIRA ANDREWS

"*Mais oui.* He was supposed to leave Como the morning after the party. He certainly wasn't supposed to rescue you and sweep you along on this mission. Especially after being told to eliminate you."

"By you."

"Nothing personal, Mr. Brambani."

Sebastian snorted. "Of course not. Can't see why I would take my murder personally."

She laughed. "Well, lucky for you our plans have changed."

"I feel *so* fortunate."

"I see why he enjoys you. He doesn't enjoy much. His work, of course, but you're something altogether different."

"Thank you?"

"Yes, it's a compliment." She glanced out the window, watching Kyle go inside the station to pay. "So tell me what he's like in bed."

Sebastian choked on his soda. "I... He's..."

"A great lover?"

Sebastian's cheeks flamed. "Maybe."

"Oh, don't be coy with me. He is."

"How would you know?" Sebastian felt a twinge of jealousy. *Had Kyle and Marie...?*

"I wouldn't, but I can imagine." She turned and whispered over her shoulder. "My guess? Strong and passionate, but tender when the situation calls for it."

Sebastian blushed further as Kyle returned to the car. Kyle glanced between Sebastian and Marie. "What?"

"Nothing!" Sebastian answered, cringing inwardly at how guilty he sounded.

Marie simply laughed merrily as she pulled back onto the road, and Sebastian found himself smiling.

MARIE HAD ALREADY arranged for a hotel room for Kyle in a small, unassuming establishment. She coyly asked whether Sebastian would require a room of his own, garnering a glare from Kyle in response. Marie simply winked and handed him the key card while Sebastian examined his shoes.

The room was surprisingly large, with tall windows overlooking the sea and a small sitting area along with the queen-size bed in the corner. The marble floors were worn but clearly polished daily. Sebastian flopped down on the bed. "I wish we could just stay here all night."

"You can." Kyle removed his boots. "In fact, you will."

"With you, I mean."

Kyle began itemizing his equipment. He thought of spending the night with Sebastian in the soft bed, maybe letting Sebastian have him. It had been a long time since he'd let anyone take control, and he wondered what it would be like to have Sebastian inside him. His cock twitched, his breath hitching.

"Kyle?"

"Well, I can't stay. You know that," he added gruffly.

Giving up on the equipment for the moment, Kyle went to the bathroom, leaving Sebastian alone. He'd barely shut the shower curtain when Sebastian was there, climbing into the tub. He smiled. "Thought you might need some help washing your back."

Kyle couldn't hide his own smile as he pulled Sebastian close under the spray of water. "Very considerate."

Sebastian unwrapped the bar of soap and lathered it between his hands. He kissed Kyle once, softly. As he soaped Kyle's body, Kyle closed his eyes and relaxed into his touch. He felt so *comfortable* with Sebastian. It was a strange but not unpleasant sensation.

Turning, he captured Sebastian's lips in another kiss. A voice in the back of his head reminded him that he had a mission in two hours and he should focus on it. Yet he couldn't get enough of the sweetness of Sebastian's mouth as he swept his tongue inside. Couldn't get enough of Sebastian's firm, lithe body pressing against his. Couldn't get enough of the warmth that filled him— heat that was more than simple desire.

Enjoy him while you can. Tomorrow it's over.

Sebastian soaped Kyle's dick, lathering it thoroughly. "So you know what I used to watch while I jerked off. What about you?"

Kyle bit back a moan as Sebastian caressed his balls. "No horses around where I grew up, sorry. A few cats. Neutered."

Laughing, Sebastian smacked Kyle's thigh. "Okay. How about the last time you made yourself come? What were you thinking of?"

The truth slipped out before Kyle could think to stop it. "You."

Sebastian froze, his eyes widening. "What?"

"The night we met. Back in my room. Horny as hell." He drew Sebastian even closer, hands on his ass. "Could only think of you."

Sebastian pulled Kyle's head down for a kiss. When he broke away, his eyes were dark with lust. "How did you imagine it?"

Kyle's pulse increased, and he grew harder every second. "Like this." With a firm hand, he pressed on Sebastian's shoulder. Sebastian sank to his knees immediately, his hands on Kyle's thighs, rubbing and touching. He looked up expectantly, and Kyle ran his right hand through Sebastian's hair, his fingers tightening.

Sebastian opened his mouth, and Kyle slid inside, groaning at the delicious heat. He rocked in and out, gently at first, but Sebastian urged him on, opening wider, his lips stretching over Kyle's cock. Kyle increased his pace, remembering his fantasy that night in Como.

But Sebastian never failed to surprise him, and as he pushed a soapy finger into Kyle's hole, Kyle's moan echoed off the wet tiles.

Sebastian took him in deeply, relaxing his throat and humming. The wet heat was incredible, and Kyle rocked in, filling Sebastian's mouth. Lips parted, he breathed deeply, the pleasure building as his balls tightened. Sebastian crooked his finger and found just the right spot, and Kyle exploded, shooting deep down Sebastian's throat.

As the pleasure receded, he braced a hand on the shower wall. Sebastian swallowed around Kyle's cock, stroking with his hand to get every drop. When he finished, he released Kyle and stood, his cock rock hard. Kyle took him in hand, jerking him roughly as they kissed.

Sebastian came quickly, and he leaned against Kyle as he shuddered with aftershocks. Kyle found himself holding Sebastian close. Eyes shut, he held him as they swayed gently under the water, skin to skin.

With a sigh, Kyle stepped back. "Time to get ready." He checked his watch. "Thirty-seven minutes until I rendezvous with Marie." He turned off the water and pulled back the shower curtain. Before he stepped out, he turned back and kissed Sebastian one more time.

SEBASTIAN TUGGED ON his jeans as Kyle finished dressing. "All black, huh? Isn't it a little cliché?"

Kyle smirked. "Well, at least they won't see this cliché coming."

There was a knock, and Kyle ushered in Marie. Sebastian soon saw that Kyle had snapped into work mode. No more tender glances or touches—Kyle barely even looked at him as he conferred with Marie about another team of operatives who had arrived.

"They brought this." Marie unfolded a piece of paper from her small purse. While Kyle was dressed like a cat burglar, Marie looked as if she was headed out for a fine dinner—her dark curls cascading over one shoulder, a flowing red dress falling to her knees. The demure neckline was accented by a string of pearls.

"Where do you keep your gun?" Sebastian asked. "That clutch looks too small."

A sly smile gracing her lips, Marie lifted one leg, planting her stiletto on a chair. She slid up the hem of her dress until Sebastian could see the gun holster strapped to her thigh.

"Are we done with show-and-tell?" Kyle took the paper from Marie's hand. He surveyed it silently. "They're sure the director is here?"

Marie nodded.

"And *you're* sure? Of them? Of the section chief?"

"As sure as I can be."

"How come you've never seen the director, Marie?" Sebastian asked.

"Few have. Only the eight section chiefs worldwide, and the director's personal staff and assistants."

"So he's the big boss. The leader of the Association?" At Marie's nod, Sebastian went on. "Why would he risk coming here tonight? Just being in Positano would be suspect, wouldn't it? Even if he's not personally at the rendezvous?"

Kyle looked to Marie. "Good question."

"I've heard tales of the ever-growing size of his ego, and this seems to confirm it. He likely doesn't dream for a moment that we're on to him. He's expecting Mr. Grant to work his magic and acquire the Chimera, at which time the director's men can steal it from him and take him out, all while framing him for its theft. So when it's used God knows when by God knows who, it will be thought that traitorous Kyle Grant sold it before his death."

Kyle stalked over to his duffel and began checking his weapons, the fury radiating off him. Sebastian wanted to go to him but stayed put. "Why did the director allow the formula for the Chimera to be destroyed?"

"This way the value of the only Chimera known to be left in existence is astronomical. The process to make it was painstaking and complex. It could take scientists years to replicate it. But only such a small portion of the powder is needed for an attack that this vial could last years. Meanwhile the director will be retired on a private island in the Pacific."

Kyle slammed a box of bullets down, sending them skittering across the small table. "We're supposed to be helping people. Saving lives. Not getting rich. If we can't trust him…"

Marie squeezed Kyle's arm. "Let's rain on his plans, shall we?"

"Why me?" Kyle asked. "Of all the operatives in the world, why me?"

"I wish I knew. As your handler, this certainly wouldn't have ended any better for me. I'm sure he would have laid a trail to implicate me. Six months ago I was told I was being reassigned. I resisted, and the section chief backed me."

"They wanted me with a new handler. One in the director's pocket."

"No doubt."

Kyle's expression was unreadable. "Why didn't you let them reassign you? You must get tired of me. I get tired of myself."

Smiling, she shook her head. "And get stuck with some know-nothing new recruit? No, no. Better the devil you know, as they say." She clapped her hands. "All right, time to go."

Although he was just staying in the hotel room, Sebastian's stomach flip-flopped. "Be careful."

Kyle's expression softened, and he seemed about to say something when he glanced at Marie, waiting by the door. He was all business once more. "Remember not to open the door for anyone. No matter what they might say."

"Got it."

"I left you a gun." He nodded to a .45 resting on the bedside table. "You know how to use it. Don't hesitate."

"I'll be fine, Kyle." Sebastian picked up the weapon, flicking the safety off and on.

"I know." He shouldered the backpack carrying his supplies, following Marie out the door. Before he closed it, he glanced back. "Just...remember what I taught you. Stay safe."

Long after the door had closed, Sebastian stared at it, the weight of the gun in his hand a strange comfort. He didn't hear the floorboard creak behind him until it was too late.

OUTSIDE THE HOTEL, Marie gave him the keys to the rental sedan. "I'll be waiting. Going to check in with the other team now."

"Capture or kill?"

"Will depend on the circumstances. The section chief would like irrefutable proof. But termination is an acceptable outcome if necessary."

As he turned to leave, an unfamiliar anxiety coursed through Kyle, making his skin itch. He tugged at the collar of his shirt and glanced back at the hotel. He looked back at Marie when she made a soft tsking sound. "What?"

Her face softened. "I never thought I'd see you in love. You were always so...sensible." She straightened her dress and hair. "Time to go. He'll be fine. He's safer there than anywhere."

"I know. It's reckless. I've never..." Kyle breathed deeply. "I don't know what's gotten into me."

She laughed kindly and pressed a kiss to his cheek. "Yes, darling, it's called love. Happens to the best of us." Her expression sobered. "Rarely ends well. Now go do your job. Good luck."

"You too." As they parted, Kyle didn't allow himself to look back at the hotel again.

An hour later he leaned against the rock face of the cliff, his feet secure on a small ledge. He listened carefully for any sounds of movement. His head was two feet below the top, and he knew a guard was scheduled to patrol the bluff in seven minutes. No sign of him yet, although Kyle didn't dare take a peek.

He'd arrived at the base of the ragged cliff on schedule as the sun dipped below the horizon. The climb up had been a challenge. There were enough handholds and stepped sections of the cliff to allow for free climbing, and the crampons he'd fitted over his boots gave him traction. The night was dark, the moon having waned, and heavy rain clouds had moved in, obscuring the stars but for a few that peeked through.

It had been a long climb, and sweat dripped down the small of his back. He breathed steadily, resting before his encounter with the guard. As the minutes ticked by, Kyle thought of Sebastian. With his fear of heights, he'd have never been able to scale the cliff. Kyle himself certainly wasn't looking down. Always best to keep focus on the present.

He knew Sebastian was safe in the hotel, but worry stubbornly gnawed away at him. He'd never felt so attached to another person. He knew it had to be infatuation; surely once Sebastian was gone, beginning his new life, he would be but a pleasant memory. It wasn't possible to actually fall in love so quickly. Both of their emotions were simply heightened by the danger and the incredible sex. It couldn't really be more.

Could it?

Right on schedule, he heard a faint noise approaching. His steps muffled by the lush grass, the guard made very little noise. Kyle inched up the last couple of feet, the whiff of cigarette smoke reaching him. As it grew stronger, he coiled his body, ready to launch himself over the top of the cliff and onto solid ground.

As he did, the guard exhaled, a puff of smoke coming from his lips, the glowing tip of the cigarette visible in his hand in the darkness. The two shots from Kyle's gun—one to the head, one to the chest—were quiet enough thanks to the silencer. Crouching down by the body, Kyle ground out the cigarette and removed his crampons.

Proceeding on schedule, he approached the main villa in the shadows. All the cameras in the villa and on the grounds should have begun playing a loop of surveillance video thanks to the technical wizardry of ground support from the Association. Kyle could only trust that they were able to remotely take over the villa's servers.

Lorenzo Bruno's security had a surprising amount of holes. Entry from the main drive would be impossible, and there was a great show of fence and gate and guards. Perhaps he thought the climb up the cliff impossible, or, as Kyle suspected, he let his reputation precede him, and woe to anyone who had the nerve to attempt an assault on Bruno's compound. Ego could never be underestimated.

Crouching in the shrubbery at the side of the lavish, three-story structure built into the side of the cliff that extended above this plateau, Kyle listened. He was surprised the buyer would agree to meet on non-neutral territory, but apparently acquiring the Chimera was worth the risk.

Hugging the stucco wall of the villa, Kyle made his way in the shadows to a window in the main room. Light shone from most windows in the house, including this one, and Kyle held out a small mirror to catch a glimpse inside. He spotted Sebastian's father right away and was surprised to be hit by a wave of hatred for the man. Exhaling sharply, he refocused.

Bruno was also present, a fat man famous for his belly-rumbling laugh—which would sound jolly if one was unaware of how many men, women, and children Bruno had slaughtered in his time. He would do anything and everything for money, and for his *famiglia*. He and Brambani were speaking with heads close together. No laughter tonight.

The buyer or buyers didn't appear to be present yet. The other occupants in the room were a handful of lackeys. None appeared to be armed—although they surely were—and Kyle could spot no case or container the Chimera might be kept in. Nothing near Brambani.

Good.

Plan A was to acquire the Chimera before the meeting with the buyer. If Kyle could replace the vial with a decoy and slip out with the real thing, it would be the most desirable outcome. This of course would depend on where the Chimera was and how many guards were posted.

Keeping low, he quickly stole around the side of the villa. Creeping vines covered the side of the structure, and Kyle tugged on one as he examined the thickness. *Should hold.* With his gun safely in a holster on his back that he could access in one point two seconds, he hoisted himself up and climbed.

CHAPTER THIRTEEN

A S SEBASTIAN CRAWLED back to consciousness, he puzzled over why there was such an intense pain in his head. This wasn't the kind of headache caused by too much wine, and he was in a vehicle that rocked steadily.

Then he remembered Kyle and the last insane days of his life. He thought back, trying to make sense of the jumble of images and memories... *Kyle leaving on his mission. Their hotel room. The gun in his hands, the door locked. And then...a sound behind him, two men rushing toward him, overpowering him before he knew it. Then agony and blackness.*

He listened carefully for any sounds of movement, any clues as to his location. The vehicle slowed and made a right turn. Was he in the trunk? He didn't think so—the sounds were clearer than they'd been when Kyle had forced him into the trunk and driven out of Como.

Sebastian didn't feel ropes or cuffs around his wrists or ankles, and as he shifted ever so slightly, he realized his arms were unbound at his sides. He'd been so consumed by the throbbing pain in his head that the rest of his body was an afterthought. He was stretched out on his side and thought maybe he was in the back of a van or small truck.

He froze as a voice spoke from not far away. It was Eastern European—Serbian?—and he couldn't understand what the man said. Another male voice answered, and they spoke quietly.

Opening his eyes a fraction, Sebastian peeked out through his lashes. Night had fallen, and the van had no windows in the back. His head was toward the rear, and he glimpsed streetlights through the front passenger window. No one watched him, so he shifted his stiff limbs, biting back a wince as he lightly probed the swollen lump on the side of his head.

His hair was sticky with blood. Why hadn't the attackers killed him? Why not a bullet to the head rather than a wallop? What did they want with him? He craned his neck but couldn't see over the empty backseat. The men were silent again, and Sebastian concentrated on the feel of the road. It was smooth but now more twisting. They were going uphill.

He had a feeling he knew exactly where they were headed.

Before long the van stopped, and he snapped his eyes shut, trying to remain motionless. A new voice asked what their business was, and Sebastian realized they were at the guarded fence. The unseen driver replied in rough Italian, and Sebastian's body went rigid.

"We've got what Mr. Brambani's been looking for. All in one piece. For now." The man chortled.

Sebastian could hear the mechanized whir of heavy gates opening, and they drove on. He kept his eyes closed, concentrating on breathing evenly. He had no weapon. He had only a vague image of the men who had stormed into the hotel room, flattening him before he could even shoot at them, but he was sure he couldn't overpower them.

He took a chance and opened his eyes again, scanning for anything he could use to defend himself. Clearly they didn't see him as a threat since he was unbound, but the van was empty. No tools, no tire iron. Not even a soda can.

Taking a deep breath, he rattled off a pi sequence in his mind. As the numbers flickered through, calming him, he thought about what he was wearing, and his hands went to his belt. Heart pounding, he unbuckled it as quietly as possible.

He needed the element of surprise, and before he could talk himself out of it, Sebastian crawled forward and launched over the backseat, wrapping the belt around the driver's neck and yanking with all his strength.

The van swerved, and Sebastian kicked at the passenger, knocking the man's gun to the floor. The driver clawed at Sebastian with one hand, the other on the wheel as he slammed on the brakes. Just as the other man found his weapon, the van rocked and tipped onto two wheels, slamming over onto the passenger side.

They all went flying as the van spun to a screeching stop. Sebastian crashed into the sliding door, and he covered his head as the van scraped across the road. Then they were still, and he forced himself forward, dropping the belt and searching for the gun. The driver had landed on the passenger, and they both groaned and swore as they tried to disentangle themselves.

Sebastian's ears rang and he hurt from head to toe, but as he caught a glint of metal in the well of the passenger-side door, adrenaline urged him on. He grasped the weapon as the driver hauled him up by his collar, face scrunched in fury as he swore loudly.

Sebastian pulled the trigger.

The man exclaimed, just a noise of shock as he slumped back, blood blooming over his chest. The passenger was climbing over the seat, shouting in Serbian, and Sebastian pulled the trigger again. But the man was still coming, so Sebastian scrambled back out of his reach before shooting again.

The bullet blew open the man's head, spraying Sebastian with blood. The Serbian collapsed, suddenly motionless and silent. Gasping, Sebastian forced air into his lungs. The driver moaned, moving his arms and legs uselessly as his blood soaked into the ruined van. Scuttling backward, Sebastian found the back door and climbed out.

He stumbled a few feet and crumpled to his knees, vomiting on the side of the lane that led to Bruno's villa. Voices cut through the night, and he wheeled around, gun raised. Rubbing his eyes, he concentrated. The voices were Italian, and they were coming from up the hill.

The van had ended up facing the way it had come, half in a small ditch. There were trees on either side of the driveway, and Sebastian stumbled off the road, keeping low as he put some distance between himself and the van. Hiding behind a thick stand of shrubbery, he thought about what Kyle would do as thunder cracked overhead.

They'd expect him to run back downhill to safety, but he knew he wouldn't be able to get over the fence or past the guards. The lights of the villa shone from above. Tucking the gun into his waistband, he forced his battered body to move, stumbling upward through the trees.

There were no blinds drawn on the floor-to-ceiling windows of the living room, and Sebastian squinted across the clearing from the safety of the tree line. The place was in an uproar, everyone shouting at once, his father's face red with familiar fury. Growing up, he'd cringed at the sound of his father returning home, his strident voice echoing off the walls.

He assumed his father's rage was directed at the Serbian hit men who had failed to deliver Sebastian to him, but with a vicious shove onto his knees, the object of Arrigo's wrath staggered into view. Sebastian swallowed his cry as his father jammed a gun to the back of Kyle's head.

He wanted to dash forward, shouting at his father to stop, but that wouldn't help Kyle. Sebastian needed a plan, and he needed it fast. His father wasn't a patient man, and the fear that he would pull the trigger any second twisted Sebastian's gut. From downhill he could hear agitated voices drifting on the whipping wind as fat raindrops began to fall. A dog barked.

Sebastian had to move. Keeping his eye on Kyle through the rain, he made his way through the trees until he was within sight of the side wall of the villa. His father seemed to have been distracted and was speaking to a guard. He waved his hands, gesturing wildly with his gun. With a deep breath, Sebastian dashed across the wet lawn, sneakers slipping on the soaked grass.

As a bolt of lightning flashed overhead, he knelt in the flower-bed beside the villa. Keeping out of sight, he calculated the distance to the second floor. If he fell from that height, his weight times velocity would lead to an impact rate of—"Stop!" he muttered. *Just do it. You can do it.*

Grasping the vines, Sebastian hauled himself up. The storm was in full power overhead, the rain pelting him and making the vines dangerously slippery. He hadn't climbed so much as a ladder since the tree incident, and his heart pounded painfully. He felt strangely detached from his body, his fingers almost numb.

But he made it up, one step at a time. He didn't look down as he pried a window open and heaved himself into a darkened room. It seemed to be a library, the walls lined with bookshelves and several plump reading chairs scattered throughout the room. Dripping a mix of blood and rainwater onto the gleaming marble floor, he swiped his arm over his wet face and pulled the gun from his waistband.

He crept to the door, which stood open. No one seemed to be alerted to his presence, but he waited anyway before inching to the doorway. It sounded as if someone was noisily ransacking one of the rooms to the right, just off the curving grand staircase. His father still shouted from downstairs, ordering someone to find Sebastian before the buyers arrived. Sebastian checked the gun's clip. Three bullets left. He wasn't a good enough shot to guarantee he could make them count.

An image of the Serbian's head exploding ricocheted through Sebastian's mind, and he tamped down the nausea. *Focus.* He needed to create a distraction. He imagined the villa blueprints Marie and Kyle had pored over, trying to remember something that could help, wishing he'd paid more attention.

As thunder boomed, the lights flickered. With sudden clarity Sebastian knew what he had to do. To the left there was a small back staircase for servants that should lead all the way to the basement. He just hoped what he was looking for was down there.

CHAPTER FOURTEEN

T HE METAL PRESSED into Kyle's skull, and he allowed a moment to curse himself for the botched getaway. He'd dispatched the upstairs guards and had the Chimera in hand when a damn lapdog out for a walk had alerted outside guards to his presence in the flowerbed as he made his escape.

Getting the Chimera had been surprisingly simple, given it had been moved into a brand of secure briefcase Kyle had learned the trick to opening years ago. It hadn't taken more than a minute, and the mission should have been a success. He should be on his way back to Positano. *Back to Sebastian.*

Exhaling, he focused on his current situation. His weapon and pack had been taken from him, and a pat down had revealed the knife strapped to his thigh. They had missed the small dagger tucked into his boot. Along with the gun currently against his head, the other eight men in the room all appeared armed except the large man sitting in a leather recliner. *Bruno.*

One of the guards finished searching Kyle's pack. He shook his head. Waving the gun inches from Kyle's head, Brambani came around, his face beet red, spittle on his lips as he snarled a string of Italian expletives. "Filthy dog. You're going to pay for this. For all of it."

A guard ran in and distracted Brambani, speaking in rapid-fire Italian that Kyle struggled to keep up with. He did make out something about a van and dead men and—his heart skipped a beat—Sebastian. *Was Sebastian dead? No, not him.* Kyle's pulse raced, panic choking him.

Another man appeared. He reported that they were searching the hillside, which was a good sign. He had no idea how Sebastian had ended up at the villa, but he prayed to anyone or anything listening that it was Sebastian they were looking for. That he was still alive.

Brambani muttered, and Kyle understood every word this time. "That boy was always a disappointment. Get rid of the bodies and find him!"

Kyle couldn't hide a smile as Brambani turned back to him. "*That boy* is a man, and you've always underestimated him."

His vision went hazy as Arrigo slapped him hard across the face. "You shut up! Disgusting piece of shit. I'm going to enjoy killing you."

"Papa?" Sebastian's brother appeared. He swallowed hard, eyes wide. "What is this? You said…this is a business deal?"

"*This* is revenge." To Kyle Arrigo added, "So kind of you to deliver yourself here tonight. Saved me the trouble of hunting you down."

A breathless guard returned from upstairs. "I searched everywhere. It's gone."

Digging the tip of his gun into Kyle's temple, Arrigo shouted to his minions. "You said you searched him!"

"We did, sir. He didn't have the vial."

"Search again!"

Rough hands shoved Kyle facedown on the marble and snaked under his clothing. One of the men yanked on Kyle's boots, and made a triumphant shout when the dagger clattered to the floor. Kyle glanced back as they tipped the boots over and stripped off Kyle's socks. The guard's jaw clenched. "No vial."

"Vial? What is he talking about, Father?" Ben asked.

Arrigo ignored him as an intercom buzzed. A tinny voice announced the arrival of guests, and judging by the panicked expressions, Kyle guessed it was the buyers. Arrigo hauled Kyle back up to his knees, fingers squeezed in Kyle's hair. "Where are you hiding it?"

A guard spoke up. "Unless it's up his ass, it's not on him."

Arrigo snarled. "You'd like that, wouldn't you? Filthy faggot." He glanced around the room, his gaze landing on the ornate fireplace set into the interior wall. Surrounded by glittering stones, the white fireplace was likely rarely used, but a poker set stood by it. Arrigo gestured to it impatiently.

Kyle said nothing as a minion hurried over with the poker. Arrigo held it up to Kyle's face. "Maybe I should check for the vial, hmm?"

Kyle kept his expression impassive.

"I think you'd like it too much!" Arrigo's arm whipped back, and he struck across Kyle's back.

Kyle bit his tongue as he struggled to stay upright, the pain sucking the air from his lungs.

"Papa!" Ben exclaimed. "Stop. What are you doing?"

The intercom buzzed again. Bruno spoke calmly. "Take him upstairs. I'll entertain our guests for the time being. It has to be somewhere in the house or on the grounds." He nodded to one of his men, who was approximately seven feet tall and made of muscle. "Salvatore should be able to coax the location out of him."

Kyle didn't struggle as they towed him upstairs. Water glistened on the floor down the marble hallway—along with blood. It went unnoticed by his opponents, but as Kyle was thrown into a study, he considered possible candidates. Possibly Marie had reassigned one of the operatives from the Association's other teams, guessing Kyle might need assistance and hedging her bets on acquiring the Chimera.

Or it could be him. He's surprised you before. He could have escaped his father's men—could he have killed them? *He could be hurt. It might be his blood.* If Sebastian was in the villa, he could be anywhere. He was in danger. He was in over his head. *God, please let him still be alive.* Kyle needed to find him. *Now.*

He barely resisted the urge to roll his eyes as Salvatore put on his best menacing face and cracked his knuckles. "Now, my friend—"

"Where is my son?" Arrigo interrupted. "You took him. Did you kill him?"

Kyle said nothing.

Arrigo clenched his fists. "He has shamed me to my very core. He is a disgrace. He should have been born a *girl*." He spat the last word as if it was a curse.

"He's more of a man than you'll ever be." *Stop. Plant seeds of doubt.* Kyle concentrated on breathing evenly and modulating his tone. "At least he was. I killed him myself hours ago." He chuckled. "I'm not sure what your lackeys told you, but they lied. Your son is dead."

Arrigo frowned. "No. He's out there, running away. They brought him here so I could ensure the job was done properly, but now they're dead."

Kyle laughed. "And you think *Sebastian* killed them? Two professional hit men? Surely you're not *that* gullible." He felt a bloom of pride. Sebastian wasn't to be underestimated. "I don't know what their plan was, but I guarantee you that your son is not here."

Still cautious, Arrigo narrowed his eyes. "Why would you kill him?"

"He knew too much. A man in your position surely understands that. He's dead, and his body will never be found."

For a moment Arrigo's face contorted into something Kyle thought might be grief before relaxing into a smile. "Well, for that I can be grateful."

The door burst open, and Ben stared at his father in disbelief. "You can't mean that."

Arrigo waved Ben away as if he were a fly. "You'll understand one day, my son. The honor of the family must be preserved."

"*Honor?* This is honor?" His eyes shone as he addressed Kyle. "My brother's dead? You killed him?"

"Yes."

With a growl, Ben wrenched a gun away from one of the two guards that had accompanied them upstairs. His arm shook as he pointed it at Kyle. "My brother was good. Basi was...*good.* He can't be dead. He can't!" He inhaled sharply. "You're going to pay."

Arrigo lowered Ben's arm with a gentle push. "Later. First we need the vial."

"Vial of what? What *is* this business deal, Father?"

"Shh, shh. Just be quiet and learn, Beniamino. Watch. You will understand everything in time."

With an electronic whine, the power snapped off and the room plunged into darkness. Kyle rolled toward the desk against the wall to his right, grabbing the letter opener he'd spotted when they brought him in. One of the guards lumbered toward him, and Kyle stabbed the opener into the side of the man's neck as he snatched his gun away.

He turned to fire at the advancing Salvatore, but the weapon jammed and Salvatore slammed into him, sending them both tumbling into the bookshelf against the wall. The air whooshed from Kyle's lungs as he crashed to the floor, his opponent on top of him. Almost immediately Salvatore choked him, meaty fingers crushing Kyle's larynx. He struck out with the useless gun, but it was like a fly on a horse's back. In the darkness, stars appeared in his vision, and Kyle reached out.

He flexed and grasped with his fingers, raising his knees in a vain attempt to dislodge Salvatore while he searched for something—anything—he could use. His lungs burned as his fingertips grazed the edge of the wooden desk chair, and he lunged toward it with all his strength, his fingers closing around the leg—

The shot seemed incredibly loud in the darkness, and Kyle gasped in a breath as Salvatore's hands loosened reflexively. As Salvatore's bulk collapsed on top of him, the man choking and twitching in what Kyle guessed were his last moments, Kyle shoved against the weight and squirmed out. He felt for Salvatore's waist and yanked a gun free.

Blinking, he tried to clear his hazy vision. In the dark he could see the shapes of several people and hear harsh breathing. A man stood in the middle of the room, and Kyle raised his gun toward him as lightning flashed through the cracks in the heavy curtains. He breathed in sharply and tried to say Sebastian's name, but his vocal cords were too bruised. He felt a mess of emotions as he watched a blood-spattered Sebastian: concern, guilt, pride. *Love.*

But there was no time for emotions. He scrabbled backward and tugged on the curtains to let in more light. Sebastian still stood with gun raised, his father and one of the two guards—the other slumped over by the door—keeping their distance in the corner to Kyle's left. From downstairs shots suddenly rang out. It was all going south, the buyers likely feeling as if they'd walked into a trap.

"Basi?" Ben still held a gun, but his arm dangled at his side. He addressed Kyle. "You said…" He looked to his brother, shell-shocked. "Basi, he said he killed you."

Sebastian trained his gun on his father and the guard, his lips quirking up into a half smile. "Apparently I'm hard to kill."

More gunshots echoed through the villa, making Ben jump. They needed to get the hell out and fast. Sebastian's gazed was zeroed in on his father. "He's the one who's really responsible. For all of it. Do you know what he's doing here tonight, Ben? What horrible weapon he's willing to unleash on innocent people just to line his pockets? How can you be here?"

Ben stared at Arrigo. "Is this true, Papa? I knew…I knew you were involved in some…unsavory things, but…" He turned to Sebastian. "He told me he sent you away. To get help."

"Help? For what? To *fix* me?" Sebastian's laugh was harsh.

"I told him there was nothing wrong with you! I told him that he'd accept it if he could just understand. Open his mind. He said he would try." To Arrigo he added, "You promised you would try."

Arrigo only smiled grimly. "To think I once believed you would follow in my footsteps. Be a worthy heir. Too much of your mother, both of you. Nothing but a disappointment to me!"

Stricken, Ben shook his head. "You're the disappointment, Papa."

Sebastian took a step toward his father. "You're never going to hurt anyone again. I'll make sure of it."

"*You?*" Arrigo laughed again. "Useless little faggot. Weak, pathetic—"

Kyle saw the shadow in the doorway a moment before all hell broke loose. He launched himself toward Sebastian, shoving him to the floor as bullets and glass flew through the air. Kyle fired at the new gunman, who fell. Arrigo broke for the door, the remaining guard at his heels, but a moment later another bullet fired and he slumped against the door frame, clutching his side. He turned back to regard his eldest son, who trembled slightly, his gun still extended.

"For our mother. For my brother. For all the years I let myself believe in you."

"Go ahead. Finish me off." Arrigo coughed, then bared his teeth in grimace.

Sebastian pushed at Kyle, sliding out and raising his gun. "I will." He aimed squarely, but a moment later his arm quivered and he took a shuddering breath.

As footsteps roared up the stairs, Kyle reeled off two shots— the first piercing Arrigo's heart, the second slamming into the guard, who'd moved to tackle Ben. Kyle slammed the door shut, Arrigo's body blocking it. He raced across the room and threw open the window, tearing the curtains and tying one end to the oak desk.

When he glanced back, Ben and Sebastian stood motionless, staring at their father's body. Kyle heaved the desk across the door as an attempt was made to push it open. Reaching out, he grabbed Sebastian's hand and tugged him toward the window, wishing he could speak.

Sebastian resisted. "No! I'm not leaving Ben."

Bruno's low voice thundered out. "Brambani!"

Ben gently shoved his brother. "Basi, go. I need to speak with Mr. Bruno. I'm in charge now, and I can't just run away." To Kyle he whispered, "Do you have this vial? This weapon?"

Kyle nodded.

"Then take it and my brother, and get them both to safety." He hugged Sebastian tightly. "I'm sorry, Basi. For everything. As far as Bruno or anyone knows, you were never here. You're dead."

Sebastian shook his head. "Come with us!"

"I need to clean up this mess. I'm in too deep to just run. I have a baby on the way."

Sebastian made a shocked sound. "Valentina?"

"I love her, Basi." Ben smiled ruefully. "Like I said, in too deep." He pressed a kiss to each of his brother's cheeks. "Now go."

Kyle pulled Sebastian with him as he swung one leg over the windowsill. Sebastian tensed but didn't fight as they grabbed on to the curtain and slid out, quickly dropping to the ground. From above Ben called out. "Mr. Bruno? My God, what's happened?"

The power was fortunately still out, and the rain had tapered to a drizzle. Kyle kept close to the side of the villa as he peeked around the corner toward the front. He was about to make the turn when an armed guard appeared, and Kyle pushed Sebastian back, slapping his hand over Sebastian's mouth as he started to say something.

He pressed Sebastian into the villa wall, listening carefully as the footsteps neared. He'd dispatch the guard if he had to, but it would be much preferable if the carnage inside distracted everyone for at least a few more minutes.

The guard neared, and Kyle wished he had one of his knives with him, or a silencer. As if reading his mind, Sebastian passed Kyle his gun, which still had its silencer attached. A moment later a distant voice called out, and the guard answered from a few scant feet around the corner of the villa.

As he hurried away, Kyle and Sebastian exhaled in unison, and their eyes met for a long moment. Then they were kissing, tongues thrusting, panting into each other's mouths. Breathing hard, Kyle pulled back an inch. He wanted to tell Sebastian how proud he was, how glad he was that Sebastian was still alive. Yet words had never been his strength, even without damaged vocal chords.

Instead he wiped some of the splattered blood from Sebastian's face and pressed a light kiss to the bump on his head. Sebastian's fingers tightened on Kyle's waist. Sebastian murmured, "I'm okay."

All Kyle wanted to do was take him in his arms and never let go, but they had to get the job done. Keeping low, they advanced, Kyle going to his knees in the trampled, muddy bed of tropical flowers. Beneath a bird of paradise, his fingers sank into the muck and closed around the vial of Chimera. He peeked into the living room window, relieved to see the room deserted but for several bodies.

After indicating to Sebastian to stay put, Kyle opened a sliding glass door. A tense argument echoed down from upstairs, but he ignored it as he grabbed his pack and dagger and slipped back outside. He hoped the guard hadn't damaged anything in the search; they were in big trouble if he had.

Kyle returned to where Sebastian waited and carefully slipped the vial into one of the secure, waterproof inside pockets of the pack. He put it over Sebastian's shoulders, making sure it was securely fastened. Sebastian's brow furrowed, but he didn't ask why Kyle didn't wear the pack himself.

Turning back in the direction of the cliff, Kyle crouched and led the way. Almost immediately Sebastian whispered, "But we have to go out over the front gate. That was the plan."

Kyle only shook his head and urged him on, crossing the rain-slicked grass toward the cliffside at a run. Chest tightening, Sebastian reached for Kyle's arm. "What are we doing?" He looked forward as the bluff neared. "We can't climb down!" His stride faltered.

One hand firm on Sebastian's pack, Kyle sped up as shouts behind them filled the air. The edge of the cliff neared, and he croaked out, "Plan B!"

With the force of their momentum, they tumbled off the edge into darkness.

Chapter Fifteen

T HE SCREAM LODGED in Sebastian's throat as his feet left solid ground, Kyle's grip on him like a vise as they plummeted. *No, no, no! God! Please!* There was a mighty tug on his back, and suddenly he jerked upward, their fall somehow slowed. Heart in his mouth, adrenaline and terror screaming in his veins, Sebastian looked up at the dark swath of material ballooning above him.

The parachute slowed their descent, a sea wind lifting them mercifully away from the edge of the cliff and the jagged rocks below. Kyle was wrapped around Sebastian's body with arms and legs, and Sebastian grasped him tightly as they plunged.

Even with the chute, they were falling far too quickly, the dark sea rising up to meet them. They hit the water as if it was concrete, the wind knocked from Sebastian's lungs, Kyle torn away from him by the force of the impact as they plunged below the surface. Kicking and reaching with his arms, Sebastian fought his way back to the top, his body screaming with pain.

He gulped in a breath in the humid night air, wiping water from his eyes as he cast about for Kyle. In the aftermath of the storm, the water had calmed considerably, and Sebastian frantically looked for a sign of where Kyle had gone under. "Kyle!" He splashed about desperately, reaching down into the water, unable to see beneath its murky depths.

Ten feet away there was a splash, and Kyle broke the surface, gasping. Sebastian paddled toward him but felt a strange resistance. *Undertow?* He kicked harder, but the pulling increased.

As he went under, he realized it was the parachute filling with water. His pulse racing, he tugged at the pack's straps, kicking violently to fight the inexorable drag of the parachute as it sank and was pulled by the current.

The pack was on too tight, and he couldn't get his arms free. His lungs burned, needing more air as he struggled to return to the surface. Mind screaming, he was pulled deeper into the sea, and he jerked, kicking and reaching out in a panic as he tried to shrug free of the pack.

He got an arm loose, and suddenly Kyle was there in the darkness, tugging at the pack and then on the ropes of the parachute. A few moments later the pressure was released, and they ascended. Coughing and spluttering, Sebastian treaded water, the pack still hanging over his left shoulder. "How?"

Kyle held up a small knife and mimed a cutting motion, the wet blade gleaming as the clouds began to clear and the moon blinked back into sight.

"Now what?" They were surprisingly far away from the shore, Sebastian realized. "Won't they be waiting for us if we try to go back?"

Kyle jerked his head in a nod. He squinted, peering out to sea. He seemed to be waiting for something, and soon Sebastian thought he could see a small boat moving toward them. He sighed, relieved. If they'd had to swim down the coast and then to shore, he wasn't sure he could have made it.

The vessel was nothing more than a fishing boat. It ran without lights, and as it neared, the outboard motor cut out. In the silence Kyle whistled in a short-long-short sequence, and someone in the boat whistled back. They swam to it, and Sebastian saw that the man on board wore night-vision goggles. He peered down at Sebastian, his face obscured. To Kyle the man said, "I have orders for one."

Kyle heaved himself up into the boat. He shook his head and

held up two fingers as he leaned back over the side, reaching for
Sebastian. Then Kyle was suddenly lunging at the man, the dagger
pressed to the stranger's throat. The man lifted his hands in
surrender, and Sebastian saw the butt of the gun he'd been
reaching for.

With a few sideways motions, Kyle rocked the boat, still holding the man at knifepoint. Sebastian lifted himself up and rolled
over the side when it swayed toward him. He took the man's gun,
and Kyle patted him down before releasing him. Kyle cleared his
throat, grimacing. "He's with us. Rendezvous point. Now." He
could barely rasp the words out.

The man nodded and pulled on the cord of the motor, which
roared to life. Sebastian and Kyle sat beside each other on the
bench at the front of the boat. They cut through the water, back
toward the lights of Positano. Sebastian looked back up at the
villa, which was still in darkness. He'd knocked out all the circuits
in the power box, which he'd found in the cellar pantry. *Ben,
please be okay. Please.*

He replayed the events of the past hours in his mind, flashes of
images appearing. *The Serbians collapsing, blood flowing into the
wreckage. Kyle on his knees, Sebastian's father holding a gun to him.
Kyle being choked almost to death. Ben's eyes shining, pulling the
trigger, their father stumbling. The bloom of red on Arrigo's chest as
Kyle finished him off.*

A moment of grief overwhelmed him, and he swallowed a sob,
blinking rapidly. Kyle's warm hand covered his where it rested
between them on the bench. Breathing deeply, Sebastian gripped
it tightly and met Kyle's eyes in the brightening night as the rest of
the clouds rolled out.

Sebastian wanted to tell Kyle he loved him. That he didn't
want to live his life without him.

But he faltered. Kyle had been kind to him, no doubt. He'd
saved his life. They'd shared their bodies. But Sebastian couldn't
fool himself into ever thinking it could be more than that.

Tomorrow it would be over, and they'd never see each other again. Sebastian let go and folded his hands together in his lap. Kyle's brow furrowed and he seemed to want to say something, but Sebastian turned away.

As they approached the harbor, the driver removed his goggles and turned on the boat's lights. They weaved among other vessels as they entered a marina in the south end of Positano. Marie stood on the end of the jetty, and as they neared, Sebastian saw she was smiling.

She looked as polished and unruffled as she had several hours earlier—not a hair out of place, her lips freshly glossed. Sebastian felt as if he'd been through a meat grinder. They disembarked quickly, and the fishing boat disappeared back into the harbor.

Marie led the way down the pier. "Mr. Brambani. I underestimated you. I saw there was a struggle in your room. I didn't expect to see you again."

"Well, I've learned a few things this week."

She smiled. "Indeed you have. It's a shame we can't keep you, resourceful lad that you are." Walking between Sebastian and Kyle, she slipped her hand through each man's arm. "So. Do you have it?"

Kyle nodded, and Sebastian remembered that the vial was still tucked away in the pack. He presumed Kyle had put it in a pocket unaffected by the parachute deployment.

Marie exhaled. "Well, that's one thing that has gone right this evening, then."

"Director?" Kyle was barely able to scrape the word out.

Marie clucked her tongue, concern sharpening her features. "Do you need medical attention, Mr. Grant?"

Kyle shook his head impatiently.

"He escaped. But the cat's out of the bag. He can't return now. We just need to hunt him down. Not that it will be easy, but every agent in the world will be on the lookout. Do you know who the buyer was?"

Shaking his head again, Kyle grumbled. His bare feet slapped on the sidewalk as they walked up to their hotel, and he seemed very tempted to kick something.

"Well, one problem at a time, yes? I have a conference call with the section chiefs in twenty minutes. Kyle, you've made arrangements for Mr. Brambani? He should be gone first thing in the morning. For now there will be more than enough confusion and topics of conversation to distract them."

"What about the Chimera? How do we get rid of it?" Sebastian asked.

"I have a courier waiting to take it to a lab. If the test is positive, they'll…deactivate it, for lack of a better term. It involves chemical compounds and neutralization and things I don't understand. But they'll render it harmless, which is all that matters."

Outside the hotel, Kyle removed the Chimera from Sebastian's pack and gave it to Marie. She smiled. "Enjoy the rest of your night, gentlemen. Mr. Brambani, it's been a pleasure. Take care of yourself, *mon cher*." She leaned in and kissed Sebastian on each cheek and then was gone.

Kyle and Sebastian garnered a few puzzled glances as they hurried through the lobby, both wet and looking worse for wear. Inside their room, Kyle ensured the door was securely locked, and Sebastian locked the large window the Serbians had jimmied. When he turned, Kyle was squatting by a few drops of blood, drying into the faded marble. His nostrils flared. "You killed them?" His voice was barely there.

"I never thought I'd be capable of that. But I was. I am. I…" He closed his eyes and tried to banish the memories from his mind. He stood up straighter. "I know they would have killed me. I did what I had to do."

Kyle nodded. They stared at each other for a long moment

before moving together as one.

One night left. Sebastian decided to enjoy every moment of it. Pressing gentle kisses to the bruises appearing on Kyle's throat, Sebastian leaned into him, tightening his arms around Kyle's waist. They undressed slowly and made their way to the shower, where they kissed softly and soaped each other's bruised bodies.

There was no fire in their caresses, and Sebastian felt that by unspoken agreement, they both wanted to make it last. His body hummed with building desire as they kissed and touched, finally making their way out of the shower. Kyle tried to speak as he ran a towel over Sebastian's back, and grimaced.

"Shh." Sebastian put his finger to Kyle's lips. "You'll make it worse. Let the swelling go down." He kissed Kyle's neck, his tongue tracing the Adam's apple. "I'll talk for you." He ran his fingertips down Kyle's spine. "How do you want me?"

Kyle groaned low in his throat.

Sinking to his knees on the tiles in the steamy bathroom, Sebastian flicked his tongue over the head of Kyle's cock. "Do you want me to suck you?" He teased Kyle's balls with his fingertips as he took him into his mouth from tip to root before pulling back. "Do you want my mouth?"

Kyle caressed Sebastian's head as Sebastian swirled his tongue around the shaft, tracing the throbbing vein on the underside. Kyle rocked forward, clearly eager for more, but Sebastian eased back, sitting on his heels. "You want that? Or do you want my ass?"

With a final kiss to the tip of Kyle's cock, Sebastian stood and turned around. He spread his arms and leaned over, his back arching. "You want this?"

Kyle moved in behind him and rubbed his cock along the crease in Sebastian's ass as he reached around to pinch Sebastian's nipples. Sebastian bit back a moan as he jolted with pleasure. Where they'd been all slow and steady, calm and gentle just minutes ago, now Sebastian felt as though a fuse had been lit, burning across his skin. "Do you wanna fuck me?" He arched back against Kyle's rock-hard cock. "I want you to. I wish you could come inside me, fill me up."

With a strangled moan, Kyle grabbed for his shaving kit, tipping it over and yanking out a foil square. Sebastian knew they had to use protection, but *God* he wanted it raw. "I wish I could feel you without anything between us." He gasped as Kyle pushed inside. He wasn't using lube and it was rough and Sebastian pushed back. "More. Fuck me hard. Make me feel you for days."

Kyle grunted as he thrust in, and Sebastian moaned loudly as Kyle stretched him. Reaching around, Kyle wiped his palm over the mirror above the sink, and as the fog dissipated, Sebastian watched himself. Pupils dilated, he panted as Kyle slammed into him, one hand on Sebastian's hip, the other wrapped around his chest for leverage.

Their eyes met in the mirror, and as Sebastian moaned, Kyle nodded. Sebastian moaned again, louder. "I love your cock. I love it inside me. I love..." He gasped for breath, and then Kyle hit just the right spot inside and Sebastian could only cry out as his body flexed and vibrated.

He felt as if he was being fucked out of his skin, and when Kyle took hold of his cock, Sebastian came, shooting all over the counter, even up onto the mirror as Kyle continued ramming him. Then Kyle was shuddering, his mouth open in a silent cry as he filled the condom deep inside Sebastian.

Both panting, they leaned against the counter, utterly spent. Sebastian tried to smile at Kyle in the mirror. Tried to keep his tone light. He wasn't sure he was successful. "Did I leave anything out?"

A bittersweet smile lifting his lips, Kyle simply pressed a kiss to Sebastian's shoulder.

Chapter Sixteen

KYLE RARELY LINGERED in bed in the mornings. He usually woke at dawn, no matter what time he'd gotten to sleep the night before, and woke fully within a few seconds. He had no need for a snooze function on the rare occasions he set an alarm.

Yet on this morning, Kyle stayed in bed, eyes closed, long after the first rays of dawn woke him. He listened to Sebastian's gentle snore and held his warm body tightly against his own. Spooned behind him, Kyle kissed the back of Sebastian's neck. Hair tickled his nose, and Kyle found himself smiling.

Of course, what he should have done when he woke was get out of bed like every other morning. Go to the bathroom. Shower. Work. Do what he was supposed to do. Put Sebastian on the morning train. Stop thinking about him. Get back to normal.

The thought of a return to routine should have been appealing. Comforting. A relief.

Yet all Kyle could think of was how much he'd miss the man sleeping in his arms. How much he'd miss everything about him. His determination. His courage. His smile. His kisses. His body. His…everything. Kyle would miss *everything*.

Sebastian stirred, and after stretching his sore, battered limbs, he turned in Kyle's arms and rolled on top of him. He smiled sleepily. "Hi." His smile faded after a moment, and he sighed. "I guess this is it."

Kyle reached up, brushing Sebastian's cheek with the back of his fingers. He gazed intently at Sebastian's face, memorizing his features. He'd never see it again—after the surgery Sebastian would be unrecognizable. *He'll be safe. That's all that matters. He deserves a normal life.*

But the thought of never seeing this face again cut Kyle down to the bone, slicing through his resolve. A burst of energy and fear and *longing* flowed through him, and he drew Sebastian down for a deep kiss. Sebastian straddled him, his tongue meeting Kyle's.

When they broke apart for air, Sebastian sat up. Running his hand through Kyle's hair, he smiled sadly. "I should get ready."

Kyle nodded but held on to Sebastian's hips. He cleared his throat, which was still damn sore. "I'm sorry about your father." His voice was better than the night before but still gravelly.

After a moment Sebastian replied. "I'm not." He shook his head. "I'm really not. Does that make me a bad person?"

Kyle shook his head and brushed back Sebastian's hair. "Your father was a bad person."

"But he was still my father. I should...I don't know."

"Fathers aren't always the men we want them to be."

Sebastian ran his fingertips across Kyle's chest. "What about your father?"

Kyle turned his head. "We should get ready."

"What did your father do to you?"

Sighing, Kyle faced Sebastian's inquisitive gaze. "It's nothing. He didn't take a hit out on me or anything. I shouldn't complain."

Sebastian's smile was rueful. "It would be hard to top that."

"All my life I wanted to be a cop like my dad. But I wasn't like my older brothers. They won all the races, joined all the teams. I used to say I wanted to be a cop, and everyone would laugh. It wasn't..." He cleared his sore throat. "They weren't trying to be mean. But they didn't think I had it in me."

"Clearly you proved them wrong."

Kyle wished he could feel satisfied about that, but there was only lingering sadness. "My brothers joined the force, and I worked my ass off in senior year to get in shape and pass the physical. I did, and I got into the academy."

"Didn't that make your dad proud?"

"Yeah." He smiled wistfully. "He was really proud."

"So what happened?"

"He caught me in the shed with Tommy Narracott from up the street." Kyle remembered it like it was yesterday: his hand down Tommy's pants, Tommy's moans hot on his neck as Kyle got him off. His father's disbelief. His rage. "He beat me black-and-blue. Kicked me out."

Sebastian watched him, sorrow pinching his features. "I'm sorry." He still sat astride Kyle, and he rubbed soothing circles on Kyle's chest.

"He told me I'd never be a cop in Pittsburgh as long as he was alive. That I'd be a disgrace to the badge. To our family."

"What about your mom? Your brothers and sisters?"

Kyle gazed at the ceiling as the memories burned white-hot. "I came back the next day, and there was a duffel bag on the stoop. Some of my clothes. A toothbrush. A wad of cash." The money had been dusted with flour; he knew his mother kept a hidden stash in the canister in the kitchen. "I know they were inside—my mother and sisters. I could hear them crying. The walls were always so thin in that house."

"I'm sure they were afraid of your father."

Kyle clenched his jaw. "They could have stood up to him. They could have done something."

"Like my mother did?"

"It's not the same. My father loved them. He would never have hurt them. They could have tried to convince him."

"Maybe they did."

Kyle shrugged. "Doesn't matter now. I left and never went back. The Association recruited me a month later. I was living in a

Y in Philly. I don't know how they found me, but that's what they do."

"You should talk to your family. They must worry about you."

"They're all fine. Lots of kids to take care of. They don't need to worry about me."

Sebastian smiled. "You totally have files on all of them, don't you?"

Kyle had to laugh. "Of course."

"If they could see you now. I mean, maybe not *right now*, but in general. You'd kick any cop's ass." He leaned down and kissed him. "Thank you for telling me."

Kyle returned the kiss. He felt strangely lighter. He'd never told anyone about his family, not even Marie. Holding Sebastian close, he rocked his hips, rubbing their cocks together. This time they didn't rush, and Kyle shuddered with desire as he watched Sebastian open himself up with lube-coated fingers. He rolled the condom onto Kyle's dick.

Sebastian had to be sore, and Kyle let him set the pace. Sebastian was hot and tight and *good*, and he rode Kyle quietly, moving up and down slowly, squeezing. They kissed languidly, tasting every inch of each other's mouths, breathing together as they stoked the fire bit by bit until they tumbled over the edge. Kyle tried to ignore the mournful voice in his head telling him it was the last time. Sebastian rested on top of him, and Kyle held him tightly.

But after a few minutes reality set in, and they silently untangled and got cleaned up and dressed. Kyle repacked his duffel and waited by the door. They left without a word.

Marie had left the keys to the rental car with the front desk, along with a note.

I'll be in touch soon, Mr. Grant. I've been called to meet the section chief in person in the morning. Unusual. Let's hope it's good news.

In the meantime, don't mope too much. It's unnerving.

M. xo

The drive to the Naples train station was largely silent. Kyle had no idea what to say, and Sebastian wasn't talking. Kyle knew this was for the best. It was inevitable. In his line of work, a...*relationship* was just not practical. He had to be realistic.

They walked through the crowded station side by side, not touching, although Kyle wanted to reach out and tangle their fingers. But he didn't. *Make a clean break.* Instead he scanned the crowd automatically. As they neared the platform, he caught a glimpse of a middle-aged man boarding ahead. Something flickered in his memory, and he stopped.

"What?" Sebastian peered into the cluster of people waiting to board.

Kyle ran through a mental file folder of Association operatives. *No matches.* Maybe he was just being paranoid. Only Marie knew he was putting Sebastian on the train. With all the confusion and upheaval involving the director, tying up this particular loose end would certainly be lower on the to-do list. And his gut told him to trust Marie.

"Kyle?" Sebastian leaned in, whispering. "What is it?"

"Nothing."

The conductor blew his whistle, and they walked on. Reaching into his inside jacket pocket, Kyle removed an envelope and passed it to Sebastian. At Sebastian's questioning look, Kyle said, "Bank account information. To pay for...everything." New papers. New face. New life. "Transfer it to a new Swiss account when you have your new name. That way..." *I won't be tempted to find you and put you in more danger.* "It'll be safer."

Sebastian swallowed thickly. "Kyle, I..."

The conductor called from the bottom of the steps ten feet away. "Gentlemen, it's time to board."

Nodding to the man, Sebastian faced Kyle and opened and closed his mouth, as if he had something to say and couldn't quite find the words. Instead, he grasped Kyle's hand as he kissed him, a final brush of lips. He turned and practically ran up the steps into the train. He didn't look back.

Kyle forced himself to walk away. *Don't stand there and watch the train leave like some lovesick schoolboy.* He put one foot in front of the other, trying to ignore the strange hollowness in his chest. If this was love, he never, ever wanted to feel it again.

In the bustling station, he examined people on autopilot, looking for signs of potential trouble, identifying various routes of escape. Something nagged at the back of his mind, and he gave his head a mental shake as he thought about Sebastian riding him that morning, moaning and so beautiful.

Stop! Stop thinking about him. He would pretend he'd never met Sebastian Brambani. It would take mental discipline to wall in the memories, but it was the most logical course of action. He needed to get his life back on track. Back to normal. He'd been out of control on this mission, and it couldn't happen again. Besides, it wasn't fair to Sebastian. Sebastian deserved a better life.

As he inspected the group of people waiting in the ticket line, his mind returned to the glimpse of the man he'd seen boarding the train. Something about him was familiar—unnervingly so. But he could think of no Association operatives that fit the description, even with a wig—

Because he's not with the Association.

The garage. Sebastian in the trunk. The hit man.

Shoving people aside, Kyle raced back through the station. The train was almost at the end of the platform, and Kyle ran, arms and legs pumping as he called out. An employee shook his head as Kyle sped by, and as the train picked up speed, it lumbered out of reach.

Cursing himself for not killing the man properly and being

too quick to escape from Brambani's estate with Sebastian, Kyle reversed course, ignoring the quizzical comments from the employee as he ran past him again. The station had grown only more crowded, and Kyle was tempted to fire a shot into the ceiling to clear the way. He leaped over a baby carriage and finally fought his way outside to the car.

Engine roaring, he thundered off. He had a train to catch.

CHAPTER SEVENTEEN

SEBASTIAN STARED BLANKLY out the window as he left Naples behind. His father was dead. His brother was embroiled in criminal business with no easy way out. He had no possessions. No friends. *No lover.*

All he had to his soon-to-be-changed name was a slip of paper with bank account information printed neatly on it. He'd hoped Kyle had included some kind of note, but there was only the string of twelve numbers that identified the account and the five-digit bank clearing sequence. *What were you expecting? Poetry? A declaration of eternal love?*

Kyle had given him the means for a new life. A fresh start. Sebastian should be grateful, and he was. Of course, one could argue that Sebastian's old life would be going along just fine if he'd never met Kyle Grant. But would it? He'd been miserable, trapped at home and subject to his father's whims. How long before his father would have decided Sebastian wasn't worth the effort? It had all been inevitable, really.

His body ached, bruises and scrapes everywhere after what he'd been through the night before, but as he shifted in his seat, there was one tender spot he savored. Squeezing his ass, it was as if he really could still feel Kyle deep inside him. He was curious to try topping sometime, but the mere thought of being taken made his stomach flip-flop and a thrill course through him.

Thinking of fickle, faithless Peter and his hang-ups now, Sebastian could only laugh. His father had done him a favor when all was said and done. Sebastian hadn't had a clue as to what sex could be. What *love* could be. Sure, Kyle didn't love him back, but Sebastian knew what he felt couldn't be called anything else. And maybe Kyle...

He mumbled to himself. "Stop it." *It's over. You'll never see him again.*

He needed to think about the future. Decide where to go. He could go anywhere in the world. Out of Europe was best, he supposed. Perhaps the man he was meeting would have suggestions. Sebastian had never been to Australia. Couldn't get much farther away than that. Or New Zealand. He could start a new life on the other side of the world.

Although he had enjoyed Boston very much. Perhaps somewhere else in the States. *San Francisco, Seattle, Miami...New York.* With eight million people, what where the odds that he'd ever run into Kyle on one of Kyle's infrequent visits home? Slim to none. *And if I did happen to see him one day, what was the harm in that?*

He was being foolish, he knew. Kyle was probably glad to be rid of him. To get back to his normal life. He knew Kyle had genuinely cared for him, but it was silly to imagine it was anything more than sex and some casual affection. They'd been caught up together in extraordinary circumstances—extraordinary for Sebastian, at least. It was only natural to be drawn to one another.

But what did they really have in common? Kyle was a *spy* for God's sake. And Sebastian was...he had no idea. *Anything I want to be.* He would go back to school, he supposed. Not Harvard, but there were plenty of good mathematics programs. Perhaps he could specialize in codes. Become a cryptographer. That would be something, at least. Not as exciting as spying, but since when did he crave excitement? He was lucky to have made it out of the past week alive, and more excitement should be the last thing on his mind.

Yet he already missed it. He wanted to stop men like his father from hurting innocent people for their own gain. He could do something to change the world. How would he ever be happy lying low and going back to school? It seemed ludicrous to go back to a classroom after what he'd learned. To go back to anything resembling his old life.

He'd spent months moping over Peter, hoping he'd come back. Hoping things would change. Hoping his father would accept him the way he was. It was futile, and this time he wasn't going to just let his life *happen*. He was in control.

He felt as if he'd aged a decade in the last week. He'd never been so weary, but beneath it all he felt a new sense of pride. Of accomplishment. He was going to be okay. Whatever happened, he would get through it.

As someone took the seat beside him, Sebastian turned away from the window. His polite smile froze on his lips as his father's assassin settled in. The man smiled himself and pointedly glanced down at the gun he held trained on Sebastian, hidden from other passengers' sight beneath a suit jacket folded over his arm.

"Mr. Brambani. How nice to see you again."

Sebastian blew out a slow breath. "I'm afraid I don't know your name. Seems I'm at a disadvantage."

The man's calm, steady smile sent a shiver skittering up Sebastian's spine. "They call me *Giaguaro*."

Jaguar. "That's comforting."

He chuckled. "You are a surprise, young man. I never thought you'd give me a moment of trouble. Of course it was your spy friend who shot me. Took me out of action for a good few days." Giaguaro rolled his shoulders back in an exaggerated motion. "Fortunately his shot was just a few inches too high. Missed my heart."

Sebastian refrained from asking whether there was actually a heart of any kind beating in the killer's chest. "Too bad."

"Yes, for you it is. And for him, of course. A measure of revenge is in order. Oh, no, no. I can see your concern. It's quite touching, really, but you needn't worry. You'll be dead and none the wiser. I will make him suffer, of course. He's been quite an inconvenience."

"My father's dead. Whatever contract you had is null and void."

Giaguaro's eyebrows rose slightly. "How interesting. But it changes nothing. I accepted the assignment, and I will see it through whether or not my employer is still invested in the outcome. It's a matter of honor."

Sebastian scoffed. "Yes, clearly."

"I have a reputation, my boy. I get the job done. In this case it's taken a week longer than anticipated, but done it shall be. I see my Serbian friends weren't successful either. I told your father not to bother with them, but he was always a stubborn man." He glanced about at the half-empty train car. "Now if you'll kindly precede me out into the aisle and move to the rear of the car. We'll be getting off at the next stop."

"And if I don't?"

Giaguaro nodded toward the middle-aged woman sleeping in the window seat across the aisle. A teenage girl sat across from her, texting intently. "Mother or daughter? Your choice."

"You can't kill them right here, out in the open."

"Oh, you'd be surprised by what I can do." He waited a moment, then nodded and started to rise. "I think daughter first," he whispered.

"Stop." Sebastian sighed. He couldn't allow innocent bystanders to get hurt. Especially since he was greatly outmatched and without a weapon. He'd thought of taking a gun that morning, but it had seemed counter to the fresh start he was making.

Sebastian desperately glanced about for options—for *any-thing*—as he walked to the rear of the carriage. He sensed Giaguaro directly behind him, could practically feel the man's breath on the back of his neck. *But if he was going to shoot you in the middle of the train, he'd have done it already.* Sebastian took his place in line behind three people who were waiting to leave the train. *Don't make it easy for the bastard.*

The lineup consisted of an elderly man and a young couple. The train slowed as they neared the station, and Sebastian craned his neck to peer past the couple and catch a glimpse of the terrain. It appeared to be a rural station, with not many buildings in the immediate vicinity, and rocky, forested countryside beyond.

Then the train was coming to a stop, and the passengers ahead were picking up their luggage. "Steady, now. Hate to put a bullet in their brains," Giaguaro hissed.

Mind whirling as he locked his plan into place, Sebastian followed as the passengers moved to the steps. The conductor nodded as they went by, and wished them a pleasant day. On the dusty platform, Giaguaro nudged him to the left, and Sebastian began walking. The train idled while passengers got on and off, and then came to life, chugging forward.

Giaguaro was at Sebastian's heels, and as the train picked up speed, Sebastian drove his elbow up and back into Giaguaro's face. The man's nose gave way with a satisfying crunch, and Sebastian kicked back, hammering Giaguaro's knee as he turned and wrested the gun from his hand. It sailed into the air and dropped over the edge of the tracks, under the departing train.

Running, Sebastian reached out, grasping for the handrail on the door to a passing car. It slipped away, and he glanced back. Three more cars, and the hit man was charging after him. Only twenty feet of the station remained before dropping off into wilderness. Sneakers pounding the cracked concrete, Sebastian leaped for the railing and swung up onto the tiny platform at the back of the old train car.

Giaguaro tried for the next car but missed. Only one car remained, and Sebastian watched, heart pounding, as Giaguaro threw himself onto the back of the train. For a moment it was as if time froze, and Sebastian waited for the man to tumble back to the platform. But he disappeared from sight, and as the train curved away from the station, the end of the platform and the track behind were empty.

Wrenching the door open, Sebastian barreled into the red-faced conductor. Ignoring him, Sebastian raced past, trying to think of a place to hide. He could only stay in the bathroom so long, and it would be the first place most people would look. The conductor shouted after him, and Sebastian could feel many eyes on him as he dashed to the next car. Glancing back, he saw Giaguaro running up the aisle. The hit man stopped and flashed what looked like a badge to the conductor. *Terrific.*

Just inside the next car was a baggage area, and without pausing Sebastian dove for the lower shelf of suitcases, squirming into the space behind the luggage. The door to the car slammed open and feet thundered by, the conductor yammering about an escaped criminal. There were five more cars ahead, and he hoped they would continue on.

Of course, the problem was that they would surely begin a systematic search of the train cars once they reached the engine and didn't find him. Sebastian couldn't simply find a nearby house to hole up in, and anyone disembarking at the next station would be closely scrutinized.

Moving quickly, Sebastian peeked past the luggage and slipped out of the train car. The vehicle had picked up speed, and the wind whipped by. A ladder led to the roof, and Sebastian clambered up carefully as the train swayed and rumbled along. He flattened onto his stomach, gripping the metal as best he could. Although the train hadn't seemed to be moving that quickly when he was inside, as he peered down at the uneven ground sloping down from the track, the thought of jumping off seemed impossible.

Holding on, he tried to think of anything else he could possibly do. Giaguaro had lost his gun—but could have a backup. Even if he didn't, he had fifty pounds on Sebastian, and the conductor and likely other train staff behind him. Sebastian would be easily overpowered.

A metallic *clank* somewhere behind him echoed over the whistle of the wind. Peering back over his shoulder, his heart plummeted as Giaguaro appeared atop the next car. Arms out for balance, Sebastian leaped to his feet and raced forward, the hit man in pursuit.

Giaguaro yelled for him to stop, but Sebastian raced onward, leaping onto the next car. He staggered and almost went down before regaining his balance. *Maybe he won't be able to make the jump.* Sebastian glanced back as Giaguaro sailed over the gap. Now they were atop the same car, and Sebastian ran onward, mind racing to formulate a plan.

As he glanced back, his heart skipped a beat as another person appeared at the back of the train. Sebastian blinked, certain his mind was playing tricks on him. But Kyle was really there, sprinting across the tops of the train cars, leaping the spaces between, seemingly without a second thought. Sebastian could have laughed with relief at seeing Kyle again. Yet the relief turned to horror as Giaguaro turned and roared, pulling out another gun from his ankle holster.

Kyle sped toward them as Giaguaro lifted his arm to fire. The train rocked from side to side as Sebastian turned and sprinted back the way he'd come. He flung himself into Giaguaro's back, knocking him flat. The man still managed to fire and was taking aim again as Kyle neared.

"No!" Sebastian jammed his knee into the hit man's injured shoulder and pinched his wrist, forcing his fingers to open. The gun landed with a *clank* and skidded over the side as the train jolted. They both scrabbled for a handhold, and suddenly

Giaguaro struck out with a knife.

Fire slashed through Sebastian's thigh as a shot rang out. Blood pumping from the wound in his back, Giaguaro faltered as Kyle jumped onto the car. After a moment of shock, a frenzied expression came over the hit man's face, and he screamed, hurling himself toward Kyle. Kyle fired again, hitting him square in the chest.

But as Giaguaro tipped over the side of the slowing train, he clutched Kyle's leg, his weight dragging Kyle off balance. Sebastian lunged forward, gripping Kyle's hands as Kyle kicked desperately to dislodge Giaguaro. He slid over the side as he shook the hit man free, and Sebastian dug in his heels, muscles burning as he held on to Kyle.

Pulling back with all his might, he hauled Kyle back up. Panting, they clung to each other for a long moment. Sebastian never wanted to let go, and Kyle held him tightly, fingers digging into Sebastian's flesh. The train jolted again, and Kyle sat back, looking over one side and then the other. He nodded toward the right. "Grassier."

They stayed low as they inched out to the edge. The ground sloped down from the track bed, a stretch of wild grass growing before a line of trees and a ravine beyond. The train was still going far too fast to jump safely, but they were undoubtedly nearing the next station and they needed to get off now. Kyle backed them up to the other side of the car. They got to their feet as the train rocked. Sebastian's right thigh screamed as he put his weight on it, but he ignored it.

Kyle said, "Three..." and Sebastian nodded, counting along. On "one," they launched themselves across the roof and off the other side. Sebastian's injured leg collapsed beneath him with a searing jolt as he hit the ground and rolled down the embankment. He came to a stop on his back in a tangle of shrubbery and tried to force his lungs to expand. Breathing shallowly, he listened to the *clackety-clack* of the train fade away.

Then there was only silence and the sound of the forest. *Too silent.* With great effort, he raised himself onto his elbows and peered around. He didn't think he had any adrenaline left, but he scrambled onto his hands and knees. "Kyle!"

Crumpled at the foot of a tree, Kyle didn't move. Dragging his right leg, Sebastian crawled to his side, his stomach roiling. *Please, please, please.* "Kyle!" He shook his shoulder, and Kyle's eyes flew open. Blood trickled down his forehead, and he winced as he prodded his head.

"Don't move." Sebastian was busy examining Kyle's limbs, which seemed intact.

With a groan, Kyle pushed himself up and sat back against the tree trunk. "We have to move. Eventually they'll get the police out there. Unless you managed not to attract any attention on board?"

"'Fraid not."

Kyle glanced down and reached for Sebastian's injured leg. Blood darkened his jeans, and he bit his lip as Kyle inspected the gash. "It'll need stitches." Taking the hem of his own T-shirt, he tore a strip of cotton and wrapped it tightly around Sebastian's thigh. "Car's about a mile back. Hid it off the road and waited for the train. Damn traffic getting out of the city; just missed you at the last station."

"How did you know?"

"Should have placed him right away when I saw him boarding, but I was thinking about who the Association might send after you. I thought I'd eliminated him."

"Thank you. For coming after me. You didn't have to."

"I did."

"Why?"

Shaking his head, Kyle smiled ruefully. "Because I'm so in love with you, Sebastian."

It was as if all the air in the forest was suddenly sucked away, and Sebastian's whole body froze. *Impossible.*

Kyle pushed away from the tree and started to get up. "We have to go."

Sebastian surged to his knees, ignoring the flare of pain in his thigh. He took hold of Kyle's shoulders, shoving him back down. "Wait."

Saying nothing, Kyle simply caressed Sebastian's cheek.

"You really...*love* me?"

"I know I shouldn't. But I do."

Sebastian's heart raced. "Why shouldn't you?"

"Because you deserve so much better. You deserve to be safe and happy, and far away from me. This is no life for you."

As he spoke, he knew it was the truth. "It's the only life I want." Taking Kyle's face in his hands, Sebastian kissed him soundly. "I don't want to go. I want to be with you. God, I love you."

Kyle shook his head. "Think of your future."

"I am. I have. I want my future to be with you. I don't care where or how. I want you."

Kyle kissed Sebastian long and hard. Resting their foreheads together, they laughed, wrapped in each other's arms. In the distance a train whistle echoed, and Kyle sighed. "We really do have to go." Pulling back, he kissed Sebastian again tenderly. "Maybe we can both disappear."

"What about your job?"

Kyle shrugged. "I'll do something else. Leave all this glamour behind."

Chuckling, Sebastian wiped a fresh drop of blood from Kyle's hairline. "But you love it." *And I love it too.* Kyle's phone rang. "Service out here?" Sebastian asked.

"Satellite phone." Kyle pushed a button. "Marie. Wonderful timing as always." He listened. "No. There was a complication. Taken care of now." He listened again. "Yes, he's here. Why?"

Frowning, Kyle passed the phone to Sebastian. "She wants to talk to you."

Sebastian answered. "Hello?"

"Mr. Brambani, so glad to catch you. I've had a very interesting meeting with the section chief."

Kyle tugged him up, and they limped along in the direction of the car, Kyle's arm firm around Sebastian's shoulders. "Define 'interesting.'"

She laughed delightedly. "We have a proposition for you."

EPILOGUE

★★🔫★★

Three months later

SURVEYING THE BALLROOM, Kyle sighed inwardly. He'd been at the gala for a tedious hour already, and they were running behind schedule. He had to wait until at least ten minutes into the sure-to-be interminable speeches before he slipped away to the service elevator and headed to the ambassador's room.

Pulling on his left sleeve, he adjusted his tuxedo jacket. *Just get on with it already.* As he glanced about, he caught the eye of an elegantly attired older woman. He took a swig of champagne to hide his grimace as she approached.

The woman smiled in a way she likely thought was extremely seductive. "Well, hello there. Are you new to Hong Kong?" She tapped her glass with a long, manicured nail. "I'm sure I'd have noticed you before."

As Kyle debated the quickest way to get rid of her, a familiar voice rang out and his heart skipped a beat. "Mr. McBride?"

He turned as Sebastian approached. He was still lean, but his tuxedo jacket showed off more defined arms and shoulders. His clipped blond hair gleamed, and his wide smile was unchanged. Kyle felt stupidly light-headed.

"Steven McBride, isn't it?" To the woman, Sebastian added, "Pardon the intrusion, madam."

She batted her false eyelashes. "Mr. McBride? We were just getting acquainted."

"Go away now." Kyle stepped closer to Sebastian, ignoring the woman's indignant huff as she went off in search of other prey, her stilettos clicking.

Sebastian stopped an arm's length away, chuckling. "Steven, you used to have such a way with words. You were a real charmer if I remember correctly."

Kyle's whole body vibrated as he kept himself in check, resisting the urge to toss their champagne to the floor and kiss Sebastian breathless. God, he'd missed him. The taste of his mouth, the feel of his body. His laughter, his smile. His…everything. It had been three long months.

He cleared his throat. "I didn't expect to see you here. I thought your business would keep you away for a while longer." Association basic training was a minimum of six months. Fortunately the European section chief had been impressed with Sebastian and, instead of eliminating him, had decided to make him an asset.

"Yes, I'm on a sort of…co-op placement."

"Things are going well? With your business seminars?"

"Very well. Quite a steep learning curve in some areas, as you can imagine."

"No regrets?" Kyle held his breath waiting for the answer, and their eyes locked.

"Not one, Mr. McBride." Sebastian moved to stand beside Kyle, the sleeves of their tuxedos brushing together.

Exhaling, Kyle looked out ahead of him at the couples gliding by on the dance floor. "Glad to hear it. How long is this placement?"

"Only temporary. One night. *All* night."

His cock twitching to life already, Kyle asked, "And your assignment?"

"Same as yours. I'm here to assist and learn from you. I'm sure the next hours will prove very educational."

"Yes. Undoubtedly. I wonder if your plan of action is any

different from mine?"

Sebastian took a sip of his champagne before speaking again, his voice barely more than a whisper. "I was thinking we could go find these documents and deliver them to the courier as scheduled. Then we go to your room and fuck every way we can think of until I have to go back to Madrid."

Kyle breathed deeply, closing his eyes as he fought for control. "Our plans are in alignment. Just need to wait for these speeches to begin."

"Shouldn't be long now." Sebastian kept his gaze on the ballroom. "Any word on the director?"

"No." Kyle's gut tightened. He'd spent countless days searching for the son of a bitch, but he seemed to have vanished without a trace. "But I'll find him."

"I have no doubt." Sebastian cleared his throat. "It's good to see you again, Mr. McBride. I expect to see you again much more regularly in the future. I'm told it shouldn't be a problem to team up. I recently met with a woman who would be overseeing both of us. French, I believe."

Kyle fought the urge to grin. "Well, we always have worked well together, Mr...?"

"Gregson. Antonio."

"Italian mother?"

Sebastian smiled. "Yes. Nice to keep one's heritage alive, don't you agree?"

"Absolutely. And it's good to see you again too, Mr. Gregson. Very good."

They shared a fleeting, tender glance, and Sebastian smiled and mouthed, *I love you.*

Kyle wasn't sure how he'd lived so long without this man. The future seemed impossible without him. He nodded and reluctantly broke their gaze. If he didn't, he was bound to do something rash that would draw attention to them, the mission be damned.

Another minute ticked by in companionable silence, an undercurrent of longing flowing between them as Kyle put his hands in his pockets to keep from reaching out. Sebastian checked his watch. "They certainly don't seem to be in any rush," he muttered.

Still fighting the urge to throw Sebastian down right there in the ballroom, Kyle grimaced. "Doesn't look like it."

A slow smile lifted Sebastian's lips. "In the meantime, do you know where the bathroom is?"

Desire pooled in Kyle's belly, hot and urgent. "I believe it's right outside."

Walking closely through the crowd in the grand ballroom, Kyle took Sebastian's hand, weaving their fingers together as they made their exit.

The Argentine Seduction

by Keira Andrews

CHAPTER ONE

WHERE WAS AN alcoholic, homicidal Russian arms dealer when you needed him?

Sebastian breathed deeply and leaned back against the bar, keeping his expression relaxed despite the rush of adrenaline. He hated waiting, and each minute that ticked by gave him more time to second-guess himself—and this mission.

Where the hell was Zhernakov? The elegant hotel rooftop terrace in Buenos Aires's Recoleta neighborhood was dimly lit, but Sebastian was positive his target was MIA. The man would surely stand out among the young, fashionable clientele. Sebastian had studied Zhernakov's picture a million times that day—his shorn silver hair, ruddy complexion, and body built like a barrel of the whiskey he consumed in staggering amounts. It was said he once stabbed a man merely for offering him vodka.

Sebastian swirled his glass, and the ice cubes clinked together. He took a swallow, wincing as the whiskey burned a path down his throat. His stomach was empty, but he'd been far too nervous to eat. A bit of liquid courage surely wouldn't hurt. He finished the drink and turned to signal for another, but the bartender placed one in front of him before he could even raise his hand. Sebastian smiled his thanks.

This March had been one of the hottest on record in Buenos Aires, and Sebastian wore only a dark T-shirt with his tight jeans. He found dark clothes brought out his green eyes, and he was confident about his trim body in a way he hadn't been as a teenager. He'd styled his short blond hair over his forehead, tousled in a careless way that made him look even younger than he was. Although he wouldn't turn twenty-one for a few months, Sebastian felt far beyond his years.

He chuckled ruefully. He supposed discovering his father was a ruthless arms dealer, going on the run with a sexy spy, and dodging assassins at every turn would make anyone grow up quickly. Now he was a spy himself. Well, at least he'd finished his six-month training with the Association.

Whether or not he could really call himself a spy would depend on the success of this mission. His role in the field would largely be cracking safes and decrypting passwords and codes, but he still had to prove he could handle himself undercover and under pressure.

The colored lanterns swayed just a bit in a cool breeze that raised gooseflesh on Sebastian's bare arms, although he thought his nerves might be the culprit. In the starless night, even the moon was obscured by thick clouds that would bring rain before dawn. The terrace was dotted with tables occupied by couples and friends, quiet laughter ringing out from here and there.

Sebastian took another drink, reminding himself to take it easy. He needed to stay sharp. He put down his glass and shoved his hands in his pockets. Focusing once more on his breathing, he wondered if his backup had arrived. He hadn't spotted anyone earlier who appeared to be an operative, but of course the point was to blend in.

Sebastian glanced around the terrace casually. By the railing to the right overlooking the hotel's pool ten stories below, a man had appeared. The last man Sebastian had expected to see. His heart skipped a beat, a smile instantly tugging at his lips. He had to tamp down the urge to close the distance between them at a run.

Resting against the rail with a beer in hand, Kyle wore dark jeans. His linen shirtsleeves were rolled to his elbows, and his top buttons were undone. His dark hair was neatly trimmed as always, and his skin was tanned. Tall and lean, Kyle was one of the handsomest men Sebastian had ever seen. At the moment he appeared the very picture of relaxation.

But they both had a job to do, and Sebastian forced his gaze back on his drink and concentrated on calming himself. Kyle hadn't even glanced his way, but Sebastian could feel the heat of his presence charging the air.

Leaving his drink, Sebastian rounded the bar and headed to the toilets. He quickly cleared the room, ensuring no one was there and that both the stalls were empty before ducking inside one. The bathroom door opened a minute later. Sebastian waited for the signal, body unclenching slightly as Kyle whistled a jaunty tune.

Once Kyle had squeezed into the stall, they stood pressed together in the small space, and all of Sebastian's questions died on his tongue as their eyes met. He was struck by a memory of their first meeting, of gazing up into Kyle's gold-flecked hazel eyes. His knees had practically gone weak, and even now his stomach flip-flopped.

Kyle cupped Sebastian's head with his hand as they kissed. They both moaned, and Sebastian lost himself in the rush of sensations—the feel of Kyle's tongue, the taste of his mouth, his scent filling Sebastian's nose, his big, hard body pressing Sebastian back against the side of the stall.

But as he gasped for air, Sebastian shook his head. "Wait, wait. Did something happen? What are you doing here?"

Kyle kissed him again, nudging his thigh between Sebastian's legs. "A month is too long."

Sebastian rocked his thickening cock against Kyle's leg. "I know. Missed you so much." He squeezed Kyle's shaft through the denim. "Can't wait to have you inside me again."

Groaning, Kyle tugged at the zipper on Sebastian's jeans and kissed him hard. Sebastian gripped Kyle's back, urging him closer, and Kyle suddenly went rigid, a small gasp escaping his lips. Sebastian felt something beneath Kyle's shirt—a bandage?

"Are you hurt? Let me see." He lifted the hem of Kyle's shirt.

Unsurprisingly, Kyle batted Sebastian's hands away. "I'm fine. It's nothing. A scratch."

"Then let me see."

Sighing, Kyle relented and lifted his shirt as he twisted slightly. "See? Nothing."

Sebastian ran his fingertips over the bandaged wound just above Kyle's right kidney. "How did it happen?"

"Dark alley. Icy. My coat took most of it. Goose feathers come in handy."

"How many stitches?"

"Just a couple." Kyle dropped his shirt and kissed Sebastian again.

"Are you sure Marie cleared you to be back in the field? She didn't tell me you'd be here." Marie was too good a handler to take a chance on any mission, even a straightforward one like this.

"I'm fine. Besides, this is your mission. I'm just the backup. You won't need me."

"You didn't answer the question. Did Marie send you? You might remember her? Small Frenchwoman, slightly terrifying when she's angry? Ring any bells?"

Chuckling, Kyle nodded. "Don't worry, she knows. I don't change plans without running them by Marie." At Sebastian's skeptical look, Kyle amended. "Well, I don't change plans often without running them by her." He brushed a knuckle down Sebastian's cheek. "Only in exceptional circumstances."

Sebastian smiled as he thought of the rules Kyle had broken and the orders he'd disobeyed to save Sebastian's life. He pressed their lips together before leaning back. "I'm glad you're here. But are you sure you're up for this?"

Kyle arched an eyebrow and rolled his hips into Sebastian's. "I'm always up for this."

Sebastian couldn't help but laugh as the worry dissipated. "I guess you're fine if you're well enough for puns." He took a shuddering breath, leaning into the warmth of Kyle's body as the anxiety returned. "I should get back out there. Target might have arrived."

"Don't be nervous. You can do this. Marie wouldn't have sent you otherwise."

"Well, Zhernakov likes pretty boys." He smiled and kissed Kyle lightly. "Sorry, old man, you don't fit the bill."

As Kyle opened his mouth to respond, the bathroom door opened with a momentary surge of music and conversation from the terrace beyond. In the hush that followed, they could hear a man at the urinal. They stood pressed together, and Kyle bent his head, his breath hot on Sebastian's ear. "This old man's going to make you come so hard your balls will ache, and then I'm going to fuck you again. And again."

Sebastian shivered. He and Kyle had only seen each other for fleeting encounters while Sebastian was in training, and they'd made the most of the opportunities. The last time they'd seen each other, in a dive hotel in Karachi, they'd spent a night in each other's arms having sex on every surface.

As the man in the bathroom finally left, Sebastian gripped Kyle's ass and ground their hips together, pulling Kyle's head down for another kiss. But his own breathy moan turned to a disappointed sigh as his phone vibrated in his pocket. Kyle glanced out to make sure they were still alone as Sebastian read the message from Marie.

New target: Zhernakov's son, Fedor. 25 years old. Same plan: he's a chip off the old block. Likes virgins.

"What is it?" Kyle asked.

"It's going to be Zhernakov's son instead. Same game plan, though. Apparently he shares his father's taste. There's a picture here…" Sebastian tapped the small image and raised his eyebrows. "Wow. He may take after his father in some ways, but he got his looks from his mother. Hot." Sebastian showed Kyle the picture.

Kyle was silent for a moment before shrugging. "Nothing special."

Snorting, Sebastian slipped his phone back into his pocket. "Yeah, only if you go in for the piercing blue eyes, chiseled jaw, shiny black hair, and six-pack abs. Other than that, sure, he's pretty average. Did you see him out there? I didn't."

Kyle shook his head. "He might be there now. Just remember what you've learned and…"

"What?" The adrenaline and nerves had returned full force, and Sebastian exhaled shakily.

"You'll be great." Hands on Sebastian's shoulders, Kyle leaned down and spoke into his ear. "Go get him."

He pressed a tender kiss to Sebastian's cheek. Ignoring the shiver of desire flickering up his spine, Sebastian nodded and kissed Kyle quickly.

Back on the terrace, he scanned the faces and felt a bolt of energy when he spotted the young and handsome Zhernakov Jr. on the other side of the roof with two flunkies. Sebastian picked up another drink at the bar and weaved his way over slowly, stopping several times to admire the view.

As he passed Zhernakov, Sebastian stumbled and sent his drink flying, splashing the man's broad chest. With a gasp, Sebastian blushed and rubbed Zhernakov's stained shirt, leaning into him. "I'm so sorry!" He hiccupped.

Zhernakov's angry expression melted. He took hold of Sebastian's arm with his strong hand. "You are American?"

"Uh-huh." Sebastian's American accent came as naturally to him as his own Italian did. "My dad's working here in Buenos

Aires. I'm supposed to be in bed." He put his finger to his lips. "Shhh. I'm not supposed to be drinking either."

The predatory gleam in Zhernakov's eyes was almost comical. "It shall be our little secret."

Sebastian grinned. "Awesome. Secrets are fun." He leaned closer to Zhernakov to look over the terrace railing. "Wow, amazing view. I've hardly been out of my room since we got here." He rolled his eyes. "Dad thinks it's too dangerous."

"Fathers. They can be…complicated." Zhernakov smiled.

"Totally." Sebastian rested his palm on Zhernakov's broadly muscled chest. The young man was tall and built and utterly intimidating, especially with his perfect cheekbones. Not to mention the two armed lackeys, who stood off to the side, gazes discreetly averted. Sebastian ran his hand over Zhernakov's thin silk shirt. "My bad. I ruined it."

Zhernakov trailed his fingertips down Sebastian's arm. "Perhaps you can make it up to me."

Gazing up under his lashes, Sebastian smiled. "Can I? How?"

Zhernakov's hand was firm on Sebastian's back as he pivoted him around. "Come, let us get you another drink where your father won't see you."

Sebastian nodded eagerly and let Zhernakov maneuver him to the elevators beyond the bar. His heart raced, but he knew Kyle wouldn't be far behind.

THE MINUTES TICKED by like hours.

Kyle pressed his eye to the peephole. The door to Zhernakov's room was visible in the periphery, and it remained closed with Sebastian inside. Kyle leaned back and paced a few steps, staying close to the door, listening carefully. Sebastian was unarmed in case Zhernakov's men searched him, but Kyle's pistol was snug and reassuring at his side. Not to mention the backup in his ankle holster and the serrated knife in his other boot. If he heard any sounds of distress from across the hall, he wouldn't hesitate.

Stooping, he checked the peephole again. No movement, and no one had been in the hallway in sixteen minutes. Not surprising since it was past one o'clock in the morning. He paced three steps, then pivoted back. Then repeated the sequence, his mind racing.

It wasn't that he didn't think Sebastian was up to the job. Since they'd met on that sultry June night in Como, Sebastian had consistently surprised Kyle, proving to be strong, smart, and resilient. Of course Sebastian could do the job. He was a math genius and a natural code breaker. Once he incapacitated Zhernakov, cracking the safe would be child's play.

It was what came before it that had Kyle on the verge of storming across the hall, kicking down the door, and beating Zhernakov senseless.

He shook his head, annoyed with his own foolishness. What did it matter that Zhernakov Jr. looked like a male model? It was a mission like any other. If Sebastian was going to be an operative for the Association, Kyle had to put their personal relationship aside when they were on a mission. He couldn't worry or hover. And he definitely couldn't play the images of Sebastian flirting with a gorgeous man in his mind on an endless loop.

Sighing, Kyle again checked the peephole and resumed pacing. In the world of espionage, seduction was only a game. Kyle had seduced dozens of women and men over the past decade or so. Sebastian himself had only been a game at first. An attractive target Kyle had enjoyed kissing and touching, a target he'd regretted having to take advantage of. A target he hadn't been able to let die.

A target who changed all the rules.

Kyle had always known love was a complication he didn't need. Or want. But until he met Sebastian, he hadn't known love was like an out-of-control freight train, and once you were on the tracks, all you could do was barrel onward. He couldn't bear to think of life without Sebastian now. Couldn't bear to think of Sebastian being hurt.

Couldn't bear to think of another man touching him.

It wasn't that he didn't trust Sebastian. He trusted him more than anyone he'd ever known, even Marie. He knew Sebastian was only acting. But Kyle still gritted his teeth, fists clenching at the idea of Zhernakov with his hands on him. Kyle was being foolish, but sometimes the game could get out of hand. Zhernakov was a strong man. Even the most experienced operatives found themselves in trouble sometimes.

Stretching his arm up gingerly, Kyle grimaced. His wound was a long, deep slash. He'd lucked out and would have been a dead man if the knife had gone in deeper. Kyle still prickled with annoyance that the target in Stockholm had bested him, even just for a moment, before Kyle put him down.

The truth was he should have taken a few days of rest. He'd lost too much blood and the wound itched and throbbed, but he'd been too eager to see Sebastian. The mission here was an easy bait and switch. The missile design Zhernakov was selling the North Koreans likely couldn't work anyway, but just in case, Sebastian would swap the USB drive with another carrying designs that definitely wouldn't work.

If the next few minutes went as planned, Kyle wouldn't have to do anything more strenuous in the next twenty-four hours than taking Sebastian to bed. A thrill of need curled up his spine at the thought. Sebastian was so passionate and eager, so fierce. Kyle swallowed hard at the memory of fucking Sebastian for the first time. And the second, the third, the fourth…

With a shake of his head to focus, he checked the empty hallway. He knew Sebastian would only go as far as he had to, that he'd make sure Zhernakov was drugged quickly. Still, it had been—Kyle glanced at his watch—eighteen and a half minutes. What if something had gone wrong? What if Zhernakov had discovered Sebastian's agenda? Overpowered him? As Kyle paced uselessly, Sebastian could be hurt, could be in danger, could be—

He heard a door open in the hallway, and he looked through the peephole. He exhaled as Sebastian emerged, appearing uninjured. Sebastian closed Zhernakov's door quietly and disappeared from sight.

Slinging his duffel bag over his shoulder, Kyle slipped out to the balcony of his room. He didn't know where Zhernakov's minions were, and he couldn't risk being seen on the heels of Sebastian's exit.

With quick movements, he swung over the balcony ledge with a short rope. As he dropped down, his wound flared white-hot. For a moment it was agony, and his lungs froze. Suspended by the rope, he wavered, head spinning dangerously, eight stories above the ground. The pain seared from the wound all the way up his right arm to his fingers grasping the rope.

Then the dizziness passed and he forced his lungs to expand as he shimmied down to the balcony below. He stopped for a moment once he had his feet under him, panting as the intense burning subsided.

Yes, perhaps he should take a day or two off after all.

The room's occupants were sleeping, and Kyle silently picked the lock on the sliding glass door. Once inside he stood motionless for thirty seconds, ensuring that the couple hadn't heard anything in their sleep. Then he slipped out into the hallway and to the elevators.

The rain hadn't come yet, but the warm air hung with moisture. Although he was eager to get to Sebastian, Kyle walked slowly. He knew Sebastian would follow protocol and wait for him a kilometer to the north. If north was impossible due to a body of water or another impediment, it would be the east, and so on in a clockwise motion. North of the hotel was a large park with flower gardens and decorative ponds—the perfect meeting spot at this time of night. Anyone else who happened to lurk in the shadows would be busy with their own pursuits.

By the time he reached the edge of the park, the raw throbbing from his wound had receded to a dull ache. He scanned the area for threats and found none. Ahead in the darkness he could make out a slim figure on a small bridge that arched over a pond. Kyle sped up, his pulse thrumming. It was madness, the way he craved Sebastian like oxygen. Not just his touch or his body, but his smile, his laughter. His…everything.

Atop the bridge he reached out, but Sebastian jerked away. Chest tightening, Kyle forced a breath out. "Are you hurt?" He couldn't quite keep his voice even. "Did he hurt you?" Jesus, he was going to kill Zhernakov. Slowly.

"No. I'm fine, really."

Sebastian's body radiated tension, his hand twitching, shoulders bunched. He stared out at the pond. Kyle wanted to take Sebastian in his arms but reluctantly kept his distance. "Are you sure? Did something happen? It's… You can tell me. Whatever it is. I won't be angry."

"I know you won't. But I'm mad at myself."

Heart sinking, Kyle kept his voice even. "It can be hard at first. Keeping perspective. Not getting…swept away. Being someone else can be powerful. Intoxicating. And Zhernakov's obviously…" The words scraped his throat like sandpaper. "Attractive, and—"

Forehead creased, Sebastian turned. "Huh? What does it matter what he looks like? The USB drive wasn't in there. Not in the safe, and not in the room. I failed, Kyle. My first mission on my own, and I blew it."

Kyle had never been so relieved to hear of a failed mission. He had to fight the urge to laugh.

"But wait, what were you talking about? Why does it matter what Zhernakov looks like?" Comprehension dawned on Sebastian's face, and his jaw dropped. "You thought...with him? Like, for real? Are you out of your mind? This was a job!"

Feeling more foolish than ever, Kyle shrugged. "I know, but things happen. Seeing you flirting with him..." He ran a hand over his head. "It's stupid. I was stupid."

Sebastian laughed, clearly incredulous. "You were jealous? I was just acting. You know that."

Kyle crossed his arms. "I know. But..."

Taking a step closer, Sebastian tugged on one of Kyle's arms until he uncrossed them. Sebastian took his hand and threaded their fingers together. "But that's how we met. So sometimes even though it's acting, there's more there."

Kyle nodded.

"Well, for the record, there was nothing there with Zhernakov except impatience for the damn drug to kick in. With all those muscles it took forever. But I played coy and innocent. So hesitant and virginal, keeping him at arm's length and making him seduce me." He grinned. "I was pretty damn good, if I do say so myself."

The tension finally leaving him, Kyle laughed and squeezed Sebastian's hand. "I bet you were."

Sebastian's smile faded. "So what do I tell Marie?"

"The truth. You performed your mission as ordered. It's not your fault the drive wasn't there. You said you searched the entire room?"

"Top to bottom. His suitcase, everything. If he has it, it's up his ass, and I'm not looking there."

They shared a smirk. "We'll leave that for plan Z. In the meantime, we'll stick to plan B."

CHAPTER TWO

L EANING INTO KYLE'S warmth, Sebastian took a deep breath. He might have failed his first mission, but he knew Kyle would help him make it right. He nodded as Kyle went through the plan B checklist. "Yep. Bugged his briefcase and the room. There's no way he'll be awake before dawn, though."

Kyle glanced at his watch. "Good. Gives us at least five hours." He brushed back Sebastian's hair. "It's going to be fine. Believe me, this isn't the first time a mission hasn't worked out as planned. Sure as hell won't be the last."

"I know. I just wanted it to be perfect. Most of the time I'll just be going along to break codes, but I wanted to show Marie that I could do it. That I'm not just the math guy."

Kyle's brow furrowed. "She knows that. You proved beyond a doubt in Positano that there's more to you than numbers. A lot more."

Sebastian wrapped his arms around Kyle's waist. He knew he had to stand on his own feet as a spy, but for the moment he was just glad Kyle was with him. "You're right."

"I know. You should get used it."

Sebastian chuckled. "A joke from Kyle Grant! Yes, ladies and gentlemen, you heard right. I think that's number three for your lifetime?"

Kyle ran his hands up and down Sebastian's back, and Sebastian shivered, desire coiling in his belly as Kyle teased his spine. "Possibly even number four. Might be years before the next one."

"Good thing you're so hot." Sebastian grew serious. "You're the only man I want. We both have to play the game, but when it's over, you're the one. The only one."

Kyle pressed their foreheads together. "Yes," he whispered.

"I don't want anyone's hands on me but yours." Sebastian kissed him slowly. "No one else's lips." He snuck one hand down between them. "Don't want anyone else's cock."

Groaning, Kyle kissed him hard, his tongue powerful against Sebastian's. Sebastian stumbled back against the bridge's railing as fat drops of rain began to fall. He raked his nails up under Kyle's linen shirt and nipped at Kyle's neck. "Missed this so much, Kyle."

Kyle grunted and dropped to his knees, yanking at the button and zipper on Sebastian's jeans. He tugged the material down Sebastian's hips until he could free his cock and stroke it with a rough palm. In the din of the growing rainstorm, Sebastian could cry out freely, and he tangled his fingers into Kyle's wet hair as Kyle swallowed him.

Rain flowed down his body, warm even in the night. The air was sweet with flowers in bloom, and Sebastian inhaled deeply before he blinked the water from his eyes, not wanting to miss a moment. The sight of Kyle on his knees *for him* had Sebastian close to the edge already. He jerked his hips, fucking Kyle's mouth, and Kyle took it, sucking deeply, his tongue working the ridge of Sebastian's cock, fingers gripping Sebastian's thighs.

It was so wet and good, and Sebastian moaned as the pleasure built. Every time he was with Kyle he thought it couldn't get better, but it did. It was like they were made to fuck each other. To love each other.

His balls were trapped by the elastic of his underwear, tugging on them deliciously as he fucked into the heat of Kyle's mouth. He cried out a warning as his orgasm rushed through him, but Kyle sucked him through it, milking every last drop as Sebastian moaned.

Kyle sat back on his heels and released Sebastian from his mouth before pressing a kiss to the tip of Sebastian's twitching cock. They were both soaked now, and Kyle was beautiful, the rain gleaming on his face. His chest rose and fell, and Sebastian could just make out the scattering of dark hair there through the soaked linen. Kyle rubbed his own cock through his jeans.

On trembling legs, Sebastian turned and peeled his jeans and underwear down his thighs. "Fuck me."

Although sheets of rain fell in the darkness, obscuring visibility, they were still in the middle of a public park. But Sebastian didn't care, spreading himself wantonly and leaning over the railing, hands wide. He could hear Kyle rummaging in his duffel, the tear of foil reaching Sebastian's ears over the rain drumming down.

Sebastian reached back with wet fingers, pushing one and then two into his hole, spreading his legs as best he could with his sodden jeans trapped around his knees. He glanced back over his shoulder. Kyle's gaze was locked on Sebastian's ass, his lips parted as he watched Sebastian finger himself.

Kyle's eyes snapped up, and Sebastian felt his gaze like a bolt of lightning. Kyle had the condom on, and he plunged forward, covering Sebastian's body and pushing at his hole, hands spreading Sebastian's cheeks. He thrust inside with his thick cock, and Sebastian moaned. "Yes yes yes. More. Give me more."

Swearing, Kyle did. He pummeled Sebastian, stretching him open farther on each thrust. Sebastian's ass burned, but he pushed back, wanting more. They panted and grunted, the rain thundering down, seeming to block out the rest of the world. Mouth open, Sebastian bent lower, Kyle's fingers digging into his hips as he rammed into him.

Kyle's breath was hot on the back of Sebastian's neck, his voice low. He pulled up Sebastian's T-shirt, the buttons of his linen shirt rubbing against Sebastian's slick skin. "Never been like this with anyone. Only you. Just you. Want you all the time. Need you." He drew almost all the way out and plowed back in. "Fuck, Sebastian."

"Yes. I'm yours." He cried out as Kyle hit just the right spot. "Oh, fuck. There. Harder!"

"Touch yourself," Kyle gritted out. "Come again."

His dick was oversensitive, and Sebastian whimpered as he jerked himself. It was too much but not enough, and he groaned, sparks behind his eyes as he stroked his cock and Kyle filled him. Kyle's motion stuttered, and he came with Sebastian's name on his lips, his hips still driving, angled to hit Sebastian's prostate.

Arm working furiously, Sebastian spurted over his hand, shuddering with his release and leaning on the railing, Kyle's warm weight lodged against him, still inside him. With a gentle kiss to Sebastian's sopping hair, Kyle pulled out and got rid of the condom with quick movements. Then he leaned heavily against Sebastian again, breathing hard—harder than normal even after their most acrobatic sex.

Sebastian frowned and glanced over his shoulder. "Are you okay?"

Kyle nodded against Sebastian's back, but he grimaced as he straightened up. "Fine." He smiled and smoothed his palm over Sebastian's ass. "Spectacular."

"If you're sure." Sebastian wanted nothing more than to find a dry place to curl up together, but he had a mission to finish. He sighed. "I guess we'd better figure out where those missile plans are."

Kyle's smile disappeared. He nodded again.

Sebastian hauled up his jeans. Time to get back to business.

"YES, I BUGGED his briefcase and room. Nothing yet." Sebastian glanced at Kyle, who confirmed by shaking his head.

As Sebastian briefed Marie on the phone, Kyle turned back to the window. Sebastian had rented a room at an adjacent hotel with a view of Zhernakov's suite—a standard plan B spies hoped never to have to fall back on. The drapes in Zhernakov's room remained shut, and the only sound on the bug was the drone of his snores.

Sebastian listened to whatever Marie was saying. "Right. Yes. Hold on a sec." He held out the phone to Kyle.

"*Bonjour.*"

"Good morning, Mr. Grant. Are you up for this? I can get a local on standby now that the mission has expanded."

"Of course." Truthfully his wound hurt more than it had since he'd received it, but he'd be fine. He'd lost himself in the sex with Sebastian, but once they captured the USB drive, he'd rest.

"Don't 'of course' me. A birdie told me that little cut you got in Stockholm was actually deeper than you mentioned. I only allowed you to go to Buenos Aires because you shouldn't have needed to do anything more than sit on a stool and sip Quilmes while Mr. Brambani completed the mission. This was meant to be straightforward." She sighed. "Story of our lives, Mr. Grant. So you're okay, *oui?*"

"It's not a concern."

Her voice softened. "I know you want to help him. All right. It's his mission, so you're still just backup. Don't fuck it up, *mon cher.*" Her tone changed once more, this time teasing. "Tell me, how did you enjoy watching your lover seduce another man? I'm amazed our Russian friend isn't already deep in his grave."

Kyle grumbled. "If that's all, we've got missile plans to intercept."

Marie's laughter came down the line. "My hard-nosed operative so spectacularly in love. It's a delight." Her jolly tone faded.

"But don't let it get in the way of the job. Sebastian can take care of himself. You know you can't always be there. He needs to be able to handle himself in the field. Now find that USB drive. *Au revoir.*"

The line went dead, and Kyle handed the phone back to Sebastian. "Let's hope sleeping beauty over there wakes soon. No movement from the North Koreans?"

"No. Word is they haven't left Buenos Aires yet. A local team is on them."

At the window, they waited. Sebastian leaned into Kyle, and Kyle was glad Sebastian was on his left. The ibuprofen he'd taken had not relieved the pulsing pain. They should be on alert, strictly business, but Kyle didn't push him away. There was nothing else they could do for the moment.

"DID YOU REALLY think I was going to sleep with that guy?"

Kyle hitched his shoulder in a shrug.

"That was never the plan."

"Plans change. You never know. The rules of the game aren't always the same. One day you might have to."

Frowning, Sebastian stepped in front of Kyle. "I'm not actually going to have sex with anyone."

Kyle caressed Sebastian's cheek. He hoped he'd never lose this lingering innocence, although it was surely inevitable. "What if it meant saving thousands of lives?"

Sebastian pondered it. "I guess…I don't know. I told Marie I didn't ever want to do that." He ran his hand up Kyle's chest, warm over the thin fabric of Kyle's T-shirt. "You're the only man I want to be with. As for women…" He scrunched up his face. "I don't know how you do that."

Kyle laughed. "It's almost easier. Pure acting. Just the game."

"I think about it sometimes. The night I met you. Well, the night I met Steven McBride. Strange to think that all I worried about was pleasing my father and going back to Harvard for a second year. My world was so small."

Reaching up, Kyle brushed his thumb across Sebastian's lower lip. "Small, maybe. But safe."

Sebastian snorted. "Yeah, until my father took out a hit on me. I may have thought I was safe, but I was just living in a dream world where my father was a 'businessman.' He was an arms dealer in bed with the mob. Safe was never an option." He stepped closer. "Either way, I made my choice." He kissed Kyle softly. "He's probably going to sleep for hours, you know."

"Mmm-hmm."

Sebastian took Kyle's hand and sucked his thumb into his mouth, tongue swirling around it before letting go with a wet, filthy *pop*. "I can think of a few ways to pass the—"

As Zhernakov bellowed, Kyle and Sebastian sprang apart. They listened intently, although Sebastian couldn't speak Russian well yet. Another voice joined Zhernakov's, a cowering minion by the sound of it. Kyle smirked. "He wants to know why they didn't wake him."

Kyle translated roughly in his head. His Russian was competent, although his accent wouldn't fool a native. But in this case all he had to do was listen as Zhernakov blathered on, berating his men and seeming in quite a hurry.

When Kyle tensed, Sebastian raised an eyebrow. Kyle answered, "He just asked..." Kyle swore. "He doesn't have the USB drive. He's meeting a courier..." He waited. "The next ferry to Montevideo."

Sebastian swiped at his phone and tapped his thumbs. "Leaves in forty-five minutes. We need to beat him on board."

They made it to the lobby in thirty seconds and hailed a taxi. The pain in his back blazed, but Kyle ignored it. Fortunately

Sebastian hadn't noticed in the dark of the park that Kyle had bled through his bandage. A couple of stitches had popped, so he'd had to wrap the wound tightly. He wore a black T-shirt just in case, but it should hold until he could see a doctor. He'd had worse, and he wouldn't let Sebastian down. He was fine.

At the pier, they fell into line for tickets and then passport control. The ship carried hundreds of people, and the deck was crowded in the morning sunshine, children laughing and playing, their parents sipping iced coffees.

"Should we look for the North Koreans?" Sebastian murmured.

"Sounded like he's meeting them on the other side, but we'll keep an eye out."

"He'd better hurry." Sebastian scanned the pier. "Ah, there he is. All right, I'll get the drive."

Kyle fought the urge to handle it himself and keep Sebastian out of harm's way. But no, he was the backup. This was Sebastian's mission. He pressed a timer on his watch as the ship blew its horn and the engines rumbled to life. "You have three hours. What's the plan?"

"Pick up where we left off last night. Wish me luck." Sebastian disappeared into the crowd.

Kyle watched him go, reminding himself again that Sebastian could take care of himself.

CHAPTER THREE

"**O**H MY GOD, hi!" Sebastian grinned.

Decidedly unimpressed, Zhernakov Jr. grunted. "You." Even with what had to be a hell of a headache, Zhernakov had coiffed his hair and was dressed impeccably, his formfitting clothes showing off his physique. Sebastian wondered what Zhernakov Sr. thought of his son and the amount of time he must spend at the gym.

Sebastian squeezed past a family and joined him at the ferry railing. Zhernakov hadn't moved for the entire journey, and the ferry was due to dock in twenty minutes. Either his plan to meet the courier had changed, or he was leaving it to the last minute. Sebastian needed to act.

Zhernakov wore mirrored sunglasses, and Sebastian caught a glimpse of himself. He almost lifted a hand automatically to straighten his tousled hair before remembering that with his surfing T-shirt and jeans, the hair contributed to the teenager look. He affected a concerned expression. "Are you feeling better?"

Zhernakov was silent for a moment, unreadable with his eyes hidden. "Yes. Better."

"Oh, good. We'd only had one drink, and you said you had a headache. I don't know what you took, but you were out like a light. I thought... Never mind."

"What?" Zhernakov tilted his head. He shifted his body toward Sebastian with a slow smile and oily charm. "What did you think?"

Sebastian glanced away, blushing. "I thought maybe you didn't like me after all." He put his hands in his pockets. "I mean, you're so sophisticated and I'm just a stupid kid. At least that's what my dad says."

"And where is your father?"

Sebastian nodded toward the direction of Buenos Aires across Río de la Plata and grinned. "He's got meetings all day, so I'm running away. I'm going to stay out all night and come back in the morning."

"All night? How brave."

"I know. He's going to kill me, but whatever. I want to have fun for once."

"And where are you going to stay if you're out all night?"

Shrugging, Sebastian smiled coyly. "I dunno. I'll figure something out."

Zhernakov tsk-tsked. "It can be dangerous out in the city by yourself. Perhaps you should stay with me. I'll take you to a club." He ran a fingertip down Sebastian's cheek. "Wouldn't want anything to happen to this pretty face."

Sebastian shivered, eyes wide. "Okay."

One of Zhernakov's men appeared and murmured in Russian, too quietly for Sebastian to pick up any words, although he could guess what the man said.

Zhernakov smiled tightly at Sebastian. "I have some business to attend to. Stay here."

"Sure."

He waited until Zhernakov was almost out of sight before following. He knew Kyle would be watching, but couldn't spot him. Thankful for the crowd, Sebastian slipped down to the lower level. Zhernakov disappeared into the bathroom. Sebastian watched the door from a distance, breathing deeply to calm his racing pulse.

No one else went in, but after two minutes, a short, balding man walked out. The courier. Sebastian sprang into action before Zhernakov left as well. Inside the bathroom, Zhernakov and his two men wheeled around as Sebastian walked in. It was a small room with only two stalls and two urinals.

One of the flunkies leveled his pistol at Sebastian. Sebastian raised his arms. "Oh! I didn't...I'm sorry." He gazed at Zhernakov beseechingly. "What's happening? Did I do something wrong?"

Zhernakov stared with a narrowed gaze. He gave a minute nod of his head, and the other flunky went to Sebastian and patted him down thoroughly. When the minion stepped back and nodded, the other put his gun away.

Zhernakov smiled. "My friend, I thought I told you to stay upstairs?"

"I just had to pee. I didn't mean to interrupt or anything. Are you, like...gangsters or something?" He kept his tone breathy.

"Or something."

Sebastian raked his gaze down Zhernakov's body and bit his lip. "Wow."

With a flick of his head, Zhernakov dismissed the men. "What is your name?"

"Eric." Sebastian drew his brows together, feigning hurt. "Don't you remember?"

"Forgive me. That headache last night was a...doozy, I think you Americans would call it."

Sebastian smiled. "Uh-huh. Sure, no problem." He took a few steps toward Zhernakov and glanced at one of the empty stalls. "You said last night..." He shook his head. "Never mind."

"What? What did I say?"

Sebastian lowered his voice. "You said you'd teach me how to kiss."

"Did I?" He laughed, sounding truly amused for a moment before pitching his voice low. "And do you still want to learn?"

Nodding, Sebastian licked his lips.

Zhernakov waved his arm toward the stall. "After you."

Heart pounding, Sebastian squeezed inside. He thought of being with Kyle the night before. How different it had been! Instead of excitement and lust and affection, Sebastian felt nauseous. His throat was dry, and he struggled to stay focused. All the training in the world wasn't the same as the real thing.

He leaned in toward Zhernakov, all sloppy eagerness, but Zhernakov pushed him to his knees with a firm hand and a sly grin. Sebastian blinked up. "I thought you were going to teach me to kiss?"

"First you're going to learn how to take my cock." His smile disappeared, and he tightened his fingers painfully in Sebastian's hair as he unzipped his trousers and pushed them down his hips to release his cock and balls. "Then you'll beg for it in your tight ass."

Nodding, Sebastian reached up. In one movement, he surged to his feet and grabbed Zhernakov's genitalia with one hand, twisting and pulling while slamming the blade of his other hand up into Zhernakov's throat. Despite the blow to his throat, Zhernakov howled loudly—too loudly—in agony and smashed Sebastian's head back against the wall, sending a burst of pain through Sebastian.

Hesitate and you're dead.

Trying to remember all he'd learned, Sebastian wrenched free and kicked viciously at Zhernakov's knee, sending him crashing to the faded tile floor. There was little room to maneuver in the stall, and Sebastian slammed his knee down against Zhernakov's windpipe.

He registered the bathroom door opening and one of the flunkies shouting for their boss before there were sounds of a struggle beyond the stall. But he kept his focus on Zhernakov, whose face became redder and redder as his free arm grappled for Sebastian, the other trapped below him on the floor. Zhernakov managed to get hold of Sebastian's throat, but Sebastian held his breath. He put all his weight into his knee where it pressed against the other man's airway—right in the right spot to knock him out but not kill him.

Finally Zhernakov lost consciousness and his arm flopped down. Sebastian stayed put for a moment, gasping shallowly and concentrating on keeping control. *I can do this. I've got this.* He forced a deep breath into his lungs and patted down Zhernakov, searching for the USB drive.

His fingers found a telltale rectangular bulge in a small pocket sewn inside Zhernakov's light jacket. Zhernakov would be out for another few minutes, but there was no time to lose. He checked his watch. The ferry docked in two minutes. Perfect. He listened carefully and peeked through the crack in the stall door.

At least one of Zhernakov's thugs was slumped on the floor, and Sebastian could hear only harsh breathing that sounded like Kyle. He edged open the stall door. Sure enough, the other minion was also knocked out on the floor, and Kyle stood with one hand braced against the wall, his boot on the man's neck. He held his duffel with his other hand.

Kyle tried to smile but didn't quite make it. "Got it?"

"Yeah." Sebastian held up the stick before slipping it into his pocket, the brief rush of elation at succeeding washed away by a wave of concern. "You're pale." He stepped over the unconscious men and reached for Kyle, putting his hand on Kyle's back. It was wet, and he lifted his hand to see blood dripping from his palm. "Jesus!"

One of the men stirred, and Sebastian slung his arm around Kyle's waist, bringing Kyle's arm around his shoulders. The ship was shuddering to a halt, and Sebastian led the way out of the bathroom, pausing to drag a yellow cleaning sign in front of the door. Most passengers were on the upper deck, so the stairs were fortunately empty.

Kyle staggered, and Sebastian tightened his grip. "A couple of stitches, huh?" Irritation warred with worry.

"Maybe a few more." Kyle grunted as they reached the upper deck and joined the throng of people disembarking.

Sebastian was grateful they'd already gone through passport control before boarding, and fought the urge to scream for everyone to get out of the way. Kyle leaned against him, swaying slightly. A few people frowned in their direction, but Sebastian ignored them, concentrating on getting Kyle to safety and making sure Zhernakov and his men didn't follow.

Finally they made it off the ferry, and Sebastian spotted the signal from the driver of a waiting car. Kyle was clearly in pain as he clambered into the backseat, pressing his lips together. Sebastian climbed in after, and the driver zoomed off.

Sebastian saw no sign of Zhernakov as they left the pier behind. He rooted through Kyle's duffel and pulled out a fresh wad of bandages to press against the wound beneath Kyle's stained shirt. Kyle winced but didn't complain. He'd bled onto the seat cushion, but Sebastian thought ruefully that the driver had likely seen it all before.

Once they left Montevideo behind, Sebastian was able to relax, at least for the time being. The windows were open in the old car, and Kyle leaned back against the seat, eyes closed. It would take an hour and a half to get to Colonia and the safe house—and doctor—there, and Kyle was breathing evenly, so Sebastian let him rest.

He'd give him hell later.

SITTING BACKWARD ON a chair, Kyle kept his gaze on the harbor as the doctor restitched his wound with steady hands. Sebastian watched from a few feet away, leaning against the door to the patio, arms crossed. Their little villa was nestled in a hillside, sweet-smelling flowers climbing the walls and old palm trees casting shade as the sun inched toward the horizon.

When the Association doctor finished and packed up his equipment quietly and efficiently, Sebastian saw him out. Kyle braced himself.

"Seventeen." Sebastian stood in front of Kyle's chair, arms still crossed. "For future reference, seventeen and 'a couple' are not the same thing."

Kyle sighed. "I know. I just—"

Sebastian held his hands up, eyebrows raised. "Didn't think I could do it on my own?"

"Wanted to see you."

Exhaling noisily, Sebastian shook his head. "I wanted to see you too, but not bleeding out."

Kyle gave him a look. "It wasn't that bad."

"It could have been! You just had a blood transfusion, might I remind you."

"Yes, and I'm feeling much better now."

"Not the point. Don't lie to me like that. If you're hurt, I want to know. We're supposed to be..." He huffed, laughing just a bit. "I don't know, actually. We never really gave it a name. Gave this a name." He motioned between them.

Part of Kyle was surprised Sebastian had to ask. He thought it had been obvious. "Partners. In work. In everything."

The rest of Sebastian's anger seemed to drain away, and he gazed at Kyle with tender eyes. "So that means we're equals. That means you don't lie to me."

"Okay. You're right. I just..." He blew out a long breath. "I've never felt like this before. Not for anyone. I hate the thought of you being hurt."

"And I feel the same way about you."

"I've been doing this for more than a decade and—"

"And you're a big tough guy, yeah, yeah." Sebastian knelt in front of the chair and squeezed Kyle's knees. "But I hate seeing you in pain. You were in no condition to be taking on two goons. I know this was all supposed to be easy and you shouldn't have had to do anything. Just…you can't protect me all the time."

Kyle covered Sebastian's hands with his own. "When you were training, it was fine. In Hong Kong, I was there. But this…I know it was foolish. I should have let another agent be your backup. But I couldn't stand the thought of not being here if you needed me."

Sebastian smiled. "That's because you're a huge control freak. But I love you anyway."

"Lucky for me." Warmth bloomed in Kyle's chest, and he brushed back Sebastian's unruly hair.

"You bet your ass you're lucky. Now come on." He tugged on Kyle's hand. "Maybe I'll kiss it better."

Laughing, Kyle followed Sebastian into the bedroom. A large ceiling fan beat overhead, the windows open to the balmy afternoon as it gave way to evening. Sebastian nodded to the bed before peeling off his T-shirt.

"Now lie down."

"How did I fall in love with someone so bossy?" Kyle unzipped his jeans and kicked them off with his underwear. He was only too eager to comply, stretching out gingerly and propping a few pillows under his right side.

Sebastian knelt between Kyle's legs and nudged them open. When Kyle spread them wide, Sebastian's eyes darkened, and he licked his lips. He ran his hands up over Kyle's legs, caressing his thighs. Kyle made a noise of complaint when Sebastian stopped just short of Kyle's balls.

With a wicked smile, Sebastian leaned down to lick and suck at the sensitive skin of Kyle's inner thighs. His hands explored, coasted up to Kyle's belly and back down, but just barely skimming his cock and balls with the barest touch no matter how much Kyle arched his hips.

By the time Sebastian finally took Kyle's dick between his lips, Kyle thought he might come right then and there. He tangled his fingers in Sebastian's hair. "So good."

Sebastian swirled his tongue around Kyle's shaft, head bobbing up and down. His mouth was so hot and wet. He slipped a finger into his mouth as well, and Kyle watched his lips stretch before he pulled it out and reached down to tease Kyle's hole.

As Sebastian pushed it inside, Kyle groaned, his legs flopping open even farther. He'd never been one to relax during sex, to be as free and open as he was with Sebastian. Sometimes it frightened him how much he trusted Sebastian, but right now he reveled in giving himself over. He moaned and muttered Sebastian's name as Sebastian worked his cock and his ass, inching in another finger.

Then Sebastian hit the perfect spot and Kyle's orgasm ripped through him, leaving him trembling in its wake, eyes heavy. Kyle petted Sebastian's hair as he licked him clean. He felt like he could sleep for days, but Sebastian needed to come. As he reached for Sebastian's cock, he couldn't hide a wince at the shooting spark of pain from his wound.

Kissing his way softly up Kyle's chest, Sebastian pressed in against him on his side. "It's all right. Go to sleep."

"I don't want to sleep." Kyle sucked at the skin over Sebastian's collarbone. He breathed deeply, filling his senses with the musky scent of Sebastian's sweat and faint cologne. He wished they could bottle the combination.

Sebastian chuckled. "Liar."

They kissed, tongues winding together slowly. Kyle tried to reach for Sebastian's cock again, but Sebastian batted his hand away and began jacking himself. Their kiss deepened until Sebastian was panting quietly into Kyle's mouth, his hips thrusting.

Kyle pulled back so he could watch. His gaze lowered from Sebastian's darkened eyes to his parted, wet lips. Sebastian's nipples were red and hard, and Kyle reached out to pinch and tease them, enjoying the flush that spread over Sebastian's skin and the moan that escaped his lips.

Sebastian's cock was straining and leaking, and their eyes met as Sebastian gasped Kyle's name and came, streaking both of their bellies. Sebastian sighed against Kyle's throat as he nuzzled there, milking himself and pressing little kisses to Kyle's skin. Kyle moved without thinking to hold Sebastian closer, but his fresh stitches protested and he grimaced.

Sebastian lifted his head and kissed Kyle's chin before rolling out of bed. He returned with a damp cloth and a glass of water. After he cleaned them both up, he disappeared into the main room and came back with the two bottles of pills the doctor had left.

"Two for infection and two for pain." He shook them onto his palm and knelt on the bed with the glass of water. "Don't even think about hiding them under your tongue because you're too tough for antibiotics."

Kyle swallowed the pills dutifully and rested back against the pillows. "You'd better make sure I didn't hide them."

With a smile, Sebastian stretched back out beside him, bringing the sheet over them. He kissed Kyle softly, his tongue slipping into his mouth and making a thorough inspection. "Now go to sleep."

"It's too early to sleep." But Kyle's eyes shut even as he protested.

"Rest. That's an order."

"Really, you were never this bossy before." Kyle smiled at the touch of Sebastian's fingertips caressing his chest and the warmth of his breath as he settled in, and Kyle drifted away.

A STRANGE BUZZING noise invaded Kyle's dream about a strange mission where he couldn't find his pants. As he opened his eyes, the buzz repeated, and he blinked at Sebastian in the faint early morning light. Sebastian was reaching for his phone on the bedside table.

"Marie? What's wrong? Is it Zhernakov?"

Kyle mumbled, trying to clear his fuzzy mind. "Tell her we already handed off the USB drive to her courier."

He listened and relayed to Kyle. "Oh. Zhernakov is already on his way out of Uruguay. Seems like he's making a run for it after messing up Daddy's arms deal. Then why…" Sebastian listened and glanced at Kyle, his expression suddenly serious. "Where? When? Are you sure?"

Kyle rubbed his face. "What?"

Sebastian held up a finger to Kyle as he listened. "Yes. We'll see you then." He ended the call and met Kyle's gaze intently. "It's the director."

Suddenly Kyle was awake, all vestiges of sleep and sedatives evaporating. He pushed himself up on his left hand. "Is she sure?"

"As sure as possible. They think he went through customs in Sydney an hour ago. Disguised, but they got a hit on the new facial recognition software."

The director. The man who had betrayed the Association. The man who had almost ruined Kyle's career and gotten him killed. Almost gotten Sebastian killed. The man Kyle wanted to take down more than any other scum on the Earth. Kyle's pulse raced, his injury forgotten in an instant. "When do we leave?"

Sebastian's eyes gleamed. "Now."

With a last kiss, they were off.

THE END

About the Author

Keira aims for the perfect mix of character, plot, and heat in her M/M romances. She writes everything from swashbuckling pirates to heartwarming holiday escapism. Her fave tropes are enemies to lovers, age gaps, forced proximity, and passionate virgins. Although she loves delicious angst along the way, Keira guarantees happy endings!

Discover more at:

keiraandrews.com

Printed in Great Britain
by Amazon

40659935R00142